HEAD IN THE SAND

A John England story

To Chrissie
with thanks and best wishes

R.A. Jordan

By *March 2025*

R. A. JORDAN

ISBN: 9798343975543

This book is dedicated to my brother Ian,
with whom I spent many happy days in Mottram St Andrew.
Also, to my great friends and lifelong pals Anthony and Rodney,
who enjoyed coming to our house and cycling with me on the Rec.

Tis'strange – but true, for truth is always strange;

Stranger than fiction: if it could be told,

How much would novels gain by the exchange!

George Gordon Byron, 1788-1824

OTHER NOVELS BY R. A. JORDAN

THE WALLS SAGA:

Time's Up
England's Wall
Laundry
Cracks in the Wall
Secret Side

CHARITY BOOKS IN AID OF NHS CHARITIES:

Match Day Murder
The Family Lie

A JOHN ENGLAND STORY

Tower of Strength
Failed Redemption
Reflections Of Death

All my books can be obtained from Amazon
Visit my website – www.rajordan.uk

CONTENTS

PROLOGUE

O n 4th January 2000, John England had been working at the firm of solicitors, Bennetts in Chester, over Christmas. He received an urgent call from Sandra Wall to attend Long Acre Farm after the body of Peter Wall, her father, was discovered on New Year's day. Peter's decapitated body was found in the old farm Land Rover. It had run into the gate post of the access to the sloping Long Meadow. Initial investigations indicated the cause of death to be suicide.

John England went to Long Acre Farm, Tarporley, as soon as possible to meet Peter's two daughters: Sandra, a commercial lawyer, and Sienna, a chartered surveyor. John felt a tingle of attraction towards the latter, despite the nature of the visit, and they maintained prolonged eye contact when they shook hands.

John was hardly away from Long Meadow in the following days and weeks. Peter Wall's estate was complex. The police, aided by forensic examinations, eventually decided a murder had been committed which was a great help to John. The life insurance policies that could not be claimed against in the event of suicide were now in play.

The police discovered the murderer was Peter's business partner, Roger Whiteside. He, too, was eventually found dead floating in the river Dee. Sandra left her job in Liverpool to take over the running of Wall's Civil Engineers. Sienna likewise left her career with a firm of chartered surveyors in Chester to start up and run Wall's Developments. Peter had purchased land, which was a helpful

1

starting point for Sienna's next venture.

After a romantic holiday skiing in the Swiss Alps, John and Sienna became even more attracted to one another and soon a wedding was in the offing. Frank Stringer, the family doctor and Sienna's godfather, was available to give her away despite being the fact he'd been imprisoned for murdering Roger Whiteside.

The property market was on fire in the early twenty-first century, especially for houses and flats. The enthusiasm for buy-to-let by private individuals was a great help in increasing sales of properties constructed and developed by the now-renamed group Wall's Holdings.

The demand for buy-to-let property was such that two local estate agent negotiators and entrepreneurs spotted an opportunity in the market. Michael Fitzallen and Wayne Lamb formed a new company to buy, furnish, and lease property for new landlords who had purchased properties as an investment. They teamed up with Wall's Developments and offered package deals for inexperienced investors. What the pair needed most was finance to get them going. Michael recalled that he had once met an Irishman at a professional dinner who had invited him to make contact with him to see if he had any deals that would interest him.

Michael approached his contact in Ireland, Niall Phelan, who lived at Dunmore Hall; he invited the pair to come to Ireland to discuss the deal. A deal was struck though it was not what the pair ideally wanted, but beggars can't be choosers. Phelan was to take 75% of the profit. The arrangement was that all proceeds had to be sent the day they received money from a sale transferred to a new bank account in southern Spain. Wayne, Michael and Niall Phelan were signatories to the bank account but only one signature was required. The deal allowed many new houses and flats to be sold to investors. After commencing this new enterprise, over £5m was sent to the Spanish bank account. As time passed, more money was transferred to the Spanish bank and Wayne was posted permanently to Spain. He kept an eye on the bank account and any withdrawals and credits.

2

Then Wayne was killed in a car crash in Malaga. Michael was getting tired of doing all the work and visited Niall in Ireland to try to renegotiate the deal. He was unsuccessful. Michael wanted to withdraw a significant amount of cash from the Spanish bank. When he went to Spain, he discovered that Niall had transferred all the money to his Irish account. It soon became clear that Phelan, who pretended to be helping drug addicts, was a drug supplier and pocketing a small fortune from his drug trading. Michael was at a loss to know how he might recover his money. He was concerned that he might be liable for money laundering if he went to the authorities.

Michael was introduced to a man called Goose. He owned a super yacht and was thought to be a smuggler of contraband of one sort or another. Michael told Goose of his predicament and Goose said he would help. Goose arranged to sell Niall Phelan a significant amount of cocaine and heroin. He needed to be paid five million euros in cash for the load. It was agreed that the drugs would be transferred to Phelan at sea in a location to be decided inside the fishing zone known as the Irish Box. The drugs were loaded onto Phelan's boat with cash at handover to Goose. Once the deed was done, Goose sped away from the area in his super yacht, Flying Goose, en route to Turkey. Goose had collected five million euros from Phelan at sea once the drugs had been handed over. In a roundabout fashion, Michael eventually received three-and-a-half million pounds. Niall Phelan got his drugs but on opening them, he and his chemist were killed by an exploding package of fake drugs.

Michael sold up in the UK and moved to Puerto Banus. He had briefly been in touch with Goose, who said he had sent most of the money, three million pounds, to his bank in the Cayman Islands. He explained to Michael that it was impossible to swan into a European bank and deposit millions of pounds or euros.

Michael received three hundred thousand euros to allow him to live in Spain. The financial crisis hit the UK and most of Europe. Wall's Holdings were fortunate that they had sold most of their property, except Peter's Tower in Manchester which wasn't finished. The bank demanded Wall's Holdings make a repayment of the three million loan secured on Peter's Tower. After numerous failed attempts to raise the money to pay off the bank, Sandra Wall placed an advert in the Sunday Times. Michael Fitzallen responded from Spain; he agreed to pay the three million for half the tower and half the rent.

As a lawyer and not entirely trusting Michael Fitzallen, Sandra drew up a contract for the loan, embodying the payments due to Fitzallen. To be safe, she included a clause which protected her from Michael. Suppose he committed a crime and was sentenced to over ten years in jail? He would forfeit his share of Peter's Tower and lose the money he had paid into the scheme.

One afternoon, under severe pressure from the authorities, Michael arranged to collect an extra ten thousand pounds from Sandra to enable him to leave the country and avoid jail for a recent crime. Sandra thought she knew what he was up to and said she would tell the police if he absconded. No one was around as they were on her farm which was currently being renovated. Michael murdered Sandra to prevent her from telling the authorities.

John was the remaining beneficiary because of the deaths of Peter Wall and, subsequently, Ann Wall, Peters's widow, and now Sandra. Then Sienna, his wife, died with their children in a car crash with a tram in Manchester. John inherited considerable sums of money, insurance payouts, and Peter's Tower. It was fully tenanted and debt-free and now belonged to him. He sold the family home. As a consequence of all these deaths, he became extremely wealthy.

Through his legal training, he decided to operate as a pro bono lawyer and leave the solicitor's practice in Chester.

Due to circumstances where John had been summoned for using excessive force on a man who attacked him in the underground car park of Peter's Tower, he met Fiona in the waiting area of the court, where she was sobbing. Eventually, due to his skills as a lawyer, Fiona was acquitted of the crime she was alleged to have committed. She was delighted.

They met and discussed plans with Goose, who had kept in touch. Goose had now purchased a new superyacht, *Brave Goose*. John and Fiona accepted an invitation to go to Ireland on holiday with Goose on the yacht. Relatives of Michael Fitzallen pursued them, intent on recovering the £3m he had lent Sandra years before on behalf of Michael Fitzallen, who was still in prison.

John and Fiona were preparing to fly back to Manchester from Cork when a rogue taxi driver offered them a lift to see the countryside. They thought this was a sightseeing trip but they were taken to Dunmore Hall. They soon realised that the intention was to lock them up and they were threatened at gunpoint. John tried to fight their attackers off. Fiona picked up the gun and fired – John thought she had killed the man who had fallen backwards when hit by the bullet. The small calibre round had run out of power when it found its way through his wax jacket and mobile phone.

Their attackers were imprisoned, and John and Fiona were allowed home. Fiona was fined a thousand Euros and bound over to keep the peace.

They returned to Manchester on the next plane.

Due to a complex set of circumstances ending with the assassination of Goose while *Brave Goose* was in Mallorca, John, who had acted as Goose's lawyer, found that he was able to purchase the superyacht. Various failed attempts to recover the money on behalf of Michael Fitzallen persuaded John and Fiona to move *Brave Goose* to Greece.

John and Fiona decided to send *Brave Goose* with her crew to Corfu, where they planned to join the boat. The route from Mallorca to Corfu took them via Sicily, the home of one of the assistants to the Fitzallen family, Georgio. The family was still trying to recover the three million euros from John England. Sicily is the home of the Cosa Nostra, who came to the aid of the Fitzallen family. Georgio orchestrated the capture of *Brave Goose* in Sicily. The mafia team Georgio had assembled held the yacht and her crew hostage until

John England paid a ransom.

John had to pay the ransom to save his loyal crew, which he did except for two hundred thousand pounds which had been extorted from a group of pensioners in Manchester by Georgio. John re-paid the pensioners their pension pots from the two hundred thousand that he had retained.

John and Fiona believed they were safe from the extortion rackets and free to continue cruising in *Brave Goose*.

*

The fictional story in these pages occurs in real places and recalls events in the nineteenth, twentieth and twenty-first centuries. The reader can visit these places, but please do not trespass! Although based on historical facts, the surrounding story comes from my own imagination. As such, the whole story is a work of fiction.

The geographical setting is the county of Cheshire. The recreation ground (the Rec) was in Mottram St Andrew, a hamlet two miles from Alderley Edge. The original name for Mottram St Andrew was Kirkley Ditch, as shown on old Ordnance Survey maps of the area. In view of the up-market nature of housing, it is little wonder that this name was changed to Mottram St Andrew. The Rec has subsequently been developed and now a large house sits on the land. The mines and caves exist to this day, but access is totally restricted, and permission must be sought to enter. There is no access to the mines now in Mottram St Andrew.

PREFACE – FACT

In 1750, William Wright built Mottram Hall. This splendid building is set on about 310 acres of land. The site incorporated the Old Hall, a traditional black-and-white Cheshire building. Mottram New Hall was built of orange brick using Flemish bond and sandstone dressings. It has a Kerridge sandstone roof and nine chimneys. There are projecting 'pavillions' on either side of the main hall. It has been substantially extended to make a hotel, golf course and football pitch for footballers' training. The building and the old hall still stand. The Hall is now Mottram Hall Hotel.

Mottram St Andrew is now an attractive place to live. House prices are at the upper end of the scale in the area. The hamlet is surrounded by farmland. There are redundant copper and cobalt mines accessed from near the Wizard Inn. The mines were first exploited by the Romans and the Bronze Age people. A Bronze Age shovel was discovered in the mines by the author, Alan Garner. Then, copper deposits were discovered and exploited in the mid-eighteenth century. The primary operator at the time was Charles Roe of Macclesfield. He took the copper and combined it with zinc from Derbyshire to make brass.

When the copper was exhausted, Roe turned to Anglesey and the Parys Mountain for supplies. The mountain overlooks Red Warf Bay. The bay gained its name as the copper from Parys Mountain ran via a stream into the bay. The bay became a solution of copper sulphate. A stream that passed through the copper deposits allowed diluted copper to enter the bay. Ships' timbers took up the copper solution, providing them with an antifouling, preventing fouling of the hull by barnacles and other marine life which can slow a vessel when at sea. Many ships would moor in the bay.

Another mineral was cobalt, mainly from the Mottram St Andrew mine, which used to be accessed through padlocked wooden doors at the back of the spoil heaps on Oak Road. The Mottram St Andrew mine enjoyed a surge in demand and price for its cobalt, chiefly due to the Napoleonic blockade which prevented cobalt from being imported, principally from Germany. The Mottram cobalt had a vivid blue colour, thought to have been used by artists such as J M W Turner, Impressionists such as Pierre-August Renoir and Claude Monet, and Post-Impressionists such as Vincent Van Gogh, and by glass makers, mainly in Bristol. The increase in demand and the reduction of supply from abroad were also factors in cobalt's price increase.

The Mottram St Andrew mine had a waste dump of sand and clay in an area outside the entrance to the mine. The opening was a wooden door with a brick surround which was bricked up in 1980. The site of the sand spoil heap has been redeveloped with a dwelling.

Mottram Hall was constructed by Lawrence Wright of Offerton. A direct descendant and ultimate heir to the now substantial estate was Julia Catherine Wright, who married a bombastic Army officer, James Frederick D'Arley Street, who changed his name to Wright.

Wright of Offerton and Mottram St. Andrew.

LAURENCE WRIGHT, of Nantwich, gent. [Said to be the son of Thomas Wright, of the same place.) Died 5 Aug., 1603. *Inq. P.M.* 1623. === MARGARET, dau. of Robert Pickering, of Nantwich. Marr. *c.* 1574. Surv. her husband. Died 18 Feb., 1617-18.

Authorities: Old pedigrees. Registers of Stockport, Mobberley, and Prestbury, &c. Inqs. p. m. Information of the family, &c. &c.

LAURENCE WRIGHT, of Nantwich and of Offerton, *jure uxoris*, Æt. 48 in 1613. Bur. at Stockport, 21 Feb. 1649-50. Will dated 11 Feb., 1649-50. === ANNE, dau. and coheir of Ralph Winnington, of Offerton, gent. Marr. at S., 21 March, 1595-6. Bur. there, 9 April, 1617. (*First wife.*) | LYDIA, dau. of . . . . . . Living 1650. Named in his brother's will. (*Second wife.*) | Roger Wright. Living 1650. | Robert Wright. Marr. to Katherine Birch. He died 14 Jan., 1616-17. | Thomas Wright, M.A., Rector of Wilmslow, co. Chester, from 1610 to 1661. Marr. Anne, dau. of Francis Hobson, of the Pasture, in Alderley parish. Died 20 Oct., 1661. Bur. at W., 23 Oct. | Margery Wright. Marr. to William Newton, of Pownall, Esq. (See vol. I. p. 128.)

Arms: Sable a chevron between three bulls' heads caboshed Argent, a crescent for difference.

Crest: Out of a ducal coronet Or, a bull's head Argent.

(These arms do not appear to have been registered at the Herald's College.)

LAURENCE WRIGHT, of Offerton, gent. Bapt. at S., 17 Dec., 1596. Marr. *c.* 1628. Bur. at S., 14 Feb., 1659-60. === MARGARET, dau. of Robt. Robinson, of Mobberley, by his wife Margaret, d. and h. of Ralph Lowe, of Mile End, Stockport. She is said to have been the widow of Thomas Legh, of Northwood. | Thomas Wright. Bapt. at S., 23 Jan., 1600-1. Bur. there, 24 April, 1601. | Thomas Wright. Bapt. at S., 6 July, 1602. Living 1650. ? Marr. to Elizabeth .... ? Bur. at S., 30 Dec., 1671. | Henry Wright. Bapt. at S., 20 June, 1603. Living 1631. Marr. to Richard Wright. Bapt. at S., 5 July, 1612. Bur. there, 20 May, 1613. | Edward Wright. Living 1631 and 1650. Bur. at S., 17 Aug., 1667. | Anne Wright. Bur. at S., 18 Jan., 1597-8. Katherine Wright. Bapt. at S., 14 Dec., 1599. Died young. | Anne Wright. Bapt. at S., 2 Aug., 1607. Died young. Elizabeth Wright, Bapt. at Chadkirk, 2 Jan., 1608-09. Living 1631. | Dorothy Wright. Bapt. at S., 23 June, 1613. Living 1631. | Margaret Wright. Bapt. at S., 7 May, 1615. Marr. *c.* 1636 to Peter Radcliffe, of Mellor, co. Derby, gent. Living 1650.

1. Laurence Wright. Bapt. at S., 3 Jan. Bur. there, 8 Jan., 1629-30. | 2. THOMAS WRIGHT, of Offerton, gent. Bapt. at Mobberley, 8 Feb., 1630-1. Living 1676. === MARY, dau. of John Hignett, of London. | 3. Laurence Wright. Bapt. at S., 13 March, 1635-6. | 4. Roger Wright. Bapt. at S., 3 Dec., 1637. | 5. Henry Wright. Bapt. at S., 25 May, 1640. | Anne Wright. Bapt. at S., 23 March, 1631-2. Bur. there, 6 April, 1632. | Anne Wright. Bapt. at S., 6 Aug., 1641. | Margaret Wright. Bapt. at S., 23 April, 1643.

LAURENCE WRIGHT, of Mobberley and Offerton, Esq. Succ. to Mobberley on the death of Miss Elizabeth Robinson, the heiress of Nathaniel Robinson, brother of his grandmother, in 1676. High Sheriff of Cheshire, 1701. Bur. at M., 9 July, 1712. === ELEANOR, dau. and coheiress of the Rev. Samuel Shipton, B.D., Rector of Alderley, co. Chester. Bapt. at A., 10 Nov., 1652. Marr. at Prestbury, 17 June, 1677. | HENRY WRIGHT, of Clifford's Inn, London, and Offerton, Esq. Died at Offerton, 28 Sept. Bur. at S., 13 Oct., 1711, *æt.* 48. === ELIZABETH, dau. and coheiress of William Block, of Essex, co. Middlesex, Esq., and grand-dau. of Judge Wylde. ? Bur. at S., 9 Feb., 1676-7. | Nathaniel Wright. Bur. at Mobberley, 27 Oct., 1662. | Mary Wright. Marr. to Francis Newton, of Mobberley, gent., of the family of Newton, of Pownall. She was buried at M., 16 Feb., 1691-2.

1. Nathaniel Wright, Bapt. at M., 1681. Bur. there, 29 Feb., 1699-1700. Unmarr. | 2. HENRY WRIGHT, of Mobberley, Esq. Born 17 Feb. Bapt. at M., 25 Feb., 1688-9. Died 12 Oct., 1744, *æt.* 56. Bur. at M. Tombstone there. === PUREFOY, dau. of Sir Willoughby Aston, of Aston, Bart. (his 19th child). Marr. 22 Nov. 1712. Died 30 Jan., 1768, *æt.* 78. Bur. at M. Tombstone there. | 1. Elizabeth Wright. Bapt. at M., 25 March, 1680. Bur. there, 30 May, 1681. | 2. Eleanor Wright. Bapt. at M., 25 May, 1682. Died unmarr. | 3. Penelope Wright. Bapt. at M., 8 July, 1683. Died unmarr. in 1712. | 4. Theodosia Wright. Bapt. at M., 26 Feb., 1684-5. Bur. there, 4 Oct., 1699. | 5. Elizabeth Wright. Bapt. at M., 15 Aug., 1686. Bur. there, 14 Dec., 1686. | WILLIAM WRIGHT, of Offerton, Esq. Purchased Mottram St. Andrew in 1738. Built St. Peter's Church, Stockport. Died without surviving issue, 3 Dec., 1770, leaving Henry Offley Wright, his next heir. === FRANCES ALICE, dau. of Randle Wilbraham, of Townshead, Esq. Marr. 14 Feb., 1720. | Henry Wright, of Offerton, gent. Died at Offerton Hall, 21 April. Bur. at S., 24 April, 1725, *æt.* 26. S.P. (See vol. I. p. 360.)

1. Laurence Wright. Bapt. at S., 16 June, 1718. Bur. 16 March, 1721-2. | 2. (Rev.) HENRY OFFLEY WRIGHT, of Mobberley, Offerton, and Mottram St. Andrew. Vicar of Derby. Bapt. at S., 17 Oct. 1719. Died 17 June, 1796, *æt.* 80. Bur. at M. Tombstone there. === JANE, 2nd dau. and coh. of Ralph Adderley, of Coton, co. Staff., Esq. Died 19 March, 1779, *æt.* 59. Bur. at M. Tombstone there. | Eleanor Wright. Bapt. at S., 18 Dec., 1713. Marr. at M., 16 Feb., 1733-4. to Geo. Lloyd, of Hulme, near Manchester, Esq. Bur. at M., May, 1735. | Theodosia Wright. Bapt. at S., 30 March, 1715. Marr. to Sir Wolstan Dixie, Bart., of Market Bosworth. Died May, 1751. Bur. at M. | Mary Wright. Bapt. at S., 15 June, 1717. Bur. at M., 3 March, 1721-2. | 1. Henry Wright. 2. Randle Wright. 3. Laurence Wright. Mary Wright. Elizabeth Wright. Frances Purefoy Wright. Wright. All died young, for dates of birth and death, see vol. I.xc vol. 1

3,1. LAURENCE WRIGHT, of Mobberley, Mottram St. Andrew, and Offerton, Esq. Born at Hame Hall, co. Warwick, 14 July, 1732. Of St. John's Coll., Camb., M.A. 1778. High Sheriff of Cheshire, 1802. Died 19 Jan., 1842. Bur. at Mobberley. S.P. === MARIA, dau. of John Waterhouse, Lieut.-Col. of the 1st Surrey Militia. | 2. (Rev.) William Henry Wright. Born at Coton, 2 Sept., 1753. Of St. John's Coll. Camb., M.A. 1779. B.D. 1786. Fellow of his College. Vicar of North Stoke, Newnham Murren, and Ipsden, co. Berks and Oxon. Died 1828. Unmarr. | 3. (Rev.) Thomas Wright. Born 1 Nov., 1756, at Derby. Of St. John's Coll., Camb., B.A. 1779, and of Emm. Coll., Camb., M.A. 1782. Rector of Market Bosworth, co. Leicester, for 52 years. Died 29 Nov., 1840. Bur. there. === Mary, dau. of William Dilke, Esq., of Maxstoke Castle, co. Warwick. Born 1 Nov., 1758. Marr. 24 Aug., 1789. Died at Lee Hall, Mottram St. Andrew, 8 Oct., 1844, *æt.* 85. Bur. at St. Peter's, Stockport. | 4. Henry Adderley Wright. Born 14 Dec., 1761, at Derby. Lieut.-Colonel 25 Reg. Died 7 April, 1838. Marr. Alice, dau. of Robert Sclater, of Horfield, co. Lanc., and widow of Major-General Rigby. | Francisca Wright. Marr. at Prestbury, 13 Jan., 1785, to Francis Parry Price, of Bryn-y-Pys, Esq. | Letitia Wright. Marr. at Prestbury, 24 June, 1789, to the Rev. John Watson, M.A., Vicar of Prestbury. (See p. 210.)

4. (Rev.) HENRY WRIGHT, of Offerton and Mottram St. Andrew. Born at Market Bosworth, 22 July, 1791. Of Emm. Coll., Camb., B.A. 1815. Incumbent of St. Peter's, Stockport, 1816-1842. Died at Cadeby Rectory, 22 Nov., 1864. Bur. at St. Peter's, Stockport. === MARY CATHERINE, dau. of the Rev. Thomas Adnutt, Rector of Croft, co. Leic. Born 24 Oct., 1789. Died 29 Dec., 1807. Bur. at St. Peter's, Stockport. | THOMAS WRIGHT, of Mobberley, co. Chester. Born 9 Sept., 1796. Died 1845. Bur. at Mobberley. S.P. | William Wright. Born 25 Sept., 1797. Died at Prickleton, co. Leicester, 5 May, 1834. S.P. | (Rev.) Charles Wright, M.A., of Hill Top, co. Lanc. Born 6 May, 1799. Marr. Lucy, dau. of Robt. Faux, of Cliff House, co. Leicester. Died 6 May, 1865. Bur. at Belmont, co. Lanc. | Francis Wright. Born 18 Nov., 1800. Died at Lee Hall, Mottram St. Andrew, in 1853. Bur. at Belmont, co. Lanc. S.P. | Laurence Wright. Born 10 Nov., 1801. Died at Cowes, 28 Jan., 1838. S.P. | Mary Wright. Born 28 Feb., 1794. Died 1794. | Jane Wright. Born 8 April, 1795. Marr. 12 March, 1827, Blakiston, Esq. Bur. at Market Bosworth, Esq. Major of Reg. Of Bell House, co. Leic. (2nd son of Sir Matthew Blakiston, Bart.)

Laurence Wright, only son. Born 25 Feb., 1818. Died at Cowes, 2 July, 1839. Unmarr. Bur. at St. Peter's, Stockport. | Maria Wright. Born 31 May, 1819. Died 11 Dec., 1843. Bur. at St. Peter's, Stockport. | John Spencer Ashton Shuttleworth, of Hathersage Hall, co. Derby, Esq. === Mary Jane Annabella Wright. | Charles Richard Bonastre Legh, of Adlington, Esq. === 5. JULIA CATHERINE WRIGHT. Heiress to her father. === JAMES FREDERICK D'ARLEY STREET, now WRIGHT, late Capt. Royal Artillery, of Mottram St. Andrew, Esq. Born 24 Nov., 1827.

One dau. | 6. Julia Mary Catherine Wright (only child).

9

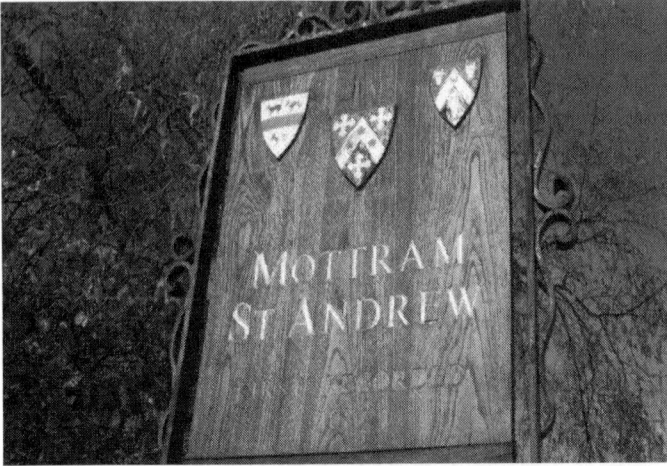

CHAPTER 1

SEPTEMBER 8TH 1979

John England, aged ten, woke on Saturday, September 8th 1979, at ten past nine in his bedroom at the back of their new house, The Corner House in Oak Road, Mottram St Andrew. It was close to the end of the school holidays, so a sleep-in was allowed. He could see the end of their back garden and the paddock beyond. His bedroom window provided a panoramic view over the whole area owned by his parents. John's father, George, was a keen horseman. He had two beautiful hunters stabled at home. This morning, they were in the paddock. John was looking forward to cycling around the Rec with his friend and neighbour, Frank. It was a sunny day with a blue sky. The weather all week had been awful, raining every day. The Rec, which was opposite John's house, was a disused spoil tip from the mine. It was an excellent bike track. Four doors further along Oak Road was Franks's home.

Half asleep and half awake, John was contemplating the rides he and Frank would make on the Rec. The last thing on his mind was that by the end of the weekend, his great friend Frank Brocklehurst would probably be dead. It was a dream he had had during the previous night, but what a ridiculous idea! He got up and went downstairs for a late breakfast.

'Hi, Mum, a much better day today, isn't it? Frank and I will be riding our bikes on the Rec today, I imagine.'

'That's good, John. You look half asleep, though!'

'Yes, Mum, I had a bad dream, so I didn't sleep all that well.'

'Ah, that would account for how you look.'

'Do dreams come true, Mummy?'

'No, I am sure they don't. They are just something in our imagination.'

'Oh, that's good as I dreamed that Frank would disappear and may be killed.'

'Don't fret, John, I'm sure that's just your imagination going a bit wild. Go out and enjoy yourselves.'

After the holidays, the two boys would attend the primary school in the village of Mottram St Andrew for their final year before senior school. They could walk or cycle there. It was a post-war single-storey brick building with a large playground, a tarmac area for play, and a much larger grass area for games. This was ideal for athletics, cricket and football. Both boys enjoyed school, where there were twenty-six other students. It was a co-educational school, with more boys than girls.

Every year, there was a school fete. Many parents took part in running cake stalls, side shows and a display of country dancing, usually put on by the fathers, with some dressed as women. It soon became the highlight of the fete, an event everyone looked forward to at the end of the summer term before the summer holidays.

The old market town of Macclesfield was about five miles away and had held a weekly market since the town was founded in 1261. Macclesfield Castle was established in 1398 by John de Macclesfield, the keeper of Richard II's wardrobe. John applied to the king to allow him to crenellate his manor house. However, the request was close to the end of Richards's reign and life and he had died before the request could be granted. John found favour with Henry IV, who in 1410 granted permission for the crenellations. The castle is no more, having fallen into disrepair, and the stone 'borrowed' by others to build other dwellings and farm buildings in the area.

Alderley Edge is famous for the sandstone escarpment, The Edge, a National Trust-owned wooded area crisscrossed with footpaths and bridleways. At points on the walk, incredible vistas take the eye over the Cheshire Plain to the North and West. The walk through the woods on a quiet week day is an enchanting encounter with nature, the woodland and all its natural inhabitants. Before they broke off for the holidays, Miss Tinker, the boys' form teacher, had taught the class about the history of The Edge and the local area.

The geology of the area consists of Triassic new red sandstone, according to the Macclesfield Museum. As evidenced by their discarded tools, the Romans started mining in the region, though some items in the old workings, including a wooden shovel, are believed to be from the Bronze Age. Alan Garner, who discovered the shovel, is the author of numerous books, including *The Stone Book Quartet*, *The Owl Service*, *The Weirdstone of Brasingamen*, and many more, often using The Edge as the pallet for his stories. The boys were aware of this because their teacher, Miss Tinker, had read extracts from *The Weirdstone of Brasingamen* during an English lesson before the school holidays. She also told of the mine where Garner had found the Bronze Age spade and explained that the mine had been in production from the Bronze Age until the beginning of the twentieth century.

'What did the mine produce, Miss?'

'Good question, Frank. The mine produced copper and cobalt.'

'What were they used for?'

'I gather that copper was a critical alloy used in buildings and was also used in the manufacture of brass. Cobalt was used in glass making to give it a blue colour; it was also used by famous artists such as Turner, Renoir, Monet and Van Gogh. Blue was the most important colour for the impressionists.'

Once the lesson was over, the children, including John and Frank, were excited about the mine.

'Do you suppose we could find our way down to the mine, John?'

'Well, Frank, the door at the back of the Rec must have something to do with getting into the mine. The mine is where all that sand has come from to form the banks we cycle around.'

'Yes, but it's all locked up.'

It didn't require any great planning as Frank and John would cycle around the Rec most days. The old wooden door the boys believed led to the mine had been locked for ages. Today was no different, except it was a Friday and the last weekend before school started again on Tuesday. It had rained heavily most days that week, preventing the two boys from their cycle adventures.

By ten that morning, the two boys and their bicycles met up and started to cycle around, up and over the hillocks made from the spoil produced by the mine. This was their chosen track, one they cycled on most days, weather permitting.

Frank had a nearly new Raleigh Chopper in red with a gear stick on the crossbar. He had been given the bike by his parents at Christmas. His aunt and uncle had given him a battery-operated light, front and back. John had a blue second-hand bike with no lights but at least the brakes worked.

The boys started over the road to what the Rec. As soon as they arrived, they were so pent up that they were off. It had been a week since they'd been there, thanks to the bad weather. They weaved around the piles of sand and gravel at the base just as fast as they could.

The racing around did not last long as Frank stopped his bike near the summit of one of the hillocks.

'Hey, John. Look what I have found. Come and look, quick.'

Standing with his bike at the top of the mound on the track they had made, the rain had washed some sand away, revealing a smooth round object, nearly the same colour as the sand.

John altered his cycle route, joining Frank as soon as he could on the top of a mound.

The two boys studied in detail Frank's 'find'. They scraped away some sand from the domed object poking out of the sand. The ceaseless rain had uncovered it during the week.

'It's a skull!' Frank said.

'Do you think so?'

'It looks very like it. Keep digging.'

'It *is* a skull! My god, I had better get my mum. You stay here, Frank, and mark the spot. My mum will know what to do.'

*

John raced home to discover his mum in the back garden.

'Mum, Mum! Come quick!'

'What is the problem, John? I'm busy. I have a great deal of gardening to catch up on – the season's over for many plants, and they all need cutting back.'

'We've found a skull on the Rec.'

'What sort of skull, John?'

'A human one.'

'Oh heavens, are you sure?

'Yes, Mum, very sure.'

'I'd better come and have a look.'

John's mum, Audrey, put on her anorak, keeping on her wellies, and came over the road to see what the two boys had discovered. She scrabbled up the sandy mound to where Frank was watching the 'find'.

'Is this it?' Audrey said, looking at the light brown dome protruding from the sand.

'Yes, Mrs England. The rain must have washed it out of the sand this week.'

'Well, there is no doubt this is a skull, Frank. There are some questions to be answered now. First, where is the rest of the body, then who is it, and how old is it?'

'How do we find out, Mum?'

'Well, boys, this is a matter for the police. They will work out what has happened. I will give them a ring when I get home. Don't touch it or ride up here until the police give it the all clear.'

'Okay, Mum, we will guard the site by riding around the bottom of this mound.'

To everyone's surprise, less than an hour after Audrey had called the police, a Morris Minor, with blue and white paintwork and a police sign on the roof appeared outside John's house. A young constable alighted and, following Audrey's directions, he walked over to the Rec.

'I have come about the skull that has been found. Is it here?'

'Yes, I will show you where it is,' said John. 'It's at the top of this mound, Sir.'

The constable walked to the location of the skull, up the mound, as directed by the boys, which he found more challenging to do than he had expected. The young PC scraped even more sand away from the skull, which was clearly human.

'Where are the other bones of the body?' he wondered out loud. 'Is it male or female? I wonder how long it's been here.'

He confirmed it was indeed a human skull and returned to John's house where he called the police station with his report. He was instructed to put police tape around the scene and keep everyone away from the location until forensic officers arrived. Once the tape was in place, he returned to the station.

'Oh, that's not fair,' complained John. 'We discovered the skull, and now we can't ride our bikes on the Rec.'

'Well, the police have to consider the public's safety,' said Audrey.

'The public never come onto the Rec. The only other person Frank and I have seen is the man from the caving society who occasionally comes to look at the door and goes away again.'

'I am sure the Rec will not be out of bounds for long,' she said. 'Why don't you and Frank create a cycle track in the paddock at the back? The horses are in the stables now, so the paddock is free.'

'Okay, Mum. That's a good idea.'

John burst out of the kitchen to meet Frank at his house four doors away and explained the temporary arrangement.

'That's great, John. Can we go now?'

'Yes, why not?'

The two boys rode their bikes to the end of John's garden and then into the paddock. It didn't take them long to establish a track.

CHAPTER 2

SKULL IN A BOX

A lady, assumed by the boys to be a police forensics officer, arrived in her red Mini car. Once she had donned wellies and a pair of brown overalls, she went to the site. She had an armful of tools and a cardboard box.

John and Frank looked on from the boundary to the Rec.

'Hello, boys. Was it you who found the skull?'

'Yes, Miss.'

'Well done.'

'Yes, it's exciting.'

'How did you know it was a skull?'

'We didn't at first. We pulled some of the sand away from what seemed to be a smooth oval object until we could see it was a skull.'

'Did you see any other bones around after you found the skull?'

'No, Miss. I promise you.'

'Don't worry, boys, you are not in trouble. You have done well to find it. Just show me where I need to go, then come back and wait here. Why is there so much sand and gravel here?'

'It's the spoil from the mine, Miss. The door to the mine is the old wooden door over there,' John explained, pointing to the mine entrance.

'What did they mine here?'

'We understand, Miss, that it was copper and cobalt. That is what our teacher said.'

'My, you two are well informed.'

'Will you be taking the skull away, Miss?'

'Yes, John. I will take it to my laboratory.'

'May we see it before you take it away, Miss, please?

'Of course.' The scientist ducked under the police tape and then stood looking for the probable location of the skull.

'I can't see it, boys. Will you show me, please? Then, you will have to go back to the other side of the police tape.'

'Yes, certainly. It's a bit of a climb. Can we carry anything for you?' said John.

'You certainly can.' There was a box of hand tools and another box with plastic bags. 'I will follow you.'

The two boys led the way up the giant mound, carrying a box each. They found it easy to ascend the summit of the waste tip.

'There you are, Miss – the skull,' said Frank in a proud voice. 'It was me who found it, Miss.'

The police scientist asked them to return behind the tape.

'Once I have completed the excavation, I will ask you to carry a box each down the slope. I will bring the skull.'

*

After about half an hour, the forensic scientist shouted to the boys to come up and carry the spare boxes of tools and plastic bags. The boys were up the slope in a flash. She handed them a box each whilst she carried the skull.

'Is the skull in the box, Miss?'

'Yes, boys, do you want a look?'

19

'Ooh, yes, please,' John and Frank responded in unison.

'What are you going to do with it now?'

'I will take it back to my laboratory and I will try and decide if it's a man or woman and how old it might be.'

'That sounds like you have a difficult job. Good luck. Can we cycle on the Rec again?'

'Yes, of course. I'm just going to have a look at the door to the mine.'

She tried to find more bones that could assist in defining the sex of the individual and possibly the name and age of the skull. After two hours of searching and digging in the sand in the immediate area, she gave up. There was nothing to be found.

She realised that the mound of gritty sand was the spoil from the mine. She could see an old door in a bricked-up panel set in what must have been the original entrance to the mine. Once the skull had been carefully removed and packed into a box in the boot of her car, her curiosity got the better of her. She would love to see what was behind the door.

On further investigation, she discovered that the door was locked with a padlock, which was now old and rusty. She doubted that, even if she had the key, it would open. She tried her hardest to break the lock, pulling on the door without success, but suddenly the hasp through which the padlock was placed gave way and broke away from the door. The timber it was screwed into was rotten. She now had access and gingerly opened the door, realising it had been shut for years and she was probably the first person in many years to gain access.

The door opened part of the way, then became stuck due to a build-up of sand. She might be able to squeeze in, but she didn't have a torch. The place looked filthy. A small shard of light illuminated the first few feet of the interior, which looked very muddy. She could hear the rushing water of an underground stream.

'I'll close the door and come back tomorrow, fully equipped,' she muttered to herself.

She removed all the police tape before she left the site as she had been asked to do, then she drove off in her red Mini, leaving the mine for another day and the Rec to the two delightful and polite young men.

'Frank, it's okay for us to go back now.'

'Yes! Let's go.'

The two boys raced around on their bikes. After a while, exhausted, they propped their bikes against the old door and sat down on a large stone nearby for a rest.

'Hey, look, John, someone opened the door to the mine.'

'What makes you think that, Frank?'

'The lock is loose and hanging down; it's not secured to the wooden door.'

'Hey, let's see if we can open it. We have always wanted to get inside.'

The two boys tried to prise the door, which would only open a short way due to a build-up of sand that prevented the door from opening more than a few inches.

'I can squeeze through there,' announced Frank.

'Maybe we can open it a bit further?'

'Okay, John, let's push together.'

The two boys grabbed the partially open door and gave an almighty heave. It moved a bit.

'Let's have another go, John. If we can open it as much again, we can easily get through.'

CHAPTER 3

BEYOND THE DOOR

T he two boys were anxious to discover what was behind the well-worn wooden door; they'd been curious about it for ages. They gave the door another massive heave with as much strength as they could muster. They achieved an opening of a further six inches, making it just over a foot wide.

'Can we both squeeze through, Frank?'

'I think so, John. It is very dark in the mine. Let me get the light off the front of my bike. It's easy enough to remove.'

'Okay, Frank, that's a great idea.' Frank lifted the front light from his Chopper bike. He would use this as a torch. Within a few minutes, the boys had entered the mine, Frank using his bike lamp to show them the way.

'I will go first, John.' Frank managed to squeeze through and John followed. It was very dark. Frank's bicycle light was a great help, but really only to him.

'Wow, it's dark in here. What's that sound?'

'Running water, it's a stream. It has been raining, so maybe there is more than a stream now. It is running very quickly. It sounds like a raging torrent. It's over on the left somewhere?'

'Cor, be careful, John, it's very slippy. There's mud everywhere. That noise is getting much louder, too,' said Frank.

'Can you speak louder? I can hardly hear you over this water. Gosh, Frank, the ceiling is very high. Can you shine your torch up?'

Frank did as John had requested.

'Look, what are those black things hanging from the roof?'

'I don't know. Could they be bats?'

'Yes, I think they are. I thought I saw one move. There are hundreds of them. How do you suppose they got in here?'

'There must be an opening elsewhere to allow them to fly in. Why are they here now?'

'Well, all I know is that they only fly at night. We learned that in a geography and nature lesson,' said John.

'I don't remember that, John. Let's press on. This track goes on a long way.'

'I don't think we should go any further.'

The two boys were shouting at one another so they could be heard over the noise of the stream, which was now a torrent. It bubbled and splashed until the water arrived at a stone face, which seemed to hold the water back. Despite this, water was flowing.

'We will be in trouble if we are found in here.'

'We can go a bit further, John. This is exciting. That stream is getting much louder,' Frank shouted. 'Be careful; the path's surface is slippery and wet here.'

'I don't think we should go any further, Frank. It's very dark and dangerous.'

'Look, John, we've been trying to get in here for ages. Now we have the opportunity and should make the most of the chance.'

'It's hazardous to carry on. The river sounds very noisy, and the water is running very quickly. I can only make out the edge of it. The river is very close, Frank.'

'Okay, John, but you need to shout louder. It is tough to hear. We'll go around this last corner, and I promise we will go back then,' Frank shouted back.

He led the way around a sharp corner in the path with slippy mud underfoot. The path narrowed until there was barely room for one foot in front of the other. The stone face of the mine at the side of the path now arched over, reducing the space to walk. The river's surface, which was disturbed by small waves, was running very close by.

Then it happened.

'Help, help! John, I'm sliding! I can't stop! Help, John, help me!' Frank was shouting.

John was frightened. His friend Frank was sliding out of sight, having fallen into the torrent. His torch showed his location, but John couldn't get near him, and he wasn't going around the corner, which seemed to have been Frank's undoing. There was a large splash. Frank was screaming his head off. His torch beam lit up the ceiling.

'Please help me, John, help me!'

'You stay there, Frank. I'm going to get help.'

Frank's torch continued to light up the mine's roof.

'Please help me, help me ...' was the last plaintive cry from Frank until there was silence. Frank had disappeared – silence now, except for the roar of the stream.

Frank was underwater, choking, he couldn't breathe. He hit his head on a sharp solid object whilst submerged. Unable to see, he couldn't work out which way was up.

He landed with his feet touching the ground and discovered he was in an underground lake. At the moment of impact, he was coughing his lungs up, vomiting water as far as he could tell. He just couldn't get his breath back. The water was black and with no glimmer of light, he had no idea which way to walk. He couldn't afford to drop into water deeper than himself again as he was convinced he would drown.

He was still coughing and spluttering with what he assumed was blood trickling down the side of his face from the bash he made to his head as he went through the slot in the rock. He was desperate to sit down but that was impossible while up to his waist in water. He decided to move carefully to his left. He heard John's voice echoing in his brain, saying he was going to get help. He realised he had been carried along in the stream through the gap – what could Frank do to let John know he was alive?

'I'm going now, Frank,' John said, unsure he could be heard. 'I won't be long. Hold on and stay put.'

John ran as fast as he could out of the mine and crossed the road, racing home.

'Mum, Mum, where are you? There's been a terrible accident. We need help, can you help?'

'Whatever is the matter, John, and where's Frank?'

'I will show you. Hurry up, Mummy, please, it's urgent. Frank's in danger.'

'Where on earth is Frank?'

'He's stuck in the stream in the mine.'

'What on earth is he doing there, and how have you got into the mine?'

'I will tell you later, Mum, hurry. Hurry! Bring a torch. You'll need wellies.'

Realising that this was a real emergency, John's mother decided to get cracking to see if she could help rescue Frank. She followed John to the entrance to the mine but couldn't get through the gap. She pulled and pushed as hard as she could at the wooden door, but it wouldn't open any more.

'I can't get through, John. How did you get in?'

'I squeezed in with Frank through the gap.'

'I'll have to go home, get a shovel to remove the sand blocking the door. I won't be long.'

'I'll keep your torch, Mum, and go and see if I can spot Frank.'

'Okay, but don't you get stuck.'

A few moments later, Audrey reappeared with a shovel, an extra torch, and an old washing line, just in case she could throw a line at Frank. She started moving the sand that was stopping the door from opening. After ten minutes of hard work, the door opened sufficiently far to enable her to gain access to the mine's entrance.

Shining her torch, she went as fast as possible, realising the surface of the path was very slippy due to water and mud, trying to catch up with John.

'Where's Frank, John?'

'I don't know, Mum; all I can see is his torch.'

Audrey spotted Frank's torch too which indicated his last position. They shouted as loudly as they could. There was no response.

They tried shouting again, but still there was no reply.

'Look, John, I will have to get some expert help here; you run across the road and tell Frank's mum what's happened. I'll go and get the fire brigade.'

John did as requested. Suddenly, he couldn't help recalling the dream he had had in the night as he got out of bed. *I hope I was wrong. Frank surely can't be dead?*

CHAPTER 4

THE SLOT IN THE ROCK

Audrey returned to the mine with Frank's mum, Mrs Brocklehurst. They walked very carefully along the track to the point where it became muddy and slippery. The sound of the rushing stream, which they could not see, was becoming more pronounced. They eventually found it once they came around the bend in the path.

On the opposite side of the stream, or more correctly, the torrent, she could make out a small light which seemed to be sitting on a stone ledge.

'Mum, Mum, it's me, John.'

'I'm here, John. Mrs Brocklehurst is with me. Where are you?'

'I am just around the corner near the rushing stream. Have you got help coming?'

'Yes, the fire brigade said they would be here as quickly as possible. They are coming from Macclesfield.'

'What happened, John?' asked Frank's mother.

'We wanted to explore the mine. Frank got the torch off his bike and went first, slipping on the corner. He must have lost his grip on his torch and it landed on a stone shelf.'

A loud siren sounded near the entrance; Audrey went to meet the fire brigade. It was nearly three o'clock. Blue flashing lights illuminated the area. She explained what had happened and led two fire officers, equipped with very bright torches, into the mine.

'So, what has happened here?'

Audrey gave as complete an explanation as she could.

'A torrent of water is running through the mine, and one of the children has fallen in as it rounds the corner. The pathway is very slippy with liquid mud. He hasn't been seen since. John saw him throw his bike light onto a shelf.'

'Greg, can you see anything?' the senior fire officer enquired of the fireman who had taken the lead towards the torrent. John also explained to him what had happened.

'It looks like the stream disappears into the ground under a narrow slot in the rock. The water is so deep it is impossible to see the top of the slot. It probably cascades down to a new chamber. It is impossible to see it. Even without the torrent of water, I imagine getting to the next chamber is not straightforward. I don't know this cave or mine structure but someone surely must know?'

'I will get some of my men to search this stretch up to the slot in the stone face to see if we can find anything. They will all be tied together, and an anchor point on dry land will be established.'

The chief fire officer organised the search party. One of the other firefighters suggested they send an air cylinder and mask on a rope down the stream and through the slot in the stone wall of the mine. If Frank had been sucked through, he would be at the very least winded. The air tank would allow him to breathe. This was agreed as a sensible approach.

Once the air tank on a long piece of rope was made available in the mine, the men searching in the torrent, all tied together, got to the slot where the water was flowing to a new location and tried to thread the tank through the gap.

'The rope is fifty meters. It should be long enough to find the floor on the other side,' announced the firefighter who had rigged up the air bottle. The frontman of the search crew tried to feed the bottle down to the bottom of the torrent but it kept bobbing up as it was very buoyant and crashed and banged on the face of rock. It just wouldn't go through the torrent to the passageway beyond.

'I am struggling with getting it into the slot, Sir.'

'Keep trying.' As they spoke, the air bottle disappeared. The rope paid out at lightning speed.

Then the air bottle surfaced again, still with its rope attached.

'The air tank won't go through the slot, Sir. What should I do?'

'Hold on. Don't let it go.'

After a while, over an hour since the firefighters arrived, the senior man declared that their search had found nothing. We need expert cavers who can go through water and out the other side. Let's hope Frank finds ample space to enable him to breathe.'

Francis Brocklehurst was beside herself. She was weeping and shaking.

'That's it, he's gone. What am I going to do?' Francis was beside herself with grief. 'Where is my little boy? He can't just disappear.'

'Is Jack at work, Francis?'

She responded with a pale voice in between crying. 'Yes,' she eventually managed to say.

She was a broken woman. 'My son, my darling son, has gone. But we don't even know where he's gone to.'

The chief fire officer on the scene was on the radio with his station. He realised this could be a fatality unless they had cave specialists who could traverse through the slit in the rock. If they couldn't get through, they'd have to wait until the stream dropped in level.

*

Later on in the evening, a caving team arrived from Derbyshire.

'Is this the stream?'

'It is,' indicated a fireman.

'How wide is the opening the stream goes through?'

'We don't know.'

'Okay, we will get one of our men in a wet suit and diving gear to try and inspect the opening.'

'Archie, are you okay to go in on your own?'

'Yes, boss, so long as I have a line attached.'

A few moments later, Archie took to the water. He found it challenging to stand as the water rushing by was forcing him along. Once he arrived at the slot in the rock, he dived down with his waterproof torch.

After a few moments, he was back, standing on the bed of the stream. He removed his mask and mouthpiece.

'There is no chance of a diver getting through the opening. It's only a little over a foot deep, about four feet wide.'

'The opening in the rock is the only escape for this water cascading down the depth here, which has increased due to the volume of water exceeding the capacity of the opening to take all the water. There has to be a lagoon or underground lake or river on the other side. It is impossible to see, Sir.'

'Okay, thanks, Archie. You had better come out.'

His diving partners on the bank hauled Archie back onto the bank.

'Any suggestions, Archie?'

'Yes, it must be pitch black beyond the torrent and the slot. Why don't we send two torches down the torrent so Frank will be able to see where he is, assuming he is able to stand and get the torches?'

'Okay, let's do that.' The chief fire officer instructed two of his men to throw two lit waterproof torches into the torrent. Everyone watched them float down towards the slot and then disappear.

'Is Frank about the same size as you, John?' enquired the diver.

'Yes, I suppose so. A little shorter, and quite skinny.'

'In that case, he must be the other side of the slot. The pressure of water is so fierce it would have pushed him through to the other side.'

'How can we make the slot bigger, Archie?'

'Well, you would first need a mining engineer to blow the slot open with explosives.'

'That sounds a bit extreme. It could bring the whole roof down, and we would never be able to gain access.'

'Yes, I understand, boss, but if they could blow a couple of feet from the top of the slot, we could gain access. First, it would be a good idea if we could rig up a communications link with the inside of the cave. If Frank is not badly hurt, he could then speak to us. We could also make sure he is not close to the slot if we blow it.'

'Sounds like a plan. We would also know that he was still alive.'

'Okay, Archie. Have we any kit with us to do that?'

'We have,' said the chief.

Another hour went by as the arrangements were made to send a microphone/speaker through the slot in the hope Frank would see the equipment and hear the message.

CHAPTER 5

THE FACE IN THE LAGOON

F rank was soaking wet from his head to his feet. His head was sore where he had hurt it on the rock as the torrent forced him through the slot in the stone. The restriction in the rock with water pushing through the slot made even more noise, and the rate at which the water was flowing increased significantly. Blood was coming down his face. He could tell it was blood as it was sticky and wet.

As he'd exited the slot, the torrent of water had pushed him forward. Coughing and spluttering, not having been prepared to dive, he fell, sliding down a slope which he thought was a waterfall. Then he felt solid ground under his feet. He was able to stand, but he was suffering from a racing heart; it felt like someone was hammering quickly on his chest. He couldn't stop coughing, and he started to cry. His unexpected immersion caused him to shake uncontrollably due to the cold water and fright. He wasn't sure if this was a lagoon or a bottomless lake. He felt carefully with his feet in case there was a very deep area. The water level dropped as he moved to his left with the torrent behind him. He kept going until he was on land. It was muddy and slippy, but he was out of the water.

'Phew,' he said to himself. 'Where am I? I can't see.'

John, his mum, and his own mum would be very frightened. Frank knew he'd never be able to tell them what it was like down here as he couldn't see anything.

No sooner had the thought passed through his mind than he saw two lit torches floating in the torrent, down the slide from the gap in the rock into the lake. The lenses were uppermost, so the cave ceiling was now lit. Frank thought the water was just like the log flume at Alton Towers, which they had visited earlier in the holidays.

Frank waded back into the lake to retrieve the torches. He was delighted to see where he was and would have skipped for joy, but he couldn't as he was up to his waist in water. Wading back to the shore as far as he could go onto drier mud, he was amazed at the size of the cavern that appeared to him.

The light from one torch was sufficient to light up the whole cave. Frank turned the other torch off to save the batteries. He could see the slot in the rockface with water cascading through it. 'My access point,' Frank said to himself.

On the other side of the 'lagoon', he could see two different openings. One was where the water was feeding into, and the other was a cave-like opening and relatively dry. The question was, where would that passageway lead?

He was unsure how long he would be in the cavern. Swinging the arc of the light gently around from the waterfall below the slit in the rock through which he had come he saw what he thought was an air tank danging in the waterfall. He didn't realise it was communications equipment, but it had stuck in the waterfall, and he certainly was not going to climb up to investigate the equipment. He then gently lit up the walls at the back of the lagoon. Eventually, he found two more openings in the rock walls. One was the route taken by the water from the lagoon flowing out of the cavern, the other at the back of the beach was just a black opening and a pathway. Frank couldn't see where that might go.

'I wonder where that goes?' he scratched his head to assist with his thought process. As he did so, he moved the scab that had formed on the top of his head and blood started to trickle again down the side of his face. He realised that the lagoon was very still by the beach. He could look at the surface, using it as a mirror at the edge near the beach. With the aid of the torch, he was able to see his face. He was right – blood was trickling down his face. He knew it would dry up in a moment. He moved his position to get a better look at the wound.

Frank was suddenly frightened to his boots! As he looked at his face in the mirror-flat water, he saw another face alongside his, reflected in the lagoon.

Frank's heart stopped. He jumped back in fright. He was sure this was a dream. It couldn't be a real person.

He then saw the owner of the other head standing right by him. He hadn't heard him come. The rushing of the torrent through the gap masked the sound of Frank's new companion.

'Hello, what's your name?' came a deep, thundering voice. The man stood at Frank's side, although slightly further away now since Frank had jumped in fright.

Frank shined his torch at the tall man, who had long black hair and a long white beard. His face had a dirty yet bronze appearance. He was tall. Much taller than Frank. He was probably twice as high and more. He wore a dark blue shirt which Frank realised needed washing. His trousers were jeans, blue but as dirty as his shirt. He wore large leather boots with thick soles. He looked like a giant to Frank.

'Oh – I – am – Frank...' he said in a trembling voice. He was very scared of the man. I am not supposed to be here, Sir. I fell into the river. I was washed through the slit in the rock that the water was pouring through. That's when I banged my head.'

Frank was convinced this man was the wizard mentioned in the story Miss Tinker had read to the class before the end of term. He certainly *looked* like the wizard Miss Tinker had talked about. The wizard who had forty knights lying low, waiting for an attack. The wizard who had bought the white mare from the farmer, who had failed to sell the horse at the Macclesfield market. The wizard who had explained he had forty knights but only thirty-nine horses. This new mare meant all forty knights would now have a horse.

'You must be the wizard in the story? Where do you keep the knights and their horses, Sir?'

'No, no.' The man laughed a deep, throaty laugh. 'You shouldn't believe everything you are told. That was a fairy story, I suspect. So what is your name, young sir?'

The laugh frightened Frank. He was expecting the wizard to say something like 'Ho ho'. But he didn't.

'Oh, well, I just thought that's who you might be, Sir. I'm Frank. Who are you, Sir?'

'I live in the mine with my wife and my two children. It was the only place we could find to sleep when we first came to the area. I was an out-of-work farm worker. We had no money, so we came to live here. Well, young Frank, you have had a bad time and are soaking wet. Come with me, and we shall see what we can do for you.'

Sensing Frank's anxiety, the man spoke again to Frank.

'Please don't be frightened. I have two children of my own.'

Frank was not sure if he should go. Where might they go, and who was he to meet?

He couldn't help but recall the beginning of *The Weidstone of Brazingaman*, which Miss Timker had read to them over the last month of the summer term. Initially, the two children staying with Gowther at his farmhouse were told to be careful when walking on Alderley Edge. The story told of The Edge, a prominent escarpment of black rock six hundred feet high and three miles long.

'You are not by chance called Gowther?' asked Frank.

'No, lad, where did you get that name from?'

'Well, sir, my school teacher read us this story before we broke up for the summer holidays. It had a character called Gowther. You are not him by chance or even the wizard that bought the white horse from the farmer for pockets full of jewels?'

'No, lad. I am not. I wish I were. Why did the wizard buy the white horse?'

'The wizard had forty knights all waiting to defend him, but he had only thirty-nine horses. That's why he bought the white mare from the farmer.'

'No, I regret I have very little. I am destitute, and so are my wife, daughter and son.'

'So where do you come from, Mr ... err?'

'Now, young Frank, you are full of questions. The question is, what are we going to do with you? Now you have come through the *letterbox*. That's what we call the slit in the stone wall that lets the torrent through. Normally, there is only a trickle of water in the little stream. The heavy rain all week has meant the stream has turned into a foaming torrent.'

'That's interesting, Sir. I have never been through a *letterbox* – until just now, that is.'

'Come with me, Frank, we need to walk this way. It's quite a long walk. It's good you have a torch. I have got used to the dark and can remember the way even if I can't see it. But now I can see it. The stone is riven with different colour seams of copper and cobalt. Very interesting, don't you think so, Frank?'

'You have not told me your name. What is it, please, Sir?'

'You have excellent manners, Frank, so I will tell you my name. It's Eric, Eric Frederick Wright, to give my full name.'

'And are you sure you are not the wizard, Sir?'

'No, no, I'm not a wizard.' He chuckled to himself. 'I live down here. When I arrived here two years ago, my family and I couldn't find anywhere to live. We had to leave the cottage we were living in on a farm on the Mottram Estate. I lost my job as the farmer was hard-up. I had heard of the old mine and caves years ago when we lived on the Mottram Hall estate. I was part of the Wright family.

When I was a small boy, my father fell out with the son of the then-owner of the estate. He was not a real Wright but had changed his name to Wright when he married the heiress to the estate. He apparently was not a nice man. He pressed all the farmers and the mine workers for more rent and a share of the proceeds from the mine. My father lost his job as the farmer could no longer afford to pay him. So we came here as I recalled the area, and my heritage is here. If I had been a wizard, I could have cast a spell on the men who wanted to put me in a small lodging with my family in a different location far away. Now, enough of this. I will take you to my wife, and she can dry you and your clothes. I will show you a way out that will be drier than how you came in. How is the bump on your head?'

'It's okay, thank you, Sir.'

Eric held Frank's hand and they walked along tunnels and through caverns. At one point, train tracks for a narrow gauge railway became evident on the floor.

'Yes, I think the last miners here before us set down these tracks to help get the waste spoil out of the tunnel. I don't think there were any railway engines. They may have used ponies to move the trucks, or they may have been pushed by hand.'

'Would that be how the sand was tipped in the area outside? That area is where my friend John and I cycle. We call it the Rec.'

'Yes, that is quite possible, Frank. I think that is why they made another opening.'

'It is a long way, Eric. Are we nearly there?'

'About halfway.'

As the conversation between Eric – or Fred as he said he preferred to be called – continued, Frank began recalling what had happened to him. He realised his mum and dad must be really anxious.

He was feeling very uncomfortable in his wet clothes and was becoming distraught. His thoughts were focused on John and his mum and dad, who would have no idea where he was or if he were still alive. Would Miss Tinker be cross because he would surely miss at least a day of school? The more Frank thought of the consequences, the less keen he was to get home.

'That is interesting, Eric. When we last cycled around after a great deal of rain, we found a skull sticking out of the sand.'

'Wow, that was quite a find, Frank. What did you do then?'

'I told my mum, and she rang the police, who came to look at it.'

'What happened then, Frank?'

'A lady scientist came who had a special name which I can't remember. She took it away in a box she had brought for the purpose. She rummaged around where the skull had been but found nothing else. She then went away in her car.'

'Were you boys watching?'

'Well, we saw her from the other side of the road. It was too far away to see what she was doing. She took all the police tape away. Before she left, she tried to open the door to the mine. She broke the hasp holding the padlock. The screws pulled out of the door as the wood was rotten. She tried to open the door, but the sand jammed it. She left, leaving the broken door.'

'So what did you do then?' enquired Eric.

'I went home to get my spade. It's the one we take on holiday to the beach. John and I dug and dug until we could open the door wide enough to let us squeeze through. We both went through but it was so dark I came back out to get the lamp off the front of my bike. We could see what we were doing then. I tripped and fell in the torrent as I arrived at a bend. The stream was in full spate and pulled me in. I tried to fling my light to John but it went the wrong way and became lodged on a stone shelf. That is when I got washed through the gap in the stone, as you call it, the *letterbox*, banging my head in the process. It was like a log flume at Alton Towers, where we went earlier in the holidays.'

CHAPTER 6

THE FAMILY IN THE CAVERN

A long way down the unknown muddy track through several more tunnels interspersed with caverns of various sizes. The two travelled slowly but easily as the torch now lit the floor. When Frank shot through the *letterbox*, he'd found nothing as big as the cavern they were in now. Down another tunnel, they suddenly arrived in a dry, warm cave. A fire was lit in the centre. It was a circular space, dry and very comfortable, thought Frank, as caverns go!

A lady and two children approached him.

'This is my home, Frank. This lady is my wife. Her name is Emelda, and these are our children. Karen and Edward.'

'Hello, my name is Frank. I got washed down here when I fell into the torrent. I came through the *letterbox*, as you call it.'

'Hello, Frank,' the family replied. The children were keen to discover all they could about him.

'Before we do all that, let me dry your clothes, Frank. You will catch a cold if you stay in those wet things. You can wear some of Edward's clothes for the time being,' said Emelda.

'That is very kind.'

'Come with me to this ingle where Edward sleeps. It's his bedroom. Oh, bless you, Frank. You have a nasty cut and bruise on the top of your head. I will put some antiseptic cream on that.'

'You are very well equipped down here. How do you manage?'

'Oh, we have a much drier way of getting here than the way you chose. We go shopping in Alderley. Also, we have an arrangement with the postman that if he has mail for us, he should leave it in a split in a tree near the road.'

'Oh, I see. So you must have a surname?'

'It's Wright.'

'Oh yes, of course. Eric, er, Fred told me on our way here. So you have an address?'

'Yes, Frank, it's The Beech Tree, The Wizard, Alderley Edge.'

'So it's as if you were living in a house but not a house. Do you live in the mine or cave?'

'We call it a cave, but it is really a mine.'

'Wow, it must be fun living here?'

'That is a way of putting it but ideally, I would prefer to live in a house. Are you hungry, Frank?' enquired Emelda.

'Yes, I have lost track of time. What day is it?'

'Well, Frank, it's two o'clock on Monday afternoon, September 10th.'

'I am not surprised I am hungry.'

'How about a glass of milk and a cheese sandwich?'

'Ooh! Yes, please, Mrs Wright.'

'Just call me Emelda, Frank. You are most welcome. We never get visitors.'

'I don't want to appear ungrateful but I think I should be going home when my clothes are dry.'

'I fully understand, lad. Where is home?'

'I live with my parents in Mottram St Andrew. My house is opposite the recreation ground on Oak Road where my friend John and I live.'

'Oh. That's quite a long way from here, Frank. Do you know your way home from the Wizard Inn?'

'Yes, it's mainly through the wood on The Edge and then down to the Mottram Road, past the old quarry, then past the entrance gate to Clock House Farm, then past the smithy up to the village store, then along Oak Road to home.'

'Well, as soon as you have finished your sandwiches and glass of milk, put your dry clothes back on.' They had been drying from the fire in the centre of the cave.

'I will take you to Mottram Road, just in case your wizard is wandering around. From there, you will be able to make it home. It would be good to take your torches with you as it might be near sunset when you reach Oak Road.'

Frank was intrigued to find the way out of Eric's cave by a short, twisty tunnel which emerged inside a small stone building with a door in the wood just opposite the Wizard Inn. Frank held onto Eric's hand as they crossed the busy road that ran from Alderley to Macclesfield. The air was heavy.

'It could rain any time soon. Will you be alright walking home should the rain come, Frank?' enquired Eric.

'Yes, I am used to the rain and getting wet.'

'Oh yes, I forgot about that.'

The two progressed slowly through the forest along well-trodden paths. There were no other people in the forest. Not even a dog walker. The trees were heavy with fully mature leaves, and oak and horse chesnut fruits were already falling to the ground. Frank spotted a few conkers. He wished he could stop and collect them but felt he should continue the walk undisturbed. The light was dim in the forest, although there were shafts of sunlight in the few clearings they passed. Clouds were few, but the ones Frank could see were dark and heavy.

Eventually, the forest path began to slope downwards which would have taken them toward Alderley, the wrong way to get to Mottram St Andrew.

'Frank, we must go off the path here and down the slope to Mottram Road. Once we get there, can you find your way home?'

'I can, thank you, Eric. I pass the quarry after the narrow part of the road. I walk along the path behind the wide grass verge until I get to the smithy once I have passed the gate that leads to Clock House Farm. After that, I climb the gentle hill to the crossroads near the shop and post office. I will be home in no time then. Thank you for showing me through the forest, Eric.'

'It has been a pleasure meeting you, Frank. Go carefully and come back to see us, won't you?'

'Yes, I will. I shall bring my friend John if I may?'

'He'd be most welcome.'

Finding the pavement on Mottram Road, Frank waved goodbye to Eric and jogged along Mottram Road to get home.

It was late afternoon when Frank passed John's house. He wondered how he was but he had to get home. Three houses along, he ran up the drive and burst into the kitchen through the back door.

Frank flung himself towards his startled mother, who burst into tears the moment she saw him. She hugged him until he asked her to stop as he could hardly breathe.

'Oh, Frank darling, where have you been and how have you got back to us? I must stop the caving people and tell the police and fire brigade.'

'Gosh, Mum, you haven't got all those people involved?'

'Yes, darling. We didn't know if you had survived, and no one knew how you might get out if you *had*. There was no telling when the torrent would abate.'

'Have you seen John?'

'No darling, he's been gated. His parents were worried he might get into trouble. No one else can enter the mine now that the council has bricked up the entrance.'

'Any news about the skull?'

'No, darling, it's you we have been concerned about.'

'Can we still ride bikes around the Rec?'

'Yes, I don't see why not. I must ring Dad. He has been worried sick that you might have drowned.'

'Well, I didn't. I'm fine, but the torches through the *letterbox* were fantastic and saved my life.'

'What do you mean, *letterbox*?'

'That is what the locals call the slot the torrent forced its way through and pulled me through with it. I got a bang on my head for my mistake, but otherwise, I am fine, Mum, honestly.'

'I must phone these people so they don't waste their time.'

'As you are going to be on the phone, can I go and see John?'

'Yes, by all means.'

Frank found his bike and cycled to The Corner House, John's home. He rang the bell. John came to the door with a long face and then screamed for joy at the sight of his great friend.

'Whatever's the matter, John?' his mother called out.

'Frank is at the front door with his bike. Can we go to the Rec for a cycle?'

Audrey ran to the door. 'Frank, how wonderful to see you! How on earth did you escape?'

'It's a long story, Mrs England, but I found a way out thanks to the torches. Can John come with me to the Rec for a cycle? We can't get lost this time. I understand the council has bricked up the entrance.'

'Yes, okay, you two. Don't get into any trouble.'

43

R. A. JORDAN

The two boys cycled to the Rec.

'Tell me all about it, Frank. My parents thought you must just have drowned.'

'No, I was washed through a narrow gap in the rock. I banged my head. It was very, very frightening. The water was flowing really fast. Luckily, I made it through the gap, which the locals call the *letterbox*. I was in a shallow lagoon. I scrambled to the side of the lagoon. It was so dark I couldn't see where I was going, so I had to move by touch.'

'Blimey, Frank. That sounds very frightening.'

'It was. My lifeline was when you sent two torches through the *letterbox*.'

'I didn't send them, Frank. It was the firemen.'

'Oh, I need to take them back to the fire station. They were excellent and saved my life. I had to wade out into a shallow lagoon to pick them up. They sent them down with the lights on. They made everything so much easier.'

'What did you find underground, Frank?'

'When I recovered my senses, I started to look around. The torches were great and allowed me to look at areas of rock that had been mined long ago. There were copper streaks, all green now with verdigris. Quite often, a layer of cobalt would lie beneath the copper. This looked like coal. I need to discover how it was used to get the colour blue out of the rock.'

'We should try and discover that, Frank.'

'Yes. When I had the torch and looked about, I realised that the lake in the cavern was still and smooth in places. I needed a mirror to look at my head. It's strange how still the water was in areas despite the torrent forcing its way through the *letterbox*. I looked at my reflection in the lake with the aid of the torch. I could see the blood had dried on my face. Then I nearly had a fit.'

'Why, what happened, Frank?'

'I saw another face peering into the water.'

'My God. Who was it?'

'To begin with, I screamed. I was terrified. It, or he, was a giant of a man. He was very tall when he stood up. He had black hair and a grey beard. He wore a blue shirt and brown trousers, which were very dirty. I was convinced he was a wizard. *Don't be frightened, little man*, he said in a much softer voice than I had expected. *Who are you?* he asked. I told him my name and asked him if he was a wizard. But, no, he said he wasn't a wizard but he'd made his home here.'

'How did he know you were in the cavern?'

'He said he heard a great deal of noise and sirens blazing. There was no issue at his end of the mine, so it had to be here. That is how I managed to escape. Eric, that's the wizard's name, took me all the way out of the mine.'

'You said he *wasn't* a wizard.'

'I know. He *said* he wasn't a wizard, but I don't know how he came down there and found me.'

'You said he heard the sirens.'

'I know, but thinking about it whilst I was walking home, his living area was miles away from where I was. He couldn't possibly have heard the sirens on Oak Road, Mottram St Andrew, from where he was.'

'So Eric lives in the mine?'

'Yes, John. His wife and two children live there as well.'

'Do they go to school, Frank?'

'I don't know, but maybe they could come to our school?'

'I had a police officer come to our house last night. He started to question me about access to the mine and how we were able to get in. I told him that we had always wanted to look inside. There was a door with a strong padlock that provided access to the mine. I told him we had sat down on a rock near the entrance to the mine when I saw the padlock and hasp had been broken away from the door, allowing access. The policeman asked if I knew who had broken the lock. Well, I said I had no idea. In fact, I think it was the police scientist in the red Mini who pulled on the door, breaking the lock due to the rotten timber on the door but I didn't tell the police that.'

'Good, John. She was a nice lady and allowed us to help her. Anyway, I'd like to go back to see Eric and say thanks again. I'll ask Dad to have a word with Miss Tinker about his children coming to our school.'

CHAPTER 7

A VISIT TO THE WRIGHTS

John and Frank received permission from their parents to visit Eric to say thank you for saving Frank's life. They were also hoping Eric and his wife would agree to send their children to their school. The two boys set off towards Alderley Edge the following morning.

'We must park our bikes at the bottom of the forest just off Mottram Road. We can hide them so they wouldn't be seen by anyone wanting to steal them,' said Frank. 'I don't have a bike lock.'

'I do,' announced John. 'We can lock them together with my chain and padlock. If we leave them behind a bush, no one will see them; if they do, they will not be able to take them away.'

The two boys arrived at the foot of the forest off Mottram Road. It only took a quarter of an hour from home. They found a rhododendron bush a few yards off the road.

'That will be an ideal spot to hide the bikes, Frank.'

John removed the chain and lock from his saddle bag. The two boys manoeuvred their bikes to the bush they had selected. They put one next to a large branch at the bottom of the bush. The other bike was the other way around, so the back wheel of one bike was adjacent to the front wheel of the other. The chain went through the wheels of the bikes nearest to the thickest branch and passed around the branch. Once done, the ends of the chain were brought together and padlocked tight.

'That's great, John. Follow me up the hill.'

The two boys scrambled up the steep hill through the forest until they made the path to the Wizard Inn. Puffing and panting, they were glad when the path appeared.

'We are not far from the wizard, Frank. Where do we find the entrance?'

'Oh, you won't see it. We have to find it on the opposite side of the main road.'

Frank took the lead once they had their breath back.

'I think it's around here, John.'

The two boys were scrambling around in the undergrowth of the forest. There was no obvious opening to be found.

'Where is the opening, Frank?'

As John posed the question, he and Frank both saw the small white-washed building.

'John, we need to go in here!' shouted Frank.

'I'm here!' John shouted as his head appeared just above the grass.

Frank soon joined his friend. He recognised the place now, but it was well hidden in the undergrowth.

'Wow, Frank, this is quite a place,' said John as the two boys made their way through a door and along a tunnel. The daylight flooded in from the door that John had inadvertently left open.

'Hello? Hello? It's Frank,' Frank shouted as they walked further along the tunnel.

There was no reply. The two boys continued as far as they might before running out of natural light. A twinkling light met them as they rounded a corner in the tunnel. As they proceeded, the light in the tunnel increased.

'Hello! Hello. It's Frank.'

Back came the response, 'Frank, what are you doing here?'

'Oh, Eric. I am sorry, but I didn't mean to startle you. This is my good friend, John. He was keen to see where I had been. I hope you don't mind?'

'No, but this is our house. Hardly anyone knows we are here, and as far as I know, you are the only ones to have ever found the entrance.'

'We wondered if Karen and Edward were around. Would they like to come and play?'

'Play. Play at what?'

'Well, we could play hide and seek in the forest or collect conkers.'

'They are not used to playing with other children.'

'Can we ask them if they want to come out with us?'

'No. What happens in my house is up to me. They don't make decisions.'

'Can I ask, Eric, why is this room not full of smoke? There is a large fire in the centre, yet no flue exists. Normally, that fire would have filled the area with smoke.'

'You are a bright spark, John, and that's the truth.'

'Sorry, Sir, I didn't mean to be rude. I am just curious as it should be choking in here with smoke.'

'I will give you this, John: you are a bright lad and just as polite as Frank. So if you don't go and play, what would you be doing otherwise?'

'Next week, Sir, we are back at school. Frank and I wondered if Karen and Edward would like to attend our school?'

'Now, why would they want to do that?'

'Well, Sir, we learn stuff, play games and meet our friends.'

'Who would pay for that?'

'As far as I understand, Sir, it is free.'

'I never heard of such a thing. It might be better than Emelda and me trying to teach them. That's a fact.'

At that moment, the two Wright children ran into the cavern.

'Hello, you two. This is Frank, who you know, and John who is his friend. They came to ask if you would like to go and play outside, but I told them it was not your choice.'

As the two Wright children started to plead with their father, Emelda came down the tunnel. She had been shopping and had a basket full of food items. She had heard most of the conversation about playing.

'We need to have a chat about that, boys. Why don't you come tomorrow around three thirty and we can give you a decision.'

'John, before you go, your question about our fire. The answer is that there is a flue, so the room is not full of smoke. How did you know that was required?'

'I learned all about fires at school, Sir,' answered John.

'So they teach you useful stuff at this school of yours?'

'They do, Sir.'

'I am convinced your children would enjoy it and learn a great deal as well.'

'I will discuss this with my wife, John. Can you pop back in a couple of days and we'll tell you our decision?'

'Yes, Sir, we can do that.'

CHAPTER 8

COLD CASE

'Mrs England?'

'Yes, whose calling?'

'I am Judy from the Police Forensic Department.'

'I guess you are phoning about the skull?' Audrey laughed to herself. 'Sorry, Judy, I was laughing at myself. I never thought I would ever utter those words.'

Judy laughed. 'I understand. It's a phrase I utter from time to time! I just wanted to advise you of the progress of the examination of the skull.'

'Has the news got through to you that Frank, the boy who was washed down the stream, is fine and back home?'

'That is wonderful. How did he manage to get out?'

'Apparently, a family living in the big cavern opposite the Wizard Inn looked after him and showed him how to escape from the mine.'

'I bet everyone is so happy.'

'They are indeed. Please tell me what you have discovered?'

'We think the skull is pretty old. Possibly nineteenth century. We can see that it was removed from the body by a sharp blow to the neck, severing the skull from the torso. It may be associated with a crime that occurred between the end of mining operations and now.'

'That is very interesting. Will you be making further enquiries?'

'Yes. There will be a cold case review undertaken.'

'Okay, I would appreciate it if you could tell me what turns up.'

Judy, the police forensic scientist, explained that she was fairly sure the skull belonged to a male, aged between 30 and 40 years old.

'I think as the skull is so old, it is unlikely *we* will do the cold case review. We will pass the details and the skull to the Manchester University Archaeology Department. They may come up with something.'

'Thanks for calling. Maybe we shall hear something in the future. Thank you for letting us know.'

CHAPTER 9

PERSUADING ERIC

Returning in September 1979 for their last year school in Mottram St Andrew, John and Frank couldn't wait for the opportunity to tell their teacher about their exploits during the holidays. It was a tradition that after the long summer holidays, the children were instructed to write in their English exercise book a paragraph or two about their holidays and any exciting or unusual activities they had enjoyed.

'Frank, you write about your trip to the mine. I will do the run-up and afterwards,' whispered John who sat behind Frank.

'Okay,' came the response.

John wrote:

I live in a house on Oak Road, opposite the recreation area or Rec as we call it. Frank and I ride our bikes there. In the last two weeks, we were doing that as often as we could. The rain had stopped us for a few days. One day, after a particularly heavy rainstorm, we found what turned out to be a human skull.

My mother called the police. A forensic officer, Judy, from the police, excavated the skull and took it away for analysis. Before she left the site, she tried to get through the door to the mine in case there were any clues there in relation to the skull. In attempting to gain access, she broke the fittings holding the lock on the old door. She still couldn't get through because sand was blocking the door. Before she left, all the police tape around the site was removed and taken away.

Once the police had gone, Frank and I decided it was the ideal opportunity to have a look into the mine. I shovelled some sand away so we could open the door sufficiently wide for us to get in.

Frank will complete the adventure.

'John, thank you,' said his teacher when she'd read it. 'That sounds like a real adventure. Did you find anything of interest in the mine?'

'Yes, Miss, but you need to read Franks's part in the adventure, which is far more exciting.'

I entered the mine with John. I took the light from my bike, so I led the way. It was very spooky. The ground was wet and slippery. There is an underground river running alongside the path. Due to the recent heavy rain, the river was running very quickly. The roof of the mine was covered in bats, asleep and hanging upside down.

I had to go around a bend in the path, but I slipped, losing my light, which landed on a ledge on the opposite bank of the river. I was in the water. Before I knew what was happening, I was washed through a slot in the rock. I was underwater, yet I was washed through this narrow gap, hitting my head on the rock as I did so. I emerged in a sort of lagoon, shaken and very wet. I didn't think I would survive.

Eventually, two waterproof torches with lights on were washed through the slit in the rock. I didn't know then that these were pushed through by the emergency services.

I had to walk through a shallow lagoon to retrieve the torches; they made everything so much easier. I made my way back to the sandy beach at the edge of the lagoon. The water was very calm there, and I could see my reflection in the still water. Bending down to inspect the bang on my head, I suddenly realised there was another face looking into the water alongside my own. I was terrified. I jumped back and shouted, 'Who are you?' I thought it was the wizard.

The man was not a wizard, although with his long beard he looked like one. We made friends, and he escorted me to the dry pathway out of the mine.

'There is quite a lot more to tell, Miss Tinker, but that will do for now, I hope.'

'My word, you two. What an adventure, and on our doorstep as well! I don't think anyone will be able to beat that. I guess the door which had been locked was there for a purpose?'

'Yes, Miss. The council have bricked up that entrance now. We have some questions to ask you, but perhaps we should wait until class is over.'

'Alright, John and Frank. When the break bell goes, you two stay behind, and I will try to answer your questions.'

As arranged, the boys stayed in class when the bell rang. Once all the other children had departed, the two boys explained Frank's encounter with Eric and his two children who would now be very interested in coming to school.

Miss Tinker said she would discuss the proposition with the head and let them know later that day.

Before John and Frank went home, Miss Tinker said they could suggest to the parents of the two children that they would be most welcome to spend a week at school to see if they liked it here.

If the two children enjoyed the school, arrangements could be made to allow them to stay on as permanent pupils.

'We have a job to do now, Frank,' said John.

The two boys raced home, and each gave the news to their parents about the invitation for Karen and Edward Wright to come to school for a trial week. They needed to go and see Eric and his wife to see if they would agree to let the two children come. John persuaded his mother to collect them on Mottram Road and taxi them to school with John for a week.

John and Frank received parental permission to cycle to Mottram Road and then scrambled up through the woodland, eventually getting to the footpath that would lead them to the Wizard Inn.

On arriving at the little stone building, the door was open, so the two boys went in. They called out several times but received no response.

After the third attempt to attract someone's attention, they walked down the twisting path.

They soon came to the threshold of the Wrights's living quarters.

'Hello?' said John loudly.

'What are you two doing here? enquired Mr Wright in a gruff voice.

'You said it would be okay for us to come back and see you. So here we are.'

'Mr Wright, sorry, Eric, our teacher has asked us to say that Karen and Edward would be most welcome to come to school if they would like to.'

'Why would they want to come to your school? My wife and I can teach them all they need to know.'

'They would meet other children and make friends, learn new things, play games. That sort of thing. I love school; it's great.'

At that moment, Mrs Wright down the twisting path from the little stone building. She was laden with more shopping.

'Hello boys, to what do we owe this visit?'

'They have come to ask if the children would like to go to their school for a week. I can't afford that; where would we get the extra money from?'

Before Mrs Wright replied, the boys said in unison, 'It's free.'

'That can't be right. You have to pay to go to school.'

'No, Sir, I promise you the school won't charge.'

'Alright, but how would they get there? It's a good mile and a half to two miles, and you have to go through the woods.'

'My mum said she would collect them for the first week and bring them back at the end of the day. If they want to stay on, there is a bus that goes down Mottram Road to the school. It is a bus especially for school children.'

Karen and Edward heard the whole conversation from their little caves off the main cavern.

'Oh, let us go, Daddy, just to try anyway!' the two children implored their father.

'What do you think, Emelda?'

'I think it would do them both good. They need to have contact with others. It will be the making of them.'

After some further consideration, Eric said, 'Okay, I am happy for them to try it for a week. We will need to find a way of getting them there if they want stay on. We will need to look into this bus.'

All four children jumped for joy and ran around in circles, shouting.

'My mum said she would collect Karen and Edward on Mottram Road at half past eight on Monday morning and for the rest of the week.'

'That is very kind of her, John. What about getting back?'

'School finishes at three fifteen in the afternoon. I am sure Mum will bring them back. If there is any change to that, Frank or I will come back and tell you.'

CHAPTER 10

FEBRUARY 2000

The head of the forensic anthropology department at the University of Manchester was alerted to the arrival of the 'Mottram St Andrew skull', as it was now referred to. Peter Oldroyd, head of the department, was keen to look at it. It was 2000 and the department now had all sorts of equipment which would allow Peter to find out exactly how old the skull was and confirm the sex. Peter, a senior lecturer at Manchester University, had been in the post for ten years. An amiable man and an expert where forensics were concerned. To look at Peter, you would not give him any credit for the work he did. His was very casual in his attire. He wore an open-necked checked cotton shirt in the autumn and winter, a period when he would generally wear a pair of dark blue corduroy trousers with a fisherman's blue sweater. To add to the ensemble, he wore a Manchester University scarf, the main item of clothing he used to keep warm. If the weather, as it can be in Manchester, were raining, he would wear his sailing anorak. He liked to wear his Hush Puppies and coloured socks. Clearly, his academic expertise had not transferred to his wardrobe.

After a few weeks of undertaking tests on the skull, including modern DNA tests, he had concluded without doubt that the skull belonged to a male who would have been sixty years old at time of death. He was a local person: Peter had identified his locus as being in the North West of England.

Why he had been decapitated was the one question his tests could not reveal. They did reveal, due to residue still in the skull for over a hundred years, a minute particle of iron.

'Tell me, Bursar, why has it taken so long for this skull to be handed over to us?'

'As I understand it, the police put it into a store at Macclesfield Police Station once the forensic officer had indicated it was very old. There was insufficient staff to look at the skull and carry out more tests. As time went by, the skull was forgotten. Some spring cleaning recently turned it up again, and it was decided to hand it over to us.'

'Well, all we have done is ask more questions than provide answers.'

*

John England, having served time as a lawyer in the Army, had left early due to an injury caused by a bomb when serving in Croatia after the Balkans War. He had gone on holiday for a year to Greece, Spain, Morocco and eventually back to the UK.

He chose to seek employment in Chester, as it was the closest city to his parents, George and Audrey, who were now retired and living in Tarporley. He joined a firm in Chester called Bennetts as a junior partner. He was involved mainly in conveyancing and bought and sold houses and flats during a busy period of house sales on behalf of his clients.

John bought himself a beautiful flat just on the Chester inner ring road. It had magnificent views over the Roodee Race Course. He knew of it by its reputation as being the oldest horse racing track in the world. This new flat enabled him to walk to work. He had hoped to spend some time after Christmas and the millennium celebrations sorting out his flat and acquiring some more furniture. It transpired that events interfered with his plans.

John arrived at his parents' house just after eleven o'clock on Sunday. He had plenty of time to help his father with any jobs that needed two people or heavy lifting. After that exercise, he would enjoy Sunday lunch with his parents.

Sitting at the dinner table while his father carved the beef, as requested, he opened a bottle of claret. Living in Chester, he was close to his ageing parents should they need help. It was a very convenient arrangement. He got a roast dinner from time to time as compensation for log splitting in the winter and grass cutting in the summer.

'Look, Dad, I will happily pay for a gardener for you to do the heavy lifting in the garden. That will allow me to use my weekends as I wish, and you can deal with your vegetable garden and flower boarders.'

'That is more than appreciated, John. I will try and find a gardener.'

'When you do, let me know the cost, and I will reimburse you.'

'No, you will do no such thing. It's a good idea, but it should be at my cost!'

'Okay, Dad, that's fine by me. I hope you don't mind me suggesting this, but I am getting busier and busier at work. The only time I can see daylight is at the weekends.'

'I fully understand, son. I am delighted the business is doing well, and you are flourishing.'

*

On January 4th, John was in the office with one other staff member, Donna, the receptionist, who looked after the phone calls. She allowed John to get on with a mass of paperwork that had been left over from 1999, last year.

John was interrupted in the middle of the morning. It was the Cheshire Police.

'Mr England, I am DI Shaw, cold case reviewer.'

'Oh. How can I help you?'

'I am reviewing a case from 1979, when you and a friend of yours,

Frank Brocklehurst, found a skull in a sand pit at the copper mine in Mottran St Andrew.'

'Yes, that was me, aged ten! That was twenty-one years ago."

'Yes, Sir, we have been able to submit the skull for DNA testing now that the procedure has become available to us. It has gone to Manchester University.'

'Are you going to tell me the name of the person to whom the skull belonged?'

'We have a name, Sir, but as one of the two people who discovered the item, and you are now a solicitor, we thought it was best to talk with you first.'

'I see. So, what's the name of the skull?'

'We have established it was a man called Wright, apparently a farm worker.'

'I recall the name in the area, but I am sorry, I don't think I will be able to help any further. Although I think a relative, possibly his brother or cousin, if he is still alive, lives or lived in Mottram Cottages on Priest Lane, Mottram St Andrew. He was a wheelwright on the Mottram Estate, if my memory serves me correctly. He lived with his sister. Neither were married.'

'Thank you, Sir. Have you any idea why the skull's owner was murdered and decapitated, and his body was never found, just his skull?'

'No, but I will consider it. Can you leave me a name and contact number so that when I have time to consider the issues, I can get back to you? It's Monday morning, and I am swamped just now.'

John wrote down the police inspector's contact details and both hung up, leaving John to ponder the contents of the call for a few days.

'I wonder what has happened to Frank Brocklehurst?' John thought to himself before being swamped with more calls.

He didn't give any further thought to the police call as he was keen to complete a mass of paperwork left over the Christmas and New Year period. It had to be finished. Eventually, the calls ceased – the receptionist had been asked not to put anyone else through to John's phone.

Until an interesting interruption: 'Mr England, I have a lady on the phone who says you know her sister. They have had a tragedy in their family. Her name is Sandra Wall; her sister is Sienna. She is distraught. Can I put her through?'

'Yes, okay. I will see what I can do for them. Please don't put through any other calls; I must finish this paperwork.'

'Hello, John England here. How can I help?'

'Yes, it's Sandra Wall. My sister Sienna tells me you have had dealings with her regarding a property owned by the church commissioners.'

'Oh yes, I recall. We managed to sort it out. What can I help you with now?'

'You may have heard the report on local radio and TV, but our father, Peter Wall, seems to have committed suicide on New Year's Day early in the morning.'

'How did this happen, Sandra?'

'It appears at the moment that he decapitated himself by using the farm Land Rover and a wire rope. It's all very gruesome. He has died leaving debts, property, insurance and a complicated agreement with his business partner. We need help. I am a solicitor specialising in corporate matters. I work in Liverpool. My father's estate could be complex. I don't want to have his details spread all over the office where I work. Would you be prepared to deal with it for us?'

John ended up travelling to Long Acre Farm in Tarporley, where the consensus was that Peter Wall had committed suicide in a most bizarre manner, which decapitated him.

Having returned to the office, John sat back in his chair, considering the chances of being advised of two beheadings. He had two to consider. One from ages ago, and the other from New Year's Day.

CHAPTER 11

SUNDAY ROAST

I t was the first Sunday of April 2020. John was back at his parents' house for lunch.

'You will never guess who phoned me recently?'

'No, we can't guess, John,' his father responded, sounding slightly perplexed as to how he would know who had phoned his son.

'It's going to test our joint memories, but the police are looking into old cases. They call it a cold case review. They told me they had obtained a DNA assessment of the skull from the forensic and anthropology department of Manchester University. Do you recall the one Frank and I had discovered at the Rec in Mottram St Andrew? With the information from the university, the police now have something to work on. They found a match on their database for someone called Wright, Fred Wright, a farm worker.'

'Good heavens, that is remarkable,' retorted John's father.

'What they can do now is very clever, Dad. However, the detailed analysis of the skull is a reasonably recent event, as they wouldn't have DNA for the deceased to match much before the 1990s. Watson and Cric's paper in *Nature* magazine was first published in 1953. Even so, the DNA matching of individuals took several decades to mature to the level it has reached today. They are improving the system all the time.'

'So what did the police want from you, John?'

'They just wanted to know if I knew anyone by this name.'

'And do you?'

'Yes, there was a tenant in the Mottram Cottages on Priest Lane. He used to be, they say, the wheelwright on the estate, and he was retired. He is most probably dead now.'

'Yes, I recall him. Didn't he live there with his sister?'

'Yes, that's correct, Dad. They say the dead man was a farm worker. I wonder why he met such a gruesome end? It is strange how things can repeat themselves. Not only did the police ring about the skull but I was instructed this week to act for the Wall family, who only live nearby here at Long Acre Farm. Mr Wall, it would seem, committed suicide on New Year's Day by decapitation.'

'Good heavens,' said Audrey, John's mother, who had overheard the conversation. 'I was in the butcher's yesterday and they were talking about the tragedy. I didn't put two and two together to link the event with Long Acre Farm.'

'So, can you think why anyone would want to kill Fred Wright? By all accounts, the analysis of the skull indicates he was beheaded. Do you think he was due to benefit from the Mottram Estate?'

'No, son. I doubt he had any money, so that couldn't be the reason behind the killing.'

'Can we have lunch first? This subject is not suitable for our Sunday roast. I waited in a queue to get this lovely piece of beef.'

'Of course, Mum. Sorry, it's my fault.'

*

'DC Cummings, this is John England. I believe you want to speak to me?'

'Mr England, I gather from the file I am looking at that you and your friend Frank Brocklehurst found a skull in a sand tip in Mottram St Andrew on September 8th 1979?'

'That's correct, DC Cummings. How can I help you now after so long?'

'Mr England, I am trying to discover a motive for the killing and I'm also trying to find the rest of the body.'

'Not sure I can help any more than I already have.'

'I would appreciate it if you thought you could give us some more information about the deceased. He was Fred Wright, a farmworker. We can't rationalise why a farmworker would have been killed. Among the reasons for murder is often financial gain in one form or another. We don't seem to be able to find anything which might have indicated he was a potential target.'

'Okay, I don't think I can help you. My mother and father are still alive and live in Tarporley now, but they used to live in Mottram St Andrew as I did. I will speak with them to see if they can recall any reason why he might have attracted a murderer.'

*

'Hi, Dad. I have had the police on the phone again, querying the cold case review of the 'Head in the Sand' murder, which goes back to Mottram St Andrew. They can't rationalise the murder by decapitation of a farm worker. They are convinced there is more to it.'

'I think they are correct, John. Leave it with me, and I will do some research.'

'Okay, thanks, Dad.'

Later in the week, John's father phoned him in the evening, knowing how busy he was during the day.

'Hi, son. I have some news for you on the potential reason for an unknown individual decapitating Fred Wright.'

'That's quick work, Dad. What have you uncovered?'

'Well, it was the internet that did the hard work. I have interpreted the information it has given me, which I think is most useful.'

'Okay, go ahead, let me know what you have, Dad.'

'I have traced the ownership of Mottram Hall back to 1750. William Wright built it for his son, Randle. Six generations of the family owned the Hall. All the transfers were bequeathed to the next generation. It seems that Randle died soon after the Hall was built. William Wright must have been mortified, as Randle was the reason he'd built it in the first place. William Wright, by all accounts, was a very wealthy man. He built St Peter's Church in Stockport as well.

'William Wright died in 1770. He had no other heirs, so the Hall was passed down to the eldest son of his cousin, The Reverend Henry Offerley Wright, who was a student at Emanuel College, Cambridge. He became the incumbent of St Peter's Stockport from 1816 to 1842. It is assumed that his uncle William Wright built St Peter's church during his lifetime. Such a family connection was, to say the least, beneficial to Rev Henry in securing this post.

'The Rev Henry Offerley Wright died on November 24th 1864, aged 73. He had a son, Lawrence, who was just twenty-one when his father died.

'So, Mottram Hall was passed to Lawrence Wright on Henry's death. Lawrence was a keen sailor. He would spend most of the summer in the south of England and spent most of his time around boats, in particular sailing yachts. He loved to go sailing, preferably racing yachts. The Royal Yacht Squadron was founded in 1815. The first 'home' of the Royal Yacht Squadron was the Thatched House Tavern, St James's, London. The qualification to become a member was that a *gentleman* who owned a vessel not less than ten tons could join. The members were entitled to fly a white ensign with the Union flag in the canton. In 1826, the club first organised races for pilot cutters and custom boats as a feature of the annual regatta at Cowes. The growing popularity of racing led to a need for regulation. In 1828, a rule was introduced requiring a yacht on port tack to give way to another yacht on starboard tack.

'The first Commodore Lord Yarborough, in his 150-ton brig

Falcon, led rallies in the 1820s and 30s to Cherbourg, where races were held, and stores of wine were purchased from French wine merchants and loaded them aboard to return the wine to England.

'In 1851, Commodore Stevens of the New York Yacht Club sailed the schooner *America* across the Atlantic to allow him to visit the Great Exhibition. As a guest of the Squadron, he was invited to take part in a race for a cup and £100. The course was to be a race around the Isle of Wight. *America* won the race. The Marquess of Anglesey was so surprised by her speed that he thought she must have a propeller. So began the America's Cup, contested every four years, and still is.

'The type of yacht sailing and racing in the Solent and elsewhere were the attractions for Lawrence Wright. The records show he died in Cowes on July 2nd 1839. It seems probable that he was severely injured while crewing on a large sailing yacht as a member of the crew. He was unmarried. He must have died quite suddenly. Arrangements were made, and he was buried in St Peter's churchyard in Stockport, the church built by his forebearer William Wright.

'Mottram Hall was passed to his sister, Julia Catherine Wright. She was married to James Fredrick D'Arley Street, who changed his name to Wright so that the name would continue and to ensure he was respected as a member of the 'Wright Clan'. He had been a captain in the Royal Artillery of Mottram St Andrew. He was born on October 14th 1827.

'James Frederick Wright (formerly Street) was known as Firey Fred, but not to his face. He was a bombast. He lorded it over the Mottram estate, the workers, the farmers, and the staff at the Hall. He took control of the estate soon after his marriage to Catherine Wright. His jealousy was increased by virtue of the fact that Frederick Wright, who was much older than him, of Mobberley, son of the Reverend Henry Wright, had become the head miner. Fred became influential in the mine and was awarded by his father a moiety of the takings from the value of the copper ore and cobalt extracted. Fred worked hard and became quite wealthy due to his success as a miner.

'Frederick, or Firey Fred, was not an attractive man. He increased rents for farmers. He also attempted to levy more from the mining operations in Mottram St Andrew.

'He and Catherine had one child, a girl, Julia Catherine Wright. She inherited Mottram Hall after the death of her mother in 1916. Her father, not of the Wright lineage, disappeared, and there was no reference to his residence after 1916. It is reasonable to expect that without Catherine alive to protect the tenants from the excesses of her husband, Frederick could have been struck down on a visit to the mine in Mottram St Andrew to levy money on the mine workers.

'Is it possible the skull discovered in the sand by the entrance to the mine could be the skull of Frederick Wright? By all accounts, it seems he had a significant disagreement with Firey Fred, who wanted more money from the mine. As he put it, 'for the estate'. Wright, the head of mine workings, a cousin of Frederick's wife, should have been the beneficiary of the Wright Estate as he was the only surviving male in the family. Frederick Wright was furious with Firey Fred, who as an ex-army officer, would have owned a sword. He had reason and the ability to kill Frederick. That would give Firery Fred a clear run for the money from the estate.'

John was intrigued by his father's interpretation of the family tree and the consequences. Could the skull be Frederick Wright, and had Firey Fred Wright decapitated him?

There was believed to have been a serious argument between the two men. Firey Fred was the younger of the two. Frederick was about twenty years older. Firey Fred took it upon himself to rule the roost despite not being of the Wright family, other than by marriage and a change of name.

John's father said he had as much information as he could find.

CHAPTER12

1979

COLLECTING THE CAVE CHILDREN

'Mum, don't forget you said you would collect Karen and Edward this week so they can get to school?'

'Yes, John. I've not forgotten.'

'I guess there could be a chance of finding them a house on the Crescent in the village,' his dad said.

'What makes you think that, George?'

'I spotted that the tenants of the middle house were moving out the other day. It could be available. It won't be everyone's idea of a home as it is not convenient for town.'

'Okay,' said Audrey. 'Tell them I will collect the children on Mottram Road at half past eight on Monday morning and return them at about half past three in the afternoon.'

So it was that Audrey England collected the two 'cave children' the following Monday morning. There was much excitement in the car with the four children. The excitement was rising the nearer they came to the school.

On arrival, the four children piled out of the car into the playground.

Audrey went into the school building to advise Miss Tinker. She explained she would be taking the two children back home at three thirty in the afternoon.

John and Frank were busy introducing Karen and Edward to their school friends.

'Is it right you live in a cave?' asked one child. 'What's it like?' and 'Why do you live in a cave?' The questions kept coming. John and Frank could see that the speed and volume of questions were beginning to upset Karen and Edward.

'Let us show you our classroom,' suggested Frank.

The four went into the school building to see their classroom.

Edward and Karen were impressed by the number of drawings on display around the walls.

'Who has drawn all the pictures, John?' she asked.

'There is a picture from every child. Some people have submitted more than one.'

'I hope I can do some drawing,' said Karen.

'You most certainly can,' said Miss Tinker, who had overheard the children's conversation as she entered the classroom. 'Hello, I am Miss Tinker. Your teacher, for the time you are with us. Now I think you are Karen and Edward Wright. Is that correct?'

'It is, Miss,' answered Edward.

'It's lovely to have you in school. You have a most exciting tale to tell about how you came to live in the cave and what you have been doing since.'

*

George England decided to call the housing department at Macclesfield Borough Council. He was enquiring if the house that had just become vacant could be applied for by Mr and Mrs Wright and their two children. George advised the children had started their first day at Mottram St Andrew school.

The housing officer explained that the family should make an application using the appropriate form. He said he would send one out. After a lengthy phone call, George managed to get the council to send him the form. He explained the family were homeless, so he had no address to send a letter to.

On Wednesday, the letter from the council, as promised, arrived at the Corner House and was addressed to Frederick Wright. George was not sure how literate Fred Wright was, so he opened the envelope to find a four-page form to be completed and returned.

Frank Brocklehurst was on hand to tell him what was happening. As Fred Wright was responsible for rescuing Frank Junior from the watery cave, George thought he would like to have the opportunity to say 'thank you' at the very least.

The two fathers sent a note with the children at three thirty to be delivered to their parents, advising that George and Frank would arrive with their boys at seven this evening as they had a surprise for the Wrights.

After supper, John and George England joined the Brocklehursts in their car for a drive to the Wizard Inn at The Edge.

Frank Brocklehurst found a spot at the front of the Wizard Inn to leave the car during their visit. The two boys escorted their fathers over the road to the concealed entrance to the cave occupied by the Wright family.

At the entrance to the cavern, John hailed Mr Wright. Nothing was heard, so they all walked further into the cavern. Frank shouted out.

'Hello, is that Frank and John?' came the booming voice of Mr Wright.

'It is Eric, and we are on our way down.'

After introductions and handshaking, Frank Brocklehurst senior thanked Eric – or Fred – Wright for saving his son and Mrs Wright for cleaning him up and drying his clothes.

'The children said they had very much enjoyed their day at school. Thank you for making the arrangements for them to attend.'

'No problem, Fred. Can I call you Fred?'

'Yes, Fred is my name.'

'What I wanted to say,' said George, 'was that I wondered how you were getting on on this cave and how you will cope in the cold of winter?'

'We are hardy folk, George. We shall survive.'

'Do you want your children to continue at the school?'

'Well, yes, so long as it remains free.'

'I don't see any reason why it wouldn't remain free. The cost will be the bus fare from here to the school.'

'As you can see, George, we are not well off. Mrs Wright and I would love the children to go to school. The issue is the extra cost of getting them to school. Ideally, we would love a house, but that has always been out of the question.'

'Fred, you have now touched on the real reason Frank's dad and I have come to see you. We think we can help you get a house. One has just come empty on the Cresent in the village. It is a council house. Rent would be due, but don't worry about that as you will probably be eligible to receive some help from the council for the rent.'

'Sorry, Frank, I don't understand what that means?'

'Well, Fred, will you and Mrs Wright come with us now? It is still light. I am sure the children will be fine here for a little while. Can we show you the house? If you are interested, I have a form here, which we can complete together if you would like to apply for it.'

'I need to pinch myself, Frank. It's not Christmas, is it?'

'No, you are not dreaming. We just would like to help you as much as we can.'

'Shall we go?' said George.

It was agreed, and the grown-ups went to Frank's car and drove to Mottram St Andrew and the crescent of council houses.

'I don't have a key, but we shall be able to look at the outside and the garden. You will get a good idea of what the house is like, and you can peep in at the windows.'

Frank parked his car on Mottram Road facing towards Alderley. They all got out of the car and walked up to the middle house on the modern terrace.

'I think these houses are about ten or eleven years old. There is a passageway from the front drive through the house to the back garden.'

'This is amazing, Fred. It is just what we need, and it is so close to the school and the local shops,' said Emelda.

'Hello, can I help you?'

The voice came from the adjoining house.

Fred didn't answer, so George stepped in and explained why they were there.

'That's okay, luv,' said a rather rotund lady dressed in a flowery house coat.

'The Jones only moved out yesterday. They still have some bits of furniture they need to come and collect. Would you like to see inside?'

'Well, if we can ...'

'I've got the key. I will let you have it. Wait there, luv. I'll fetch it. I think I know you from somewhere?'

'I live at the Corner House on Oak Road. I have a couple of horses, and I ride down here quite often.'

'That's where I have seen you, luv. Look, here is the key. Let me have it when you have had a look around.'

The four parents went to the front door. George handed the key to

Fred Wright. A beaming, wide smile split Emelda's face.

'Here we go, Mrs Wright. I am not going to carry you over the threshold. It's not ours yet, but it does look great.'

Frank and John were delighted with the Wrights' initial excitement. All four went through the front door. The ground floor consisted of a large living room and a large kitchen diner. Upstairs, there were three bedrooms and a bathroom.

Views of the back garden from the living room and back bedrooms were excellent. The garden at the back of the house was quite large, mainly laid to grass, which needed cutting.

Fred said he could soon sort that out.

'As we are hard up, where can we get some furniture?'

'Fred, don't concern yourself on that front. There are lots of charities set up to help people like you. The most important thing now is to get this form completed and back to Macclesfield Borough Council as soon as possible.'

'I think this is a definite yes, George and Frank. Can you help me with the form?'

'Certainly. Let's do that when we get back to your place. Fred and I will then take it this evening and post it through the door of the Town Hall so that they will have it tomorrow.'

John brought the two children home quite a bit later than anticipated. Frank walked home with his son. All four were delighted with the night's work, hoping like mad that the council would agree to the Wrights' tenancy of the house.

George England, the accountant in the group, penned a letter with an explanation and offered himself as a guarantor. He also pointed out that the accommodation the Wrights were currently occupying was not appropriate and would only get worse as winter approached. The letter went with the form. George indicated that as the Wrights didn't have a registered postal address, it would be best to return the council decision to himself, and he would ensure the Wrights were advised of the outcome.

While at his office on Friday, George received a call from the housing officer of Macclesfield Borough Council. George became very apprehensive as the housing officer required further information. Where were the Wrights currently living, how long had they been there, and did the Wrights have any connection to the area?

'I am able to answer all your queries. Starting with the last question, Frederick Wright is the remaining descendant of Lawrence Wright, who lived in Offerton Hall near Stockport. He was the man who built Mottram Hall and St Peter's Church in Stockport. He was the High Sherriff of Cheshire in 1802. The descendants on the male line ran out when the man James Frederick D'Arley Street changed his name to Wright on his marriage to Catherine Wright. He did this to put himself in line to inherit a small fortune from his wife's uncle.'

'That is a very comprehensive answer, Sir.'

'I did some research on him before contacting you. He is very definitely a person who belongs in Mottram St Andrew.'

'I can't help but agree, Sir.'

'Thank you. Will you be able to offer the Wright family the house on the Cresent?'

'The offer will be subject to the Wrights inspecting the house.'

'That has already been done. I, along with Frank Brocklehurst, who is the father of the boy who was washed down the mine. It was Fred Wright, who, living in the cave, rescued young Frank Brocklehurst when he got washed into a lake underground. We are grateful to Mr Wright. Well, we took Mr and Mrs Wright to see the house. While we were exploring the garden, the next-door neighbour gave us the front door key which she was holding for the previous tenants who will need to return to remove their remaining furniture.'

'That is most irregular. The previous tenants signed to say that they had surrendered all the keys to the house. It's number six, The

Crescent, to be correct.'

'I am sure this practical step by the previous tenants will not prevent Mr and Mrs Wright from moving in?'

'No, Sir. Their pedigree is exemplary, and you are to be the guarantor, so all is well.'

'So what now, please?'

'I need to get the council member for the Mottram Ward to approve the application, which will go forward with my recommendation for acceptance. It should be an automatic approval.'

'Thank you. I look forward to receiving the written confirmation. Apart from the next-door neighbour, where can I get the keys?'

'Once I have approval, I will meet you at the property and hand over the keys. When will the new tenants wish to move in?'

'They will have to move furniture into the house, then they can move in.'

'Thank you for your help, Mr England. I will be in touch.'

The following morning, the postman delivered a letter to George from the council confirming that Fred Wright had been granted the tenancy. George went to see Fred Wright and his wife to tell them what he hoped would be good news.

'Yes, Mr England, that is good news. Though we are very concerned about moving into the house. We don't have much money. We will have to pay for electricity, gas and, of course, furniture.'

'Don't worry about any of that. Mr Brocklehurst and I have a plan which I hope you will find satisfactory. The problem with living in a cave is that you don't have an address, so you are unable to claim benefits and so on. Living in a house which does have an address makes life so much easier.'

'I look forward to hearing about the plans.'

'Mr Brocklehurst can collect you, your wife and the children on

Saturday morning, say at ten o'clock. He will drop the children off at his house, and then they can play together with Frank and my son John. Then you will go to the house with a tape measure, pen and paper. You can then work out what you require in the form of furniture. I will walk down and see you there.'

Saturday came, and Frank Brockelhurst, true to his word, collected the Wright family and brought them all to 6, The Crescent. The children went wild, running from room to room, bagging one bedroom after another for themselves. They were so excited at the prospect of living in a real house.

By the end of Saturday, after visiting two large charity shops in Macclesfield, the Wrights had chosen furniture, rugs, and carpet for their new house, all of which were to be delivered on Monday by the Macclesfield charities. Soft furnishings, including cushions and curtains, had been acquired from another charity shop and taken away on Saturday.

Frank and George met at the Crescent, having collected the Wrights.

Once again, the children were thrilled at the prospect of moving to a house. They ran around outside.

'Fred, Frank and I have a proposition for both of you.'

'Oh, you had better listen to this, Emelda.'

'We are conscious that you don't have a fixed job. Luckily, Mottram St Andrew is now populated mainly by people who can afford to pay for help. Frank and I would each individually like to employ you as our gardener a day a week. Audrey would like some help in the house a day a week, which will be, say, from the time you drop the children off at school to when they need collecting. I am sure other folks in the village would like your help. Would you both be up for that?'

'That all sounds excellent. Can we just get moved in next week and then start the following week?'

'It's a deal. You may get other work from others. I will help you create a postcard advert to place in the post office.'

The Wright family were thrilled.

CHAPTER 13

SPRING 2023

THE WRIGHT FAMILY

'Hello, Edward, it's Frank Brocklehurst. I am so sorry to hear of the death of your father, Eric. Or Fred as he preferred. When did he die, and what did he die of? Do you know when and where the funeral will be?'

'Kind of you to ring, Frank. He died of a heart attack. We are waiting to hear from the undertaker. It will be a service at Macclesfield Crematorium. He was never one to go to church.'

'Is there anything we can do to help, Edward?'

'I don't think so, Frank. Thank you.'

'Okay, Edward. Please let me know when and where the funeral will be as I know John England wants to come over for it. I have more reason than most to give thanks for your father's life. He saved me from a nasty situation when I was ten.'

'I know. However, the wonderful things you and John did for our family over forty years ago meant my sister and I have been able to get a good education and go on to get good jobs. Mum is on her own now, so Karen or I will keep popping back to check she is okay. I am really pleased to speak with you after all these years. Would you be good enough to say a few words at the crematorium about my father?'

'I would be honoured to do that. We still live in the same house, but the Englands moved over to Tarporley. John used to work in Chester, but since the tragic death of his wife and children in a crash with a tram in Manchester, John sold up in Chester and took over a penthouse flat in the block his family owned in Manchester. John was the sole beneficiary. That's how he came to live there now.'

'Okay, can you let John know when the funeral is to be held? I would love to meet up with him again.'

'I will, Frank. Good to speak again. I'm so sorry it is under these circumstances.'

Later that day, Frank called John England and left a message and his phone number.

*

'Hello, Frank. Great to hear from you. To what do I owe this honour?'

'Hi John, thanks for getting back to me. It's about Eric Frederick Wright. He died two days ago. He was the man who rescued me from the mine?'

'Yes, of course.'

'I thought you would like to attend the funeral. No date yet.'

'That is a massive coincidence. I have been looking into the death of Fred's father. I am so sorry to hear he has died. A lovely man, and your saviour!'

'Yes, I will let you know as soon as I get a date and time. I look forward to catching up.'

When John ended the call, all sorts of questions came rattling back into his brain – the head in the sand in the Rec. Ultimately, it was discovered the skull was due to a beheading. The extraordinary thing, as he could recall, was that the evidence of the beheading of the skull was given to John in the same week he had to deal with the death of Peter Wall. Peter's death had left the Wall family in a state of disarray. As time had passed, John had become romantically attached to Sienna Wall, Peter's youngest daughter, whom he ultimately married. John, Sienna and their children went to live on Long Acre Farm in Tarporley. Until the fatal car crash ...

Peter Wall was also beheaded. At the time, it was assumed to be suicide. Eventually, it was discovered his business partner had murdered him.

But who murdered Fred Wright?

John recalled that he had promised to do some research into the head in the sand, but to date, he had done nothing.

He realised he had to do something about it as he was no longer on board *Brave Goose* in Greece, his large motor yacht, which was undergoing a refit in Paleros' workshop in Lefkas. John found he now had the time to investigate the head and the consequences of the death.

'What are you up to, my love?' enquired Fiona, who had returned from a food shopping trip, laden with bags.

'It's a long story, which I will tell you one day. I am trying to discover the name of a skull found in a sand pit by a great friend of mine. It was decided by forensic examination that he had been beheaded. The police forensic department and Manchester University jointly discovered the sex and age of the victim. The task was to discover who had beheaded the man, and of course, who was he? I promised I would try to find out. I never did. Until I had a call an hour ago from my old friend Frank, I had totally forgotten all about it.'

'So what are you doing to try and discover the information?'

'Since the time Frank discovered the skull, technology has raced ahead. The internet is likely to provide me with the answer.'

John's first port of call was to look for the family tree. He discovered the family tree of the Wright family of Mottram St Andrew. The family tree commenced with Lawrence and Margaret Wright. They had their coat of arms on the tree, but it was never registered with the College of Arms in London. The arms are described as a sable chevron between three bulls' heads 'caboshed' with an Argent crescent. A ducal coronet surmounted the shield with a bull's head Argent. The arms were in the shape of a shield. The coat of arms with the bull's head and the coronet probably gave the name to the local pub, The Bull's Head.

The couple had six children. Lawrence died in 1650, and his wife Margaret died in 1617. The dynasty continued to grow; the first mover and shaker was William Wright of Offerton. He had purchased Mottram St Andrew in 1738, building Mottram Hall. He also built St Peter's Church in Stockport, dying without issue in December 1770. The estate was bequeathed to Henry Offerley Wright who was the sole heir to the fortune. Henry became the Reverend Henry Offerly Wright. Henry was the Vicar of Derby. He married Jane, daughter of Ralph Adderley of Coton, Staffordshire. Their first issue was Lawrence Wright of Mottram St Andrew and Offerton. He married Mary Catherine, who died at the age of 78. Lawrence became the High Sheriff of Cheshire in 1802. He died in 1842 at the age of 73.

As previously mentioned, the only male issue was Lawrence Wright, who died in 1839 at the age of 21 as a result of a sailing accident in Cowes. He is buried at St Peter's Church, Stockport.

The skull was probably that of Frederick Wright, who was the great-grandfather of Eric Frederick Wright. He was most likely the victim of the beheading, looking at his job as mine superintendent at the time of his death. Firey Fred was taking lots of money from farmers, and he tried to collect more from the mines despite the fact that the copper franchise had finished. The killing of Frederick Wight could not be established beyond doubt. The only child of Firey Fred and Julia Catherine Wright was Julia Mary Catherine Street, who was baptised in Prestbury Church on 28th September 1858. She was thirty-one when her father died. She was nominated as the heir to the Mottram Estate, and her given name was Wright.

It seems likely that the grandfather of Eric Wright would have had everything to gain by the death of Firey Fred, who was not a Wright.

After the death of Firey Fred, the then only heir, Julia Catherine Mary Wright, married twice. Her first husband was killed in action as an Army officer. The value of the estate would have been substantial. The trustees of the Wright Estates, which was set up at the request of her mother, Julia Catherine, were a firm of solicitors in Manchester. The name of this firm was and still is unknown.

John England set about trying to discover the holder of the estate's funds.

*

By the time Fred and Emelda and their two children had moved into their house in the Crescent at Mottram St Andrew, the only property still in trust was the pair of cottages on Priest Lane. A Mr Wright was a joint tenant of one of the cottages. He is said to have been a wheelwright on the estate. His sister also lived in the cottage. The adjoining cottage was empty and derelict. The derelict cottage had been sold, along with the tenant's semi-detached cottage, in 1967. The derelict cottage was to be refurbished.

John sent a round-robin email to all solicitors in Macclesfield, Wilmslow, Alderley Edge and some of the larger firms in Manchester. His message was simple.

I am trying to discover the location of the family trust for the Wright family of Mottram St Andrew and Offerton. Many properties have been sold. I believe the last to be sold were The Cottages, Priest Lane, Mottram St Andrew. I gather it was sold in 1967. If you are the custodian of the funds or know where or who has custody of the trust's monies, please get in touch with me. I am acting for the sole surviving legatee.

John England, Solicitor.

John left his desk for the kitchen and a cup of coffee. Fiona was busy emptying all her purchases into cupboards, the fridge and deep freeze.

'That should keep us going, darling, for a week or two.'

'You are joking, John. That might last a week! So what were you going to tell me?'

John explained what had happened at one point in his childhood: the contact with the Wright family in Mottram St Andrew, the events that surrounded the temporary disappearance of Frank, and the work done by Frank and his parents to get a proper home for the Wrights in a local council house. The task was still not finished.

'So where were the Wright family living before your parents managed to get a home for them in a council house?'

'You will find it hard to believe but the parents and their two children lived in a mine. A bit like living in a cave.'

'I do find it hard to believe. Why were they living there?'

'They had to move out of the farm cottage they'd occupied. They couldn't afford the rent, so the farmer had to let Frank go as the farmer was being subjected to higher rents by the Estate. There were no other places to live on the estate. Fred Wright, the father of the two children, who has just died, knew of the mine from his childhood and came to Alderley Edge to live. I assume he would have hoped to find a house eventually. My parents and Frank Brocklehurst's parents, who lived near us, got together and found the Wrights a council house in Mottram St Andrew and they've lived there ever since. Though, it will just be Mrs Wright now her husband has died. The two children left home several years ago.'

'That is an amazing story, John. So who has just died?'

'Fred Wright is the father of Karen and Edward. It was he who helped Frank get out of the mine he found himself in when he was washed through a slot in the rock called the *letterbox*. The stream that he fell into was in full spate. He was washed away and for a while no one knew what had happened to him. It was assumed he must have drowned, but he wasn't. Eric, or rather Fred as he liked to be called, rescued Frank and helped get him home. I said I would go to the funeral. Would you come? You can meet my schoolboy friend, Frank.'

'Yes, of course, darling. You can show me where you lived as a child.'

'I can do better than that. We can go to the Bull's Head pub in Mottram for lunch or dinner, depending on the timing of the funeral.'

'That will be excellent, John. Is it the phone call that has spurred you into action?'

'Yes, darling. I suspect there is a redundant trust fund languishing in some lawyer's client account, and I am waiting for it to be identified. I can then pass the funds to the family. I guess the fund is in the name of the Wright family. The only ones surviving now are Mrs Wright and the two children, who are, of course, grown up. If I can find the nest egg for them, it may help them, depending on what money is left.'

'You are a good man, John England. The beneficiaries of any money collected will be overjoyed.'

'Fiona, I have been having thoughts. I am concerned that should anything happen to me, you would be out of pocket. I have not made any arrangements for you in that eventuality.'

'Has the death of Edward Wright triggered this thought?'

'In a way, yes. Emelda Wright will be destitute unless provision has been made for her. I suspect she will only get her old age pension.'

'I thought some time back, John, what if something happened to you? How would I manage? As it is, I own half a superyacht. I couldn't keep that going, and if you popped your clogs, say, during a refit, I would find a large bill landing on my desk with no money to pay the bill.'

'Yes, darling, that is a real issue and something I intend to rectify.'

'Oh, well, we are on the same wavelength. Let me know what scheme you devise when you make up your mind.'

'Come over here, you little angel. I have something for you.'

Fiona left her chores stacking shelves with groceries, sat on John's knee and gave him a big kiss.'

'It's morbid talking about arrangements when one of us is not here. You will be okay when I go, but the other way round, I would have quite a bit to sweep up.'

'I would like you to wear this. It's special.'

John handed her a small box coloured Boodles pink, with a Boodles B on the lid. Fiona knew it would contain a jewel. She opened it carefully. She was amazed by the contents. It was a large diamond sparkling in the remnants of the afternoon sunset.

'Wow, John! What has led to this present? It is wonderful, thank you.'

'Well, this bauble comes with strings attached. It also satisfies my requirement to sort out your financial situation in the event I pre-decease you.'

'Pre-decease? What does that mean in your legal language?'

'It means, my love, it sorts out your financial position if I die before you.'

'No, this is a beautiful ring, and I am sure it is precious, but even if I had to pawn it, I don't think it would pay for the re-fit of *Brave Goose*.'

'That is only part of my plan.'

'So what else have you in mind?'

'Will you marry me?'

'John England, wow, what a plan!' shrieked Fiona, nearly falling on the floor from his knee. 'You are my star! You are a wonderful man, John. When did you buy the ring for me?'

'Before I go into all the details, what is the answer?'

'YES, YES, YES!' she shrieked. 'I am so in love with you. Of course, I will marry you. That is wonderful!'

John went to the fridge and retrieved a bottle of Pol Roger Sec and two glasses.

Bang went the cork, bubbles overlapped the glasses, and they both drank to each other's health.

CHAPTER 14

MAY 2023

ILLEGAL ACTIVITY

John received three emails from his mailshot concerning the Wright estate. After a few calls, he was able to reconcile two firms of solicitors. One of the firms was a very old established company, Finn & Co of Levenshulme, Manchester, now part of an extensive practice in the City, Frasers & Co. The partners had all died at Finn & Co., and the partners of Frasers had bought Finn & Co. by providing the spouses of the previous, now deceased, partners with some capital from the sale. A clerk employed by Frasers called Kent Watson was an old employee of Finn & Co. He knew most of the old clients. Instead of moving truckloads of files, Frasers decided to keep the premises, with Watson to deal with any queries from previous clients.

The email from John England had found its way to Kent Watson. Despite previous strenuous efforts, no beneficiaries had been found for the Wright Estates. Time was running out. The Frasers had to monitor and search for beneficiaries. The estate accounts and client accounts showed the account still held just under £100,000. That sum would be on its way to a charity if, within the next six months, to comply with the Solicitors Regulation Authority (SRA), no one had come forward to claim the funds.

Kent was amazed to receive the email. He was aware of a male beneficiary living in one half of the Mottram Cottages on Priest Lane,

Mottram St Andrew. Despite emails and letters sent by Royal Mail and hand-delivered to the address by Watson, he had never received any response.

Kent was at the end of his working life. He had done all sorts of jobs for his employer without any special remuneration. This estate was to be his bonus. He was furious that someone had popped up to claim the money. He now had a dilemma. Should he do the right thing and give the funds away to charity, or should he construct a scheme which would give him the majority of the legacy?

After much deliberation, he decided to press on with the scheme he had already established. No one had spotted his deception. Why add to his pain and admit to his illegal activity?

He emailed John.

Mr England, I am Kent Watson of Finn & Co. You wrote to me recently about the Wright Trust. It would be helpful if you could come to my office. The address is at the bottom of this email. Wednesday morning, say ten o'clock, would be ideal for me. Please advise.

John was surprised and delighted that he had possibly unearthed the source of the information and, hopefully, money for the Wrights.

Dear Mr Watson, I will be at your office at ten o'clock this Wednesday. John England.

John decided to do some background checks on Kent Watson. He first contacted the Solicitors Regulation Authority and the Law Society. There was no reference to the firm on either register. He then tested the name of the parent company to no avail. John decided he would have to wait until Wednesday.

He then had an idea. He emailed all the estate agents in Macclesfield and Wilmslow to enquire if any had sold a property or dealt with any transfer of land or farmland in the last ten years, which would have belonged to the Wright Trust. John thought if there had been a sale, one of the agents in the area would indeed have been instructed to sell the property.

He realised this was a 'scatter gun' request. It all depended on landing on the appropriate desk to find the answer he needed.

Kent Watson was busy for the next two days sorting out the residual investments in the Wright Trust and calculating their current capital value, as well as the income derived from the residual holdings.

By Tuesday, he had created a spreadsheet itemising the capital and income receipts from the various holdings. Over the last ten years, he had concocted a scheme where he invested one £100,000 into tax-free ISAs. The value of these investments was now in excess of £200,000. The investments were in his name. The amount of £10,000 was initially paid annually at £800 a month. This month, it had increased to £1000 a month. The sums paid to Watson were management fees for the estate. Frasers' partners were content with this arrangement. They paid Watson a six-hundred-a-month salary, which had not increased in all the time they owned Finn & Co.

Watson paid the money from the Wright estate to his private ISA account. This was clearly a fee for managing the trust. He decided to allow England to know this but not to whom the money was paid, other than to admit it was the cost of administration of the Wright Trust.

*

'Mr England, please come in.'

John England had arrived at the Levenshulme office of Finn & Co. He didn't know what to expect, but he didn't expect to find a first-floor office over an Indian Takeaway shop. The door to the office was down a short passage with steep stairs to the first floor.

'Mr Watson, you are certainly hidden away here.'

'Yes, I hardly get any visitors other than a monthly visit from one of the partners.'

'How did you end up here, managing the Wright Trust and its assets?'

'There are no existing beneficiaries, or so I thought until I received your email. Many years ago the main office in Stockport was required for redevelopment. Then, the partners thought they would sell up and move the trust business here. I find it convenient. I can walk here. My flat is about a mile away. We don't get visitors as a rule, and the trust is nearly wound up. The partners decided when the trust was running down to leave all the records where they were to allow me to spend the last ten years of working and seeing an end to the estate. I have been looking after the legal issues and management of the estate for over twenty years now.'

'Well, Mr Watson, I can tell you that there have been four beneficiaries of the estate during the last ten years. The first two, a brother and sister Wright, who lived in Mottram Cottages, Priest Lane at Mottram St Andrew, have died. I think the cottages were sold in 1978. Subsequently, Eric Frederick Wright moved to a council house in the Crescent, Mottram St Andrew, with his wife and two children. I have no doubt that he was the sole surviving beneficiary. He has recently died, and his wife is still alive. I think she is the final beneficiary of the trust and is able to claim such funds as you have retained.'

John sat on a rather battered chair opposite Kent Watson, who took his chair to the opposite side of the desk. John was amused by the elderly solicitor who wore a black jacket over a black waistcoat and a white shirt with a stiff fly-away collar. His trousers were black with chalk stripes. The man looked as if he had never seen the sun. His face was white, with a sallow complexion, grey eyes, silver hair and eyebrows. It occurred to John that Watson had a face like a tennis racket: it was flat and devoid of expression. John smiled inwardly at this revelation. Watson didn't have a scintilla of a smile.

'You give me the impression, Mr England, that you expect to walk away with a large cheque for your client. If that is the purpose of your visit, I regret to advise you that there is very little money in the trust and even fewer assets.'

91

'I understand what you say. I assume you have some figures to justify that statement?'

'I do, but if you want to go back further than ten years, then you will have to come again. If you have a date, that would be helpful, as if it is a long way back, it will take me some time to put the numbers on a spreadsheet.'

'Let's see how we get on with the last ten years. Once I have seen those, I will be able to know if I need to look further back.'

Watson shuffled a set of spreadsheets he had compiled and passed them over to John.

'I may need to take some time to consider the contents. Bear with me, please, Mr Watson.'

'Take your time. I have nothing else to do. I am retiring at the end of this year. As you will discover, there is nothing left in the pot as far as any beneficiaries are concerned.'

John hoped a cup of coffee might have been forthcoming. No such luck.

'Can you please explain these figures to me?'

Watson set about indicating income from rents as opposed to capital receipts.'You see, once a capital asset has been sold, the rent stops.'

'I understand that. So if all the assets have been sold, how are you still receiving rent?'

'It is a matter of timing, Mr England. In January of this year, we sold the last asset. That was a single farm cottage in Henbury. There is no income coming into the Trust now.'

'Thank you, Mr Watson. May I take these sheets away with me? There may be supplementary questions when I have had the opportunity to study them.'

'Yes, that's fine with me,' replied Watson.

'Do you have a schedule of all the trust assets when your firm started to manage the estate?'

'Probably. That will take some finding. If you leave it at least a week before you return, I will endeavour to find the terrier for you.'

John left an hour after arriving, saying he would be in touch regarding his return.

CHAPTER 15

FRAUDULENT DEDUCTIONS

B ack at the apartment, John found it was empty. Fiona had gone out. He called the front desk by way of the building's intercom system.

'Sydney, did Fiona go out? If you saw her, did she say when she might be back?'

'No, sorry, Sir. She seemed to be in a hurry and took a taxi when she left.'

John sent a text to Fiona's phone, but no response.

A cup of coffee was required. The Nespresso machine provided what he needed. Then, the coffee and spreadsheets were taken to his office for further consideration and consumption, as the case may be.

It had just passed noon when John heard Fiona return. He went to greet her.

'Hi, darling. I see you have been shopping, but you only did that yesterday, so what have you been buying?'

'Well, when I was shopping yesterday, I didn't know I was about to get married.'

'Oh, what have you been buying? I assume clothes! But you have loads of clothes!'

'Yes, darling, but I have nothing to wear for weddings.'

'Come on, what have you been buying?'

'I have not bought a wedding dress. We are too old for that sort of thing, and anyway, I don't know how and where we might get married.'

'That is something we need to discuss. Also, there will be some documents for us to sign.'

'Oh, what will that be all about?'

'I have already instructed Bennetts to create a set of documents. When they come, I will go over them with you. They are for your protection.'

'Sounds intriguing, John.'

'We will need to go to Chester to sign them. There is nothing to worry about. It's all arranged to provide you with protection should I become seriously ill or worse.'

'Oh, John, I don't like to think of those things.'

'Too many people take that point of view. It is so simple to make arrangements when everyone is alive and compose documents. It becomes a nightmare if someone is dead and no will. Then, the government licks its lips at the sums of money coming its way. Estate planning it is called.

'Interestingly, that is what I am trying to sort out for Emelda Wright now Eric has passed away. I went to see the lawyer who administers the Wright Estate. I have a bunch of spreadsheets to pursue, and then I need to go back and see him at some point. I hope to extract some money for Mrs Wright. If nothing else, to cover her husband's funeral costs. I will help out if there is anything else. They were so helpful to Frank when he was washed away by the underground river.'

'You are a wonderful man, John. Have you had a moment to speak to Robert at Paleros to see where they are up to with the refit?'

'Interesting you should ask. I was going to phone Noel this afternoon. I will call Paleros first, then Noel.'

*

'Robert, it's John England. I wondered how you were getting on?'

'Hi, John. Yes, we have made good progress. We are waiting for some parts regarding the air conditioning. They are coming by ship from China. A large container ship stuck in the Suez Canal delayed everything for a couple of months. We have been promised the parts for next week. They will be fitted as soon as they arrive so we can be ready for the re-launch.'

'Can't you launch and fit the items when *Brave Goose* is afloat?'

'No, John, there is a water intake and an exhaust. It's annoying, but we can't launch without these parts. When are you coming out?'

'We are not sure yet. Fiona and I are hoping to get married in Lefkas and then spend our honeymoon on *Brave Goose*.'

'Congratulations! That will be a party!'

'It will, Robert. A party you and your wife Yana will be invited to.'

John's next call was to Noel.

'Noel, it's John. How are things with you? Are all the crew back now?'

'Yes, John. Great to hear from you. You may be aware there has been a delay waiting for parts from China for the air conditioning, but I hope we might get afloat again within a week or ten days.'

'That is great news. I have some other news for you.'

'Oh, what might that be?' enquired Noel somewhat apprehensively.

'Fiona and I are getting married.'

'Oh, that is marvellous news, John. Are you tying the knot in England?'

'In a way. We shall have a very quiet registry office wedding to make things legal in the UK. We then hope to come to Lefkas and have a traditional wedding in the lovely little church off the main street. Then we shall have a party, and then sail away for our honeymoon.'

'Wow, that sounds fantastic.'

'I may need your assistance in making the arrangements.'

'Of course. The crew I and will be delighted to help you.'

'Thanks, Noel. We would like to come out next week or so to make some local arrangements. I will let you know when. Let me know as soon as you are launched. Thanks, Noel.'

*

'Fiona?'

'Yes, my love?'

'What sort of wedding would you like?'

'Well, as an old lady, I guess something quiet is needed.'

'Okay, I get the message. I will call Frank to see if he knows when the funeral will be. I also need to contact Kent Watson. He has some explaining to do.'

*

'Mr Watson, it's John England. I need to come and see you. Would Wednesday this week be suitable?'

'Did you manage to understand my calculations, Mr England?'

'In a way. It seems to me there are significant shortfalls in the sum of money available to the beneficiaries. That's what I need to understand.'

'Okay, ten o'clock on Wednesday, here at my office.'

'Okay, I will be there.'

*

'Guy, it's Kent.'

'Hi Kent, what can I do for you.'

'I need a busybody sorting out and making them so afraid they will leave me alone.'

'Oh. What have you been up to, and why do you require my assistance this time?'

'I was so impressed with your work previously, so much so I was scared stiff. This man has discovered my activities in relation to a long outstanding trust. I thought all the beneficiaries had died. However, one has surfaced, with a lawyer acting for the remaining beneficiary. I need him to realise he is best leaving this matter alone and go away.'

'I see. Is the attic room still available?'

'It is; there is a substantial lock on the door, and some of your other equipment remains from the last time you used the room.'

'Good. What time do I need to appear and when?'

'The man, John England, is due here at ten o'clock this Wednesday morning.'

'Okay, I will be there at nine. I will remain in the attic. I will discuss my thoughts with you before he arrives. Do you have an address for this man?'

'Yes.' Kent Watson supplied John's address and his background.

'How much money is involved, Kent?'

'It is a matter of opinion but not less than one hundred thousand pounds.'

'Okay, Kent, I will charge ten per cent of the amount, that is ten thousand, with five thousand up front on Wednesday morning.'

'Okay, Guy. That's agreed.'

*

Aware he was going to be dealing with a slippery customer, John decided he should get all his paperwork together. He also decided to take a colleague with him.

He called his old friend, Detective Chief Inspector Jon Kim of the Manchester and Cheshire CID. It's a long story of how he got to work part-time for each force, but the arrangement worked for both forces.

'Jon, it's John England. How are you keeping?'

'I am just fine. I guess you have a problem?'

'What makes you think that?'

'You only ring me when you have a problem.'

'I am working on a *pro bono* basis for a widow who is the last beneficiary of a trust that was set up in the eighteenth century. The lawyers dealing with the trust have virtually abandoned the trust. It has been left with a firm that has not practised for many years. The man left to handle any queries is Kent Watson. The firm is Finn & Co, which is owned by Frasers Solicitors. Watson is ready to retire or possibly past retirement age. I have had a meeting with him, and he supplied me with spreadsheets to indicate the income and expenditure over the last ten years. I have also done a trawl of local estate agents seeking information on any sales the trust may have made in the previous thirty years. I discovered that two properties were sold in the 1970s by an old, established firm of agents. They sold a barn for over £100,000 six years ago and a pair of cottages, one of them tenanted in the 1970s, for £1,700. The more recent sale of the barn should have netted the trust, after fees, of roughly £180,000 as a minimum. No mention of this last sale is made on the spreadsheets. I am meeting the solicitor on Wednesday morning to try to discover what has happened to the money. Are you free at ten o'clock on Wednesday to join me in visiting the office of Finn & Co?'

'I can do that. Do you anticipate trouble?'

'I do, Jon. The solicitor is old and frail. I think he may ask a younger member of Frasers team to join him. I would like some support.'

Jon confirmed he would be at Peter's Tower at nine-thirty.

John explained to Fiona what he was going to do on Wednesday and said that his old friend, Detective Chief Inspector Jon Kim, would be with him.

'Do you think there'll be trouble, John?'

'Well, it's always possible when money is involved. I get the distinct impression that Kent Watson, the manager of the solicitors, didn't think there were any more beneficiaries. He may have plans to take the money for his retirement.'

'How do you manage to get a top police officer to come and help?'

'I have known Jon Kim for years. He is an unusual policeman. He works part-time for Cheshire and Greater Manchester forces. It was a way of allowing him to carry on after the retirement age.'

At nine-thirty on the dot, Jon Kim appeared at the reception. Sydney rang up to the penthouse to notify John.

The two men rode in John's Range Rover to Levenshulme and the office of Finn & Co.

Chatting in the car, John said that he was sure that there was a silver Ford Fiesta following them with two men inside.

'Yes, there will be. They are plainclothes officers. I thought it appropriate just in case!'

'You are a good man, Jon, thank you.'

At nine o'clock, Guy Miller rang the bell at Finn & Co. Watson knew who it would be, so he pressed the release button.

'Hi, Kent. Is everything in order? Before I check the attic, have you my up-front money?'

'Yes, it is here in this envelope.'

Guy took the envelope and proceeded up the uncarpeted wooden staircase to the attic. Miller was an ex-boxer, somewhat out of training. His scars from his times in the ring were still noticeable. A squashed and repaired broken nose, two cauliflower ears and a big scar over his left eye. His hands were like two sledgehammer heads. He was tall, over six feet two inches.

He certainly could stand up for himself if required.

*

John parked the Range Rover outside the entrance to Finn & Co in a side street. The Ford Focus parked in front of him. Before he left the car, Jon Kim checked the radio connection between himself and the officers in the Ford. All was working as expected.

'Out of interest, John, what makes you think you will meet with resistance, possibly physical, at your meeting this morning?'

'I am assuming I have hit on a source of income for Watson and possibly other partners in the firm that owns Finn & Co. If I am right, I think they will wish to ensure I give up and go away. That might involve physical threats.'

'Okay. Let's hope it doesn't turn out that way.'

John pressed the bell push on the office door; Watson, he assumed, had pressed the electronic release button to allow access.

The two men stood in the spacious and untidy office. It had a large desk with a computer and monitor resting on it. The printer was on another side of the office on a separate table. The office was festooned with piles of files, paper, old newspapers, and there were law books scattered on the desk. There was an over-full bookcase with books laid on their side on top of other books.

The ceiling was tobacco-coloured, signifying that Kent Watson was or had been a heavy smoker.

As agreed between them, John went up the stairs first, followed by Jon Kim.

The two men entered the untidy office. John was holding photocopies of the spreadsheets which he had marked in various places. He also held two letters from the estate agents, Bridgnorth & Co, who had written to him following his round-robin to agents in the area seeking information on sales of properties on behalf of the Wright family trust.

'Mr Watson, this is a friend of mine, Jon Kim.'

'I didn't think you would be bringing someone with you?'

'I find it useful when there is a disagreement.'

'Do we have a disagreement, Mr England?'

'Yes, we do. The figures on your spreadsheets are totally wrong. I am only able to prove two inaccuracies in such a short space of time. Though I suspect there are numerous inaccuracies or fraudulent deductions from a trust which has been in your sole care for years.'

CHAPTER 16

'YOU CAN'T PROVE A THING'

W atson went red in the face with rage.

'How dare you come into my office making accusations? I prepared all the information you required, but then you insult me by telling me the figures on my spreadsheets are incorrect! How dare you?'

'Mr Watson, I told you I would be here this morning. I have been doing some research. I have two letters from the agents you used to sell off the remaining property. They confirm the two cottages on Priest Lane were sold in 1978 for the sum of £1700. Then there is the recent sale of what I suspect is the last property sale, with no other properties remaining. You received the sum of £150,000 in 2021. Neither of these transactions appear on your spreadsheets.'

'Mr England. When the Priest Lane properties were about to be sold, we endeavoured to discover the whereabouts of the remaining beneficiary without success. It was not a process we needed to repeat on the sale of the barn, as we had established there were no beneficiaries left to inherit.'

'Convenient response but an incorrect one. As I indicated to you at my last visit, I act for the remaining beneficiary. Eric Frederick Wright was entitled to the proceeds of the sales. He is now dead, but his wife survives. She needs this money to allow her to live. Where is the money, Mr Watson?'

Watson's flat refusal to tell John where the money had gone enraged John.

'I will sue you and your firm for this money, and I will contact the Solicitors Regulation Authority. They will take action on my behalf.'

Watson pressed a bell button on his desk. Down the attic stairs came Guy Miller, the heavy-weight minder for Watson.

'Do you have a problem, Kent?'

Jon Kim recognised Guy Miller, but Miller didn't recognise Kim.

'Yes, this man is threatening me. He thinks I or the firm have taken money not belonging to me, and he is suggesting he will report me to the Solicitors Regulation Authority.'

Miller approached the two men who, Watson said, were harassing him over money.

'I think you two had better bugger off and not come back.'

'I don't know who you are or what your role is in this fiasco, but I will not leave until I get an answer to my question as to the whereabouts of the money, which I can prove was paid to Finn & Co, and Mr Watson in particular.'

'Are you deaf?' responded Miller. He walked closer to John in a menacing way.

'Why have you sought the assistance of this goon, Mr Watson? Is he here to ensure you don't have to pay back the client's money you have embezzled?'

Watson didn't reply. He left the heavy stuff to Miller.

'I suggest you two clear off, now.'

At that time, Jon Kim produced a warrant card.

'I suggest you two calm down and deal properly with the questions and declare where the money has gone.'

Watson said nothing. Miller stood there, wondering what he had got himself into.

'I am leaving now. This has nothing to do with me,' announced Miller, who went down the entrance stairs and away.

'So, Mr Watson. Not only have you not indicated where the money has gone from the sale of the two properties, but you have tried to threaten Mr England in order to retain the funds. You and your partner, who has just left, are trying to hide the theft of funds from the trust. You have a duty of care to maintain the funds for the benefit of the trust and its beneficiaries. What you are involved with is theft. Not an edifying end to your career as a solicitor, time in prison, is it?'

'You can't prove a thing. I have not stolen any money.'

'So where is the money that was sent to you by the purchaser's solicitors in these two cases, Mr Watson?' asked John.

Watson said nothing.

'I have the proof, Mr Watson. If you can't or won't produce the money within the next seven days, I will issue a writ in addition to referring you to your professional body. I have a perfect witness in Detective Chief Superintendant Jon Kim. If you refuse, please consider the unpleasant implications of your failure to act. You are behaving as though your head is in the sand.'

The two men left Watson's office only to find Miller standing by the silver Ford Focus police car in handcuffs. The two officers had arrested him.

Kim spoke with his plain clothes detectives. 'Have you the full details of this man?'

'We don't think we are being given the truth, Sir.'

'Okay. Take him back to the station. We need a photo, fingerprints, address details and his mobile number. Before we release him, check his records to see if we know him.'

The two detectives drove off with Miller in the secure back seat.

John thanked his old friend Jon Kim and drove him back to the police station.

*

John returned to the apartment to find Fiona sorting through her clothes.

'Now what are you up to?'

'As I am about to get married, I needed to look at what clothes I had that would be appropriate for my wedding prior and post. Obviously, I don't have a wedding dress, and I don't want a white wedding, but a smart dress for the occasion is required. I still don't know, John. What do you have in mind for our wedding?'

'It is more a case of what *you* would like for our wedding.'

'I had no idea until the other day. I didn't even know that I would be getting married!'

'Okay, so let me see if we can work something out. My thoughts are that we should get married sooner or later. In the UK, we should go to a register office and have a small service, which will be an official marriage, and a marriage certificate will be issued. We can have a few friends for dinner at a restaurant of your choice. Then I thought we should go to Greece. We should have as many friends and acquaintances as possible and spend time on *Brave Goose* as a honeymoon. What do you think?'

'That sounds like fun, John, although it will be unusual to spend our honeymoon with friends.'

'Okay, where would you like to go for a honeymoon?'

'Well, I thought it would be nice if you and I could hide away on our own for a couple of weeks. Could we go to the Maldives or Seychelles?'

'Of course, we could. I will have a look into what is available.'

'Have you heard from Paleros Boat Yard in Lefkas about the progress with *Brave Goose*?'

'No, but I did have a chat with Noel. They were awaiting some parts for the aircon system. They will be coming from China. Apparently, they have been despatched but are stuck on a container ship somewhere.'

'When do you want to arrange the registry office, John?'

'The sooner, the better. I am anxious to ensure that should anything happen to me, you are to be looked after. That is what I am battling to secure for Emelda Wright.'

'I am sure you are not going to peg out any time soon, but I love you for wanting to look after me in the future.'

'Okay, now it's halfway through May. Let's arrange to get hitched in the next week or so. That will make matters legal and straightforward. We will both need wills once we are married, but nothing is stopping us from making arrangements to have them drawn up now.'

'I am all for that, John.'

'When are you free, darling?

'I don't have any plans other than important shopping in preparation for the wedding.'

John made arrangements to go to Bennetts, in Chester, his old firm, to instruct them to draw up wills that would reflect each other's assets.

John made the arrangements and fixed an appointment at ten thirty on Tuesday next.

'Hi, Dad. It's John.'

'Hello, son, to what do we owe this call?'

'Fiona and I are coming to Chester to have a meeting with Bennetts on Tuesday next week. I wondered if you and Mum would like to join us for lunch at the Grosvenor at, say, twelve thirty?'

'Let me just check with Mum. Won't be a minute.'

John's father came straight back. 'Are you still there?'

'Yes, Dad.'

'That is an excellent offer. We look forward to seeing you at the Grosvenor next Tuesday.'

CHAPTER 17

END OF MAY 2023

LAUNCHING *BRAVE GOOSE*

John and Fiona discovered that the parts for the air conditioning had arrived and been fitted. *Brave Goose* was now ready for re-launch following the re-fit. They would fly out to Greece on Monday, 22nd May. John decided he needed to fix a date at the registry office in Manchester for when the two of them returned from Greece.

'England, this is Watson from Finn & Co. I have looked at your 'so-called' evidence. There were two sales as you say. However, a man claiming to be the remaining beneficiary of the estate said he wanted to do something with the barn. He just asked for a transfer. He then asked for a transfer of a pound. He dealt with the future of the barn from then on.

'As for the sale of the two cottages, that was quite some time ago. There was little or no profit by the time the agents and we had taken our fees.'

'Okay, I accept the situation on the cottages. I assume you must have had some proof of the bona fides of the purchaser. What was his full name, and where did he live?'

'I did see his birth certificate at the time, which proved he was born to a Maria Wright, the wife of John Spencer of Derby Wright. He was able to prove it to my satisfaction by showing me a copy of the family tree. Spencer and Maria Wright had only one child. He said he was that child!'

'Well, Mr Watson, I am looking at a copy of the family tree. There was one issue from Maria Wright and John Spencer, and that was a girl. Maria Wright, who died in 1843. So any child who turned up a girl or boy would be old, about one hundred and seventy at best. So, they could not have been a bone fide descendant. As the solicitor to the trust, effectively a trustee, you were duped, or you falsified the documents to suit you. I am sorry, but I hold you responsible for the sale of this farm barn. I demand on behalf of a legitimate beneficiary the £150,000 that the barn was sold for a month after you say it was transferred for one pound.'

Watson put the phone down to end the conversation.

John was furious at this man who clearly had been involved in a deception, possibly for his own benefit. He wrote down the name 'WRIGHT' and the name 'WATSON'. The names had six letters each, and both began with a W. Could there have been a switch of names on documents allowing Watson to claim the benefit of the sale without triggering an enquiry from the firm's partners?

If John was correct, he needed to see the original documents that had been prepared and signed for the transfer.

*

'Would you like me to book flights for our trip to Greece, John?'

'Oh, yes, please. Have you a date in mind?'

'I thought we had agreed on 22nd May? When do you want to return?'

'Let's book for two weeks. We can then decide what to do when we are there. I hope I can start unravelling this conundrum I have unearthed by then. I wonder if Fred's funeral will take place before we go?

*

'Frank, it's John. Any news about Fred's funeral?'

'Hello, my friend. It is proving difficult for the children and Emelda as the cost of the funeral is causing an issue. They have a date, which is May 19th. I don't think they will have it as financial issues are holding them back. They are trying to get the funds together to hold a funeral and a wake afterwards.'

'Look, Frank, I will send you £5000 now. Please ask them to do it or can you organise the funeral and wake on 19th? I have made some progress in getting some money from the Wright family trust. It is going to take some time. Fiona and I will be getting married in June. I hope you and your wife will be able to come to a little gathering after a registry office wedding.'

'Congratulations, my old friend. We would love to come. Thanks for the money, John.'

John sent the money to Frank as soon as he'd finished the call. He made a note in his diary for Fred's funeral on 19th May.

*

'Did you manage to get flights on the 22nd of May, darling?'

'Yes, John. They are early, so we need to be at the airport at 0600hrs on the day.'

'Ah. That will be a challenge, although we will have more of a day when we get there.'

'Yes. I am excited to see *Brave Goose* again. It seems like ages since we have been out to her.'

'I agree. I am just as excited as you.'

*

In Lefkas, Noel was busy with the rest of the crew getting ready to launch *Brave Goose* and then get her moved to her berth in anticipation of the arrival of the owners.

'Noel, can you and the rest of the crew help me with a full spring clean on the whole boat? It could take a couple of days.'

'No problem, Sally. We will all pull together once we are at our mooring. She will be launched later today.'

The launching of *Brave Goose* went without any issue, and she was moored stern-to the quay by noon. All the crew were delighted with the transformation that had occurred. She had undergone a complete re-fit internally and externally. The hull had been polished. A new coat of antifouling and a new white waterline had been applied. Even the Williams jet-powered dinghy had had her name applied – *Gosling TT to Brave Goose*. Before serious cleaning and polishing of the newly fitted cabins, saloon, bridge and engine room, Sally had served lunch.

'I wondered where you disappeared to, Sally. This is an excellent start to the new season. Well done.'

The crew all sat around the table on the quarterdeck, eating a lovely salad with fresh vegetables and fruit.

'I have opened a bottle of white wine. I think you all deserve a glass.'

'Thanks, Noel. I agree the wine sets off Sally's salad beautifully,' said Jock, who was not known for his culinary expertise or his pallet in tasting wine.

They all laughed at Jock's unexpected expertise. As the laughter died down, there was a call from the quay to the captain of *Brave Goose*.

'Can I help you?' said Noel, standing up and looking to see who was calling. He saw two port policemen and a member of the Greek Marine Customs. They were all in uniform.

'Yes, Sir, may we come aboard?'

'Certainly.'

During the ship-to-shore conversation, Sally and José moved all the empty plates and cutlery into the galley.

The three officials who boarded *Brave Goose* were invited to sit around the table.

'How can I help you, gentlemen?'

'May we see the ship's papers?' enquired the marine customs officer.

'Yes, of course. We only launched this morning, so I still need to come to the Port Office to register the fact *Brave Goose* is afloat and berthed here.'

'Yes, that would be normal. There is no immediate requirement to do that. However, you must register the vessel with us before you set sail.'

'Yes, Sir. I fully understand that.'

The customs officer read through all the paperwork Noel had provided to him.

'These papers are not complete. Where is the certificate saying VAT has been paid in the EU?'

'This is not a new vessel, she's possibly twenty-five years old, hence the re-fit she has just undergone. I have not had any request for payment of VAT at any time since we have been in EU waters.'

'Well, Sir, you have seven days to either leave Greek waters or pay IVA, the VAT on the value of the vessel. The rate in Greece is twenty per cent.'

'The owner will be here on Monday, and I will make him aware of the issue. A decision will be made either to leave Greece's jurisdiction or pay the IVA. My owner is the only person who can do that.'

'I understand, Sir. May I take these papers and make copies and return them to you?'

'I can make a copy for you now. Please accompany me to the office where the printer is.'

The three officers left without further comment.

Noel sent an email to John the minute the officers left, explaining the issue and the urgency of removing *Brave Goose* from Greek jurisdiction. Based on discussions with other skippers, it seemed the solution was to re-register *Brave Goose* in Malta.

*

John and Fiona were driving to Macclesfield for Fred's cremation, followed by a wake at the Bulls Head in Mottram St Andrew. John heard his mobile ping, but he thought nothing of it. It could wait until after the funeral. He left his mobile in the car while at the crematorium and for the wake in the pub.

It was gone three in the afternoon before he was back in the Range Rover and picked up his phone. There was only one text message, from Noel.

'My god, Fiona. We have a serious problem. The port police and Maritime Customs have been on board *Brave Goose* today and demanded to see a VAT-paid certificate, or we have a week from today to leave Greece.'

'What does all that mean, John?'

'It has to do with Brexit. Since then, boats in EU waters, mainly in the Mediterranean, have to have a VAT certificate if they intend to remain in EU waters for more than six months. That on a quick calculation, if *Brave Goose* is worth, say, a million pounds, then the tax payable will be £200,000.'

'My god. That, on top of the bill for the refit, will be very expensive.'

'You can say that again, my love. What a performance.'

John decided to call his accountant, but it was not an ideal time being a Friday afternoon.

'Paul, it's John England.' John then explained the situation though he did not expect an instant response.

'John, I have heard about this problem before, but not on the scale you are on. One answer is to re-register the vessel in Malta and pay the VAT, which is considerably less than in most Mediterranean countries. You are then free to travel anywhere in European waters with the Maltese registration, which is less costly than other one-off jurisdictions. In addition, there is a facility where you can register as Maltese citizens. I think you may have to purchase a property there to get your 'Gold' visa. It may be worth looking into that at the same time. If you do that, your income tax bill will come down quite considerably as you will then be treated as Maltese citizens for tax purposes.'

'Wow, I didn't expect you to have the answer at your fingertips. That's great, Paul. When you have a moment, can you email me with this advice?'

'No need, it's all online. Look up Maltese Yacht Registrations, and that will explain the whole process to you.'

'Brilliant. Fiona and I are flying out on Monday. Sounds like I will have some reading on the plane. Thank you so much, Paul. The perfect solution as always.'

*

Fred's funeral was a small affair. Family, a few friends and neighbours, Frank and his wife, Fiona and John. Less than twenty people.

The crematorium was booked for two o'clock in the afternoon. The entourage and mourners left the crematorium at two thirty. By the time those who couldn't make the wake said their farewells outside, it had just turned three in the afternoon when the rest arrived at the Bull's Head.

A drink in hand was the prelude to the inevitable balancing act of a plate of food and a drink, making it impossible to shake hands with folk. Several people in Fred's immediate family who knew that John had provided the funds for the event came to say thank you. John also sat for a short while next to Emelda. A delightful lady. John explained that as Fred was the last beneficiary of the Wright Family

Trust, he was trying to discover how much money was going to be available to her.

'It may take some time, but I am on the case.'

'That is very kind, John. I will be okay, as I have my pension, disability benefit, housing benefit, and I have sufficient coming in to see me through.'

'Good. I will let you know as soon as I have some news. I must go and speak with your children. Then we need to get back to Manchester.'

John spoke to Edward and Karen, and explained what was happening with the trust. He gave each of them his business card and requested that they email him so he could keep in touch as matters developed. They seemed grateful. John bade his farewell to Frank.

On the way to Manchester, Noel rang from *Brave Goose*.

'John, I have been having a chat with the captain of another UK-registered superyacht. He told me that last summer, he had to take the yacht he was skippering to Malta because they were in the same situation as you with regards VAT. I thought you would like to know that.'

'Yes, thanks, Noel. My accountant has told me much the same thing. We may need to up sticks and go to Malta next week.'

CHAPTER 18

BRAVE GOOSE REBORN

John and Fiona stepped out of the white Mercedes taxi onto Quay E, where *Brave Goose* was mooored. The crew, dressed in blue *Brave Goose* shirts and khaki shorts, were watching them from the quarterdeck.

'Hello everyone,' John waved and called out. José came down the passerelle to collect luggage, though there was only one small case for each. He was delighted and surprised at the same time, realising there would be no mountain of bags to get up to the deck.

'Welcome, John and Fiona,' Noel expressed his delight at seeing the owners again.

'Wow, it looks like you have all been very busy. When did you launch, Noel?'

'Thursday last week. We have been non-stop since.'

'Are you happy with the improvements?'

'We are, John. I hope you and Fiona will be pleased with what has happened?'

'I'm sure we shall. I can't wait to see it. Do you want to point out the changes that I may not recall?'

John, Fiona and Noel set off to examine all the work that had been carried out over the winter. The changes became immediately apparent to the owners as they entered the saloon. New carpets, curtains and blinds. New varnish or French polish had been applied to the furniture and other exposed timber elements in the saloon. They moved forward, admiring the latest light fittings, carpet and soft furnishings.

On the bridge, Noel pointed out the improved instruments.

'Oh, the bridge ceiling is a matte black now, Noel. Why did you do that?'

'When navigating at night, the glare from instruments and other lights spoils your night vision. The black ceiling absorbs stray light and allows the operator to maintain their night vision.'

'Simple job but very effective, I am sure,' commented John.

All the cabins looked as if the boat had come straight from the builders. Everything was new, including bathroom fittings. The master cabin was a sheer delight. Fiona uttered a loud 'wow' at first sight of their cabin.

The beautiful old-style wall lights had been retained in the cabin to maintain the character and the age of the boat. The lamps, in keeping with the rest of the ship, were all changed to LED bulbs to save electricity. Also, the lights in the cabins and reading lights had all been changed to LED lamps. The adjustable reading lights, as well as lights over the dressing table, all had new bulbs.

'What's that?' requested Fiona, pointing at a new grill near the skirting board between the cabin and the en suite bathroom.

'It's the air conditioning vent. This dial here allows you to set the temperature to either warmer or cooler. To start the air-con, you just need to switch on here.'

'Now that's clever. It will be excellent in the heat and, of course, when it's cool if it heats as well?'

'You are so right, darling. Is there anything we have missed here, Noel?'

'Yes, John. You are aware the carpet is new. We have named all the cabins to help with allocation. Your cabin is called Bule Whale as it's the largest mammal in the sea. The VIP cabin is called Dolphin. The following double is Puffin, after the delightful little bird who mates for life. The last single cabin, but with a Pullman berth capable of being used as a double, is called Shrimp. The significance of these names and the crew titles is for the indicator board at the aft end of the saloon. Paleros has made a beautiful teak, polished board with the cabin names and crew list: captain, engineer, stewardess, and crew. Simply slide the cover over it to indicate when someone is in or out.'

Noel explained it was only to be used in port.

'That is great, Noel. I may get teased about the whale as my stomach increases in size, thanks to Sally's wonderful food.'

'That's not all, John. Going back to the air conditioning which runs throughout the boat. There are several generators situated near the cabins, the saloon, the galley, crew quarters, and the engine room. In addition, we have a fuel polishing unit and an additional system to discharge waste.'

'I recall that Sally had asked for a trash compactor. Is that fitted?'

'Yes, John, but I was alluding to black waste from toilets. The modern waste treatment plant is in. I am sure it will be a great help.'

'Oh, so Sally now has the means to compact galley waste. That's good. So how does the black water waste work?'

'It dries the black water waste and then cleans any residual water and moisture, allowing that to be discharged overboard without any adverse effect to the environment. The dry waste material is bagged or discharged overboard. Our preference is to discharge the dry inert waste to land waste tips when we come to a larger port.'

'That all sounds very eco, Noel.'

'It is, John. There will be no issues anywhere with how we handle our waste, and quite right too.'

'While we are discussing issues, do you have any detailed

knowledge of the Maltese registration arrangements?'

'No, I have not had any dealings with the Maltese. I have been looking into their registration process, and it appears to be the sixth-largest marine registry in the world. I think they have favourable tax and VAT arrangements.'

'Do you know if we have to take *Brave Goose* there?

'No, I don't. I guess a phone call will answer that for you, John. I have details on the bridge. Let me give them to you.'

Noel handed John a wadge of paper with complete details on how to register a ship in Malta, the tax arrangements, and the VAT situation. As the phone number of the registry was available, John went straight to his office and called Malta.

'Thank you, that is most helpful. My fiancée and I will come early next week when we sort our flights. I will let you know when we shall be with you.'

'Fiona, we need to fly to Malta as soon as we can next week. I need to register *Brave Goose* there. I have made a preliminary appointment to meet with a registrar on Tuesday. Are you up for coming?'

'Yes, certainly, John.'

*

The one hour forty minutes flight from Athens at 0830 in the morning was booked. The return flight was booked for Wednesday. The short flight to Malta should take no time. John had booked the five-star Sofitel hotel near the airport in Athens for the night before.

'We need to be in Athens to book into a hotel at six on Monday evening, Noel. Can you please book a private car to take us there?'

*

Once Fiona and John had arrived in Malta, they checked into the Iniala Hotel overlooking the harbour. They had time to wander around before their appointment with the Register of Shipping at two thirty in the afternoon.

'This is a beautiful hotel, John. One to remember should we need to come again.'

'I agree. This harbour is something else. It is possible to get any number of large yachts in here.'

'Yes, and a safe place to be. It is, of course, a natural harbour.'

Walking close to the harbour, they came upon a continuous film presentation of the 'Defence of Malta in the Second World War.' They became transfixed with the story as it was portrayed on the screen. The highlight was that in August 1942, an oil tanker, the *Ohio* had been crippled by bombs. The supply of fuel for the island was essential for RAF Spitfires. Without fuel, they were useless. On the 15th of August, the badly damaged tanker carried the all-important fuel to allow the spitfires on the island to give air support during the upcoming battles. Field Marshall Montgomery was planning to attack the Rommel forces. The tanker was limping towards Malta and could have sunk at any time. Captain Mason of the destroyer *Penn* lashed the damaged vessel to the side of his ship, and the two sailed cautiously into Malta and unloaded the precious cargo. Captain Mason was awarded the Geoge Cross for this action. The people and the island of Malta were also awarded the George Cross, a symbol that occupies a place on the flag of the island.

John and Fiona were just in time for their appointment with the Deputy Ships Registrar for Malta. His office was housed in a magnificent stone building with a view of the harbour. The details of *Brave Goose* were presented. They were told they would need a maritime survey when she arrived in Malta to prove her seaworthiness. The registrar explained this could be undertaken at the port.

John accepted all the requirements and paid the registration fee for the first six months. He would now de-register from the UK, and he was given a certificate as a record to show authorities in EU countries. The final inspections by the Maltese registration service had to be completed within six months.

'Now, Mr and Mrs England.'

'No, not quite. We shall be married soon.'

'Oh, I am sorry. It was an assumption on my part. My apologies. You will be aware that a UK citizen can only reside in the EU for ninety days in one hundred and eighty. We find this to be a massive inconvenience to our owners. We have a system called the Nomad Residents Permit, which is structured by businessmen who can work remotely. We have another scheme, the Malta Permanent Residence Programme, which essentially makes you and your spouse residents of Malta and permits you to travel in the Schengen Area without restriction.

'You will appreciate there are financial implications to both these schemes. You don't need to decide now what you would like to do. However, *Brave Goose* is now a vessel registered with the Malta Maritime Registry.

'Before you go, Mr England, I now have a present for you as well as a marking note. This gives instructions to your marine engineers on how to change the location of the registration form from London to Valetta. Here is your present. A large Maltese ensign for *Brave Goose*.'

John and Fiona were excited at the prospect of registering *Brave Goose* in Valetta. They could also become European citizens, which would help them when they wanted to visit other EU countries.

CHAPTER 19

THE NEW EUROPEANS

John and Fiona landed in Athens, intending to take a taxi to Lefkas. That is until John received a message on his phone.

'John, to save a taxi ride all the way to Lefkas, ask the taxi to drop you off at the Corinth Yacht Harbour. We are at anchor outside, and I can send the rib to you. Just send me a text when you arrive.'

'Thank you, Noel. That will be a great help.'

'Did you get the drift? Noel has brought *Brave Goose* to Corinth to save us having to make a lengthy taxi ride to Lefkas Marina.'

'That's kind of him. We will get a bit more holiday on *Brave Goose* than expected.

On arriving at Corinth marina, *Brave Goose* was very obvious. John sent a text to Noel. No sooner had the text been sent than José was on his way to pick them up in the little port in the rib.

Back on board *Brave Goose,* John and Fiona were welcomed back like lost friends.

'Hello to you all. I have a present for *Brave Goose*. It's your department, José.'

José took the package with a degree of suspicion until he discovered it was a Maltese ensign.

'As you are all here, I have some news for you. *Brave Goose* is officially registered as a Maltese vessel. The implications are good for you, *Brave Goose*, Fiona and me. All of us will enjoy being Maltese 'nomad' residents. It would mean you, the crew of *Brave Goose*, Fiona and I would no longer be restricted to having limited access to EU countries in the Schengen area. That would be a fantastic benefit for you all. We shall have to make arrangements to sail to Malta to complete the registration process. I think the Maltese authorities will wish to see your passports in due course. The stern needs 'London' removed as the home port of registry and replaced by 'Valetta'. In addition, José, the UK ensign needs to be replaced by the Maltese ensign.'

'You have been busy, boss. I imagine there is still a great deal more paperwork to do?'

'Yes, Noel, you are so right. Did Paleros give you the final invoice for the re-fit? Are we all happy with it, the new equipment and so on? If so, I will pay Robert.'

*

'As we are in Corinth, where would you like to go? Another visit to Athens, hopefully a quieter visit than last time?'

'Is the canal open now, Noel?'

'Yes, John. Would you like me to arrange a transit?'

John looked at Fiona for agreement.

'Okay, Noel, yes, let's go through the canal.'

Noel set about making arrangements for the transit through the canal for the next morning.

'Okay, everyone. Sally, do you have anything we could BBQ tonight?'

'Yes, John. I have some lamb chops that will certainly feed everyone.'

'Good. It looks as though we shall have a warm, calm night. Let us all eat together on the quarterdeck this evening.'

Jock recovered the BBQ from its winter store. It needed a polish, but as he had given it a good cleaning before he stored it away, there was not a great deal to do to bring it up to specification.

John and Fiona decided to go swimming. José set the outside staircase on the starboard side and linked up the shower. Within half an hour, John and Fiona were in the sea. The two relaxed and played like two young children, swimming around the boat.

'It is hard to believe, John, the last time we were here, we were under attack.'

'Yes, my love. Let's put all that behind us and enjoy what is now looking like a new boat.'

The two owners had just showered at the bottom of the bathing steps and were starting to dry off when a rib approached the boat at high speed. John and Fiona ran up the steps in case it was someone they didn't wish to meet.

'Hello, were you running away?' said the Greek man who seemed familiar. John and Fiona had reached the quarterdeck. The driver of the rib had disembarked and was standing on the bathing platform at the bottom of the steps that had been deployed on the starboard side.

Before they knew it, he was standing on the quarterdeck, having climbed up the boarding steps.

'Do I know you?' asked John.

'You should, but it was a busy time when you were last here, so I am not surprised you don't recognise me.'

'Ah, you were one of the teams who tried to sink this boat. What are you doing here? Why are you on my boat?'

'That's not very friendly, Mr England.'

'I don't recall you being very friendly when I last saw you. I know who you are now. You were the organiser of the attack on *Brave Goose*. I have just recalled your name. Is it Vova?'

'Pretty good memory.'

'So why are you here?'

'The boat was moored here last night. I had someone tell me you were here.'

'So?'

'I never got paid by Georgio. He is still in prison. I don't think he is going to pay me now.'

'I hope you don't think I am going to pay you for organising the ambush on *Brave Goose*.'

'Mr England, Athens can be a dangerous place without security.'

'I hope you are not going to attempt to blackmail me again?'

'Blackmail is not a word I like. It's more of a security measure. I can ensure you and your crew will stay unharmed if you employ me as your security guard while in this area.'

'I see. How do you intend to ensure our safe passage as there is only one of you?'

'Oh, don't you worry about that! I have a new team as the last lot are still either in prison, hospital or dead.'

'Can I suggest we have not had this conversation? You can get back on your rib and sail away – NOW!'

'That isn't very friendly.'

'I don't feel very friendly towards you, so do as I ask.'

Vova turned and left in his rib, muttering in a loud voice that John would regret his decision.

'Whatever next? I think I will ring my friend Miron in EKAM. See what he advises. Do you remember him? He is the boss of the Greek special service unit.'

John returned to the quarter-deck dressed now in pale blue trousers and a dark blue *Brave Goose* polo shirt. He had already told Fiona the essence of the call with Miron. John now advised the crew what was to happen.

'When will the BBQ be ready, Sally?'

'Within the hour, John.'

'Can you hold it for a couple of hours?'

'Okay, that will be fine.'

'I expect it will be about two and a half to three hours before we can dine.'

'I can hold it all back, John, until you are ready.'

'We are heading off now through the canal, and Miron is arranging a berth for us in Piraeus. We can get the BBQ going when we get there.'

'So, another trip through the canal. Let's hope this trip is a little calmer than last time.'

Noel made immediate arrangements to leave. The crew brought the rib back on board the boat deck. José withdrew the boarding ladder on the starboard side.

'Weigh the anchor, please, José.'

Jock had started the engines, and they were underway.

Within half an hour, Noel reported a rib travelling at high speed towards them down the Corinth Canal.

'Yes, it could be the EKAM troops. Miron said he was going to send an escort.'

No sooner had John confirmed the arrangement than the rib was alongside.

It was crewed by four EKAM officers, two of them brandishing submachine guns. The skipper and helmsman advised Noel he was the escort.

'When we get to the far end, we will sail straight on, with the compliments of the Canal company.'

'*Brave Goose*, this is EKAM on your starboard side. Go to channel 72.'

The VHF radio on the bridge of *Brave Goose* burst into life with this message.

'EKAM, this is *Brave Goose* – over.'

'Yes, *Brave Goose*, please proceed straight through to the far end of the canal without stopping to check in at control. This has been authorised. Please keep a keen lookout if you see any suspicious movements; advise us immediately.'

'Will do. Out,' responded Noel.

'José, John and Fiona, can you please get hold of a pair of binoculars each and keep a good lookout. Please advise me immediately if you see any unusual activity. John and Fiona, can you take up position on the flybridge. José, can you go to the bow, please.'

The log on *Brave Goose* was showing a speed of eight knots. However, as there was a westerly flowing current of about two knots, the speed over the ground was six knots. The EKAM rib kept altering its position from astern to ahead and then either side as they progressed through the canal. Everyone on board was transfixed by the engineering, the towering walls of the canal carved so long ago to provide a shortcut from or into the Ionian and out to the Saronic Gulf.

As *Brave Goose* arrived towards the easterly end of the canal, the chain bridge was lifted. A message came from the VHF and from Canal Control wishing *Brave Goose* a safe onward journey.

'There will be no charge this time!'

Everyone on deck waved to the canal officers as they sailed past the office and they in turn waved back.

'That is a rare event, John. I think they were embarrassed by the lack of security when we last came this way.'

'You are probably right, Noel.'

The EKAM rib stayed with *Brave Goose* up to the entrance of Zea marina in Piraeus.

Once moored in the marina, Sally started to lay the table on the quarterdeck as it was now eight o'clock in the evening. She used the intercom to communicate with Jock, requesting him to light the BBQ. By nine o'clock, it was at peak heat with grey coals. The lamb chops smelled delicious, wine was on the table, and there was a salad and some spring new potatoes with a lashing of melted butter. Some mint sauce accompanied the lamb chops, which smelt incredible.

John had asked Noel not to run out the passerelle just yet.

'We don't want to be disturbed during dinner.'

After they'd eaten, José arranged for the passerelle to run out. A uniformed marina employee arrived with a bundle of forms.

'Sorry to interrupt, Sir, but I need some details of the boat, the crew and guest list, a copy of your VAT papers and your insurance certificate.'

'I am the owner of this vessel,' stated John. 'We have only just re-registered her in Malta. Due to time circumstances, we have been unable to get documents or make the change in registration. I shall try tomorrow with the assistance of the British Embassy and the Maltese delegation. Can all this wait until the morning? I can assure you we will not be leaving for a day or two.

'However, the crew, my partner, and I are all English but soon to be European, with a Nomad Visa from Malta.'

'Very well, Sir. Can you please bring what papers you get when you have done the rounds of the embassies?'

John agreed. The wine flowed, and John discussed the jobs for the following day, requesting that Noel and Fiona join him as there would be paperwork to complete.

CHAPTER 20

EUROPEAN RED TAPE

O nce *Brave Goose* was moored in Zea marina, and the passerelle had been run out, to John's surprise they had a visitor.

'Miron, my dear fellow! How good of you to come, and thank you for the escort through the canal.'

'The canal authorities were pleased to give you free passage due to the utter carnage the last time you passed through. I am not sure if you had time to inspect the westerly bank, but it has all been repaired wonderfully well. The gang who orchestrated the ambush are now all in prison.'

'Yes, we could see the repairs. It looks like a substantial job. I regret to have to inform you that you do not have all the culprits in prison. We were visited last evening by a guy called Vova, who was the organiser of the hi-jack.'

'Oh. I wasn't aware of anyone by that name. I thought the Scillian, Georgio, was the money and brains behind the operation?'

'Georgio was certainly the instigator of the attack, but Vova was the on-site organiser. He must have slipped away at the height of the activities. Probably when the digger fell from the top of the bank into the canal.'

'Can you recall how he looks, John?'

'I can do better than that. Since the re-fit this past winter, we have installed new CCTV cameras all around the boat. I can show you the relevant tapes now if you like.'

Miron was most impressed. He didn't recognise the individual. The video was pin-sharp, so it should be possible to apprehend him. He left, promising to return.

*

At breakfast, discussions recalled the previous evening.

'John, are we never going to be free of these people?'

'Don't concern yourself, Fiona. The authorities were of the opinion that they had caught everyone. Clearly not. I am certain Miron will sort this out. Where do you want to go for dinner?'

'I really don't mind. I would prefer to fly home sooner or later. We have a great deal to organise.'

'Shall we try and fly home tomorrow?'

'Yes, why not. I will see if I can organise tickets now.'

*

'Noel, Fiona and I will be leaving tomorrow. I have arranged tickets to Manchester for the two o'clock flight from Athens with EasyJet. I'm not sure when we shall be back, but while we are away, can you take *Brave Goose* to Malta? Please speak with the registrar to arrange a berth and a surveyor. Once the survey has been done, we will be well on the way to becoming fully-fledged Maltese.'

'What do I tell the marina officials when they come for the papers?'

'Explain we had to leave due to an emergency. The registration of *Brave Goose* in the UK has been terminated. I will leave you copies of the Maltese registration. You can copy these for the marina here. We will have the official papers next time we come here.'

'Yes, John, that is not an issue. Have you paid Paleros for the last instalment of the re-fit?'

'No, I haven't, but I will make the payment when I get back to

Manchester.'

*

The EasyJet flight had the two of them back in Manchester by early afternoon. It was Tuesday. On the flight, John and Fiona discussed their wedding arrangements. Fiona was concentrating on what to wear. By the time the plane landed in Manchester, they had a rough outline of the event. Fiona agreed to make the booking.

*

'Afternoon Sydney,' called out John as he and Fiona walked through the spacious glass reception area to Peter's Tower. There was no reply and he was clearly not at his desk.

'He must have slipped out to the shops,' suggested Fiona.

Once at the penthouse level in the southerly lift, the two bounded out full of the joys of spring, very much looking forward to their wedding and subsequent honeymoon.

'When are the cleaners due, Fiona?'

'Oh, I think they come on Thursdays.'

'They have left our front door open, but it's only Tuesday. Do you suppose they left it open since last week?'

Entering the apartment, John knew immediately they had been burgled. The whole penthouse was turned upside down. The sofas had been slashed and turned on their backs. The TV had been smashed. The bedrooms were also totally destroyed, with furniture upended. The clothes in the wardrobes had been thrown around, and the washbasins smashed.

'My god, how have these people got in here?'

'Do you think Sydney is okay, John?'

'Good thought. I will go down and see. There is no one in here now.'

John appeared in the reception area, but still no sign of Sydney. He went behind his desk. No sign but the safe door was open, and the spare keys to the penthouse were missing.

John continued on a 'behind the scenes' search of the reception area. He opened the door to the large store cupboard where there were cleaning materials, trip switches for the whole building alarm, and fire control switches mounted on the wall. He managed to find the light switch, and there was Sydney: trussed up and lying on the floor. John needed cutters to break him loose from the large cable ties. Eventually, he discovered a drawer in a unit in the store cupboard which housed some tools. Side angle cutters lay on top of the small selection of tools. Just what he needed.

'Sydney, can you hear me?' John was speaking loudly but the man was out cold. Even when John had removed his bindings, he was still unconscious.

He tried to sit Sydney up, back against the wall. He felt for his pulse then phoned the emergency services for an ambulance and the police.

He phoned the penthouse.

'Are you okay, darling?'

Apart from being in tears, Fiona was okay. John explained that Sydney had been attacked. He had been knocked out, and the attackers had opened the safe for the card key. The rest was obvious.

The ambulance crew, with a paramedic on board, came very quickly. They managed to restore Sydney to consciousness but explained they would have to take him to the hospital for a check-up. As he was being removed on a stretcher, three police officers came in.

John explained what had happened as best he could.

'We have CCTV, which should show what happened,' he said.

'And who are you, Sir?' said the taller of the two police officers.

'Can you move your police car back a couple of meters? We need to get this stretcher into the ambulance,' asked the ambulance driver.

Slightly red-faced, the tall police officer went outside and moved the car back a few meters. He left the blue lights flashing.

'I am the owner of the block,' advised John. 'Not only has my chief receptionist been attacked, but the attackers broke into the safe for the security lift pass and door key to my penthouse apartment. They have ransacked our apartment, and it's a mess. Will you come and inspect what has happened?'

'Yes, Sir. Do you have CCTV?'

'We do, officer. But first I need to phone the relief receptionist. Can you wait a moment?'

Once John was off the phone having arranged for the relief receptionist, he took the two officers up the right-hand lift to the penthouse.

The two officers marched in, frightening Fiona, who had not spotted John behind them.

'What a fantastic view,' the second officer remarked.

'Look, I have not asked you to come here to look at the view. Just look at the mess this apartment is in and the damage to furniture, bedding, bathroom fittings and the like.'

'We need to get CID onto this and a SOCO team as there could be evidence available, so can I ask you please not to touch anything here until they have finished?'

The senior police officer spoke to the station, requesting the additional services he required at the scene.

'We will go now, Sir. I will send you a crime number for your insurers as soon as I can.'

Once the two officers had left, John and Fiona returned to the foyer. The new receptionist had arrived.

'Ha, Ben, do you know the form here?'

'Yes, Mr England, thank you. Do you know how Sydney is?'

'No, but he was conscious when he was stretchered away. Please don't disturb anything in the store room or touch the safe. It is possible fingerprints and DNA could be available to the police.'

'I understand, Sir.'

*

John phone Jon Kim.

'Morning, Jon. You probably haven't heard, but whilst we were away, probably yesterday or first thing this morning, Sydney, our chief receptionist, was knocked out. The safe was opened, and the attackers took the key card for our penthouse. The intruders have wrecked the place.'

'Oh John, what a thing. I will speak with CID and SOCO to try to expedite things. Are you okay?'

'Yes, Jon, we are fine, thanks. Sydney, who they met at the front desk, got a battering. He is in hospital at the moment. I am about to phone my broker to get a loss adjuster around here as soon as possible.'

'Okay, John. If I have a moment, I will call later. If you need anything else, don't hesitate to call.'

*

'Hi, can I speak with Ian Birch, please? It's John England, and it's an emergency.'

'Sorry, Sir, I am new here. What is your name?'

'John England. I am an established client of the business.'

'Mr Birch asked not to be disturbed this morning, Sir.'

'Put me through NOW,' insisted John.

'Wait, please.'

After a few moments, the next voice he heard was Ian Birch.

'John, it's good to hear from you. I gather you have an urgent issue.'

CHAPTER 21

MORE ISSUES

J ohn phoned his letting agent to enquire if there was a vacant apartment that was available. He explained the circumstances and why he and Fiona would like to occupy it for a month or so.

'John, I am so sorry, but we have had a very successful time of late. Everything is let.'

'That's what I employ you to do. I bet at other times, there would be one or two available.'

'Yes, John. I am very sorry.'

'Don't be sorry, but keep up the good work.'

'John, why don't we go back to *Brave Goose* for a month? Help sort out the Malta registration. We have clothes and a very comfortable bed. We can get the insurance company to sort the situation out here.'

'You're not just a pretty face – brains as well!'

John phoned Robert at Paleros, in Lefkas.

'Robert, I am sorry not to have been back to you sooner. I have had an aggressive burglary at my penthouse here in Manchester. As a consequence, our apartment is uninhabitable, and there are no empty apartments in my block, so we are planning to return to *Brave Goose* later today. I am sorry I haven't paid you the balance owed. My computer has been smashed. Do you mind sending me a text with your bank details and the total amount due? I will arrange payment before I leave later today.'

After a friendly chat, Robert agreed that he would do all that.

Within the hour, the text came from Greece. John forwarded it to his bank manager with instructions on how to pay the amount due today.

'Noel, it's John. Where are you at the moment?'

'We have left Zea Marina and are heading back towards the Corinth Canal for a return to Lefkas. Then, in a couple of days, we shall be off to Malta.'

'Great. Please don't leave Lefkas before we get on board. We will join you for the trip to Malta. Can you contact the registrar to see if he can fix a berth for you? Also, can he organise the survey for shortly after you arrive?'

'Yes, no problem, John. Look forward to seeing you both in a day or two.'

*

'Ian, thanks for taking my call. We have been turned over in the penthouse. The receptionist has been attacked and is in hospital. I need a loss adjuster here and for the insurers to put the place back as it was with new furniture to replace all the furniture that has been damaged. The decorations, furnishing lamps et cetera have all been severely damaged. Can you please organise the insurers to get stuck in and make the place as it was?'

'Yes, John. You are insured on a like-for-like basis and new for old.'

'I understand, but I don't want to find the insurers have replaced expensive furniture with similar-looking cheaper furniture.'

'I understand. Will you be staying in the apartment?'

'No, Ian, the place cannot be occupied as it is now. The police forensic team are all over the place as I speak. Fiona and I are returning to *Brave Goose*. We have clothes and a comfortable bed there, so that makes sense.'

'Do you know when you will be back?'

'We will come back when we are advised the penthouse can be re-occupied. The security locks will need changing. Can I please leave all this with you, Ian? If there is an issue with the quality of furniture, beds and so on, please go for the best, and I will pay the difference between the insurance value and the actual cost.'

'John, I don't have the staff to do what you wish. I can get an interior furnishing company to handle all that. I will try to get the insurers to pay, in view of the premium income they receive each year for the block.'

John's next call was to the Corps of Commissionaires to ensure they could ensure there was a member of their team on duty at all times. John agreed to pay the extra cost as required.

'Now let us get a flight back to Lefkas.'

'John, why not try Pickford Travel to sort this for you? They can also look into the honeymoon location in the Maldives or Seychelles.'

'Great, you do that. I will book a room at the Midland for tonight and possibly tomorrow night as well. I don't think *Brave Goose* will be in Lefkas until the day after tomorrow.'

The couple hadn't undone their overnight bags. So, no packing was required.

Once they had established themselves at the Midland, they wandered around St Ann's Square in Manchester, finding their way to Waterstones book shop on Deansgate. In the travel section, Fiona saw an ideal true story about someone who lived and worked in the Seychelles. *Cream Teas to Coconuts* by Sue Hynd was the title and author. She thought it would make an excellent read whilst travelling to Malta on *Brave Goose*. It will tell me the truth about the islands rather than the usual sanitised travel guide, she thought.

That night, they had an enjoyable dinner and some excellent wine. They didn't sleep very well. John knew that the break-in at the penthouse must have had something to do with the investigations he was having with regards Fred Wright's inheritance and now Fred's wife's inheritance.

The following morning, John England had a long conversation with Jon Kim. They agreed the man who had been arrested and subsequently released when they visited Kent Watson's solicitor could have something to do with the break-in at the penthouse.

'Don't worry, John. Leave it with me. I will have a good look at the evidence and the forensic reports. You go back to Greece. If you need me, you can call me on my private number. Equally, I will let you know what we find.'

*

Jon Kim went to visit Sydney in the hospital. He was making good progress. He had received a nasty bash on his head. Sydney was unable to give much detail to Jon but was appreciative of the visit.

Later that day, a copy of the CCTV tape covering the time of the break-in and a copy of the SOCO report were provided. Jon Kim sat down, watched the video, and read the SOCO report. Both items provided him with valuable evidence.

Jon scrutinised the evidence. He realised he knew the man on the CCTV but not his accomplice. The accomplice was a tallish man with a denim jacket and jeans. He had black hair and a bronzed complexion. He looked athletic. It was Guy Miller, who had probably been sent by Kent Watson to put the frighteners on John England. Jon realised that Watson had no idea who he was dealing with. John England was a winner – he would get retribution for this outrageous attempt to intimidate him!

*

'Hi Jon,' said John England after placing a call to his friend. 'I am still in Manchester. We are leaving for Greece tomorrow.'

'I've seen CCTV footage of the intruders who broke into your apartment. The main culprit was Guy Miller, the heavy ex-boxer Kent Watson employed. The one my officers arrested outside Watson's.

We had no reason to charge him with anything at the time. He must have thought that there were no CCTV cameras in your apartment. How wrong he was. We have very clear pictures of him and his friend as they take your penthouse apart. There is a warrant out for their arrest. Enjoy your trip to *Brave Goose*. I will keep you informed of developments at our end!'

As John listened to Kim, a text appeared on his mobile to confirm Robert at Pelaros in Lefkas had received the money and thanking John for the payment.

'Thanks, Jon. My insurance broker, Ian Birch, will be obtaining a quote to repair the damage. He will be employing an interior designer and furnishing expert to put the penthouse back together.'

'Thanks, John.'

*

At seven the following morning, John and Fiona were on a tram to Manchester Airport. It took them straight to Terminal Two to connect with the EasyJet flight to Preveza.

The expected arrival time was 1300 hours Greek time. John text Noel that he expected to be in Lefkas marina by 1400 hours.

Behind them on the tram was a passenger dressed in jeans, a black T-shirt, and a blue denim jacket. He wore well-worn brown deck shoes and no socks. He didn't have any luggage; he just had an overnight bag, which he had placed on the luggage rack on the tram.

The man was sitting five rows behind John and Fiona. He had a Jeffery Archer novel, *Traitors Gate,* which seemed to occupy him for the journey.

CHAPTER 22

LEFKAS TO VALETTA

T he EasyJet flight mid-week did not carry a full complement of passengers. Just after one o'clock, John and Fiona made their way through passport and customs control. At the gate onto the main concourse was a smiling Greek taxi driver with a 'Mr England' sign on a piece of cardboard.

'Senor England, I have a taxi for you.'

'Where are you taking us to?'

'Oh, the port.'

'Which quay?'

'They didn't tell me.'

'Who is 'they' ?'

'Sorry mate, there has been a mix-up. My taxi is over there waiting for me.'

John and Fiona started to cross the airport road to a line of white taxis. Mostly Mercedes saloons.

'Sorry, Sir,' shouted the taxi driver with the sign. 'They said I have to take you out of the airport.'

'Have they paid you?'

'No, they said I would get one hundred Euros when I delivered you to the destination.'

'Sorry, mate, you are not taking us anywhere. Look, here is twenty euros for your trouble.'

'Senor, I HAVE to take you.'

'No, you don't,' insisted John. 'He and Fiona walked to the taxi rank and got into the first cab. John explained their destination.

Once in Lefkas Marina and approaching Quay E, John realised the taxi man with the sign had followed them all the way to *Brave Goose*.

John and Fiona alighted from their taxi, handing the driver fifty euros. He drove off, just missing the shadow taxi.

The crew of *Brave Goose* were lining the rail of the quarterdeck, and the paserelle had been deployed. John and Fiona galloped up to the deck. John pressed the 'retract' button, which lifted the passerelle and retracted it into the body of the boat.

The taxi driver who had been holding the sign was sitting in his seat, talking on his mobile.

'The driver of that taxi told us he had been booked to collect us from the airport. However, he wasn't sure where he was to take us, so I thought it was not quite right, which is why we got a taxi off the rank.'

'Have you had an issue with someone, John?' enquired Noel, realising he had seen situations like this before.

'Noel, this situation has nothing to do with *Brave Goose* or the crew. I am trying to recover in excess of £150,000 from a firm of solicitors in Manchester. They have managed an estate for the beneficiaries of an estate. It looks like the solicitor running the branch has embezzled the money and I've accused him. I guess that is why he is not happy with me. I have reported him to the Solicitors Regulation Authority and the Financial Conduct Authority. They will be tough to deal with. In the meantime, I have an elderly widow who could do with help with the money!'

'You do seem to attract problems that land you in a scrape!'

'You are quite right, Noel. So if we can leave in the morning for Malta, that would be good.'

'Yes, John. I have done a quick calculation. Depending on fair seas and not too much adverse weather and wind, we should make Malta in forty-eight hours, at ten knots. If you want to be more frugal with fuel, then it will take sixty hours at eight knots.'

'How soon can you be ready to sail, Noel?'

'We can be ready within an hour. We are topped up with fuel; everything is working as it should, so we can go whenever you like.'

'Okay, Noel. Let us depart at 1600 hours, which at ten knots will see us arriving in Valetta at twenty hundred hours on Friday?'

'Yes, that's correct, John. I will get everything ready for sea, and we shall be ready to go at six o'clock this evening.'

Noel spoke to the harbour master. He explained that they could be away for a month or more.

'That's okay, senor. It is your berth, and you have paid for it. Have a good trip.'

It was a calm early evening when *Brave Goose* departed Lefkas marina. They turned south, travelling along the now-widened canal out into the Ionian Sea. Their course would take them past Nisos Skorpio, the island much loved by Aristotle Onassis and Jackie Kennedy, and then south to the Meganisi Channel. Once clear of the channel, Noel altered the course to a more south-westerly one. The final piece of land, the cape of Dhoukato, is the most southerly point of the island of Lefkas. The point was marked by a lighthouse. Once through the channel between Lefkas and the northerly point on Cephalonia, marked by the little port of Fiskardho, *Brave Goose* would be able to go on her main course for the trip to Malta.

The course was set at 245 degrees magnetic. *Brave Goose* would remain on this course for four hundred and eighty nautical miles. It was anticipated it would take two full days to arrive at Valetta, where a mooring had been reserved.

As night began to close in, the magical view of the setting sun to the west had everyone on board transfixed. As the corona of the sun neared the horizon, the sky turned pink and orange. Eventually, the sun left the sky, leaving a trail of colour, a sight those on board would never forget. An hour later, the sky had turned to a dark blue velvet sprinkled with millions of stars as far as the eye could see in any direction. The final light visible was the lighthouse at Dhoukato. It flashed like a tiny Christmas tree light. It was observed about three times, then nothing. *Brave Goose* was out of range.

Noel took the opportunity to check their position on the satellite navigator. He was delighted to see that their position was precisely on the track line he had marked on the chart. The electronic track on the sat-nav also showed the exact location. Noel marked the chart in pencil with their position and distance travelled to this way-point. The sea state had become very calm.

Fiona, the most inquisitive member of the team, asked Noel, 'Why do you make a pencil note on the paper chart? The computer and sat-nav have all the details recorded?'

'I have experienced electronics failing before. We do have duplicates, but the pencil record on the chart is always there and cannot disappear even if there is a fault with the electronics. It's a safety issue, Fiona.'

'That is why we love you so much, Noel. You always ensure we are safe. Thank you.'

Sally was delighted to be under sail and cooking food, which she served on the quarter deck. She, Fiona and John lined the rail at the aft end.

'Look, wow! What causes that?'

'I don't know,' responded John. 'It is a light show the likes of which I have never seen before.'

Fiona went to the wheelhouse to tell Noel what they could see in the wash of the boat aft of the hull.

'I think it could be an ideal moment for you to go to the Portuguese bridge.' That was the area surrounded by a solid surround, forward of the bridge outside the bridge. It was possible to see really well dead ahead of the boat.

In a flash of spray and efflorescence, Fiona could see a dolphin, and then one more, keeping up with *Brave Goose*. They were covered in fantastic sparkling bubbles for the length of their bodies. They looked like some sort of aquatic act from a circus. It was a sight and display she would never forget.

She returned to the quarter deck and explained to John and Sally what she had seen at the bow. They all followed her to see what she was talking about.

'Wow, that is amazing.'

'It is, Sally. I have never seen anything like this before.' John pulled out his mobile phone and tried to video the scene. He wasn't sure this would work. If it didn't, he decided he would purchase some proper camera equipment to film sights he had never seen before and possibly might never see again.

It was eleven o'clock. *Brave Goose* had travelled five hours and covered fifty nautical miles. Just under four hundred still to go.

The crew split into watches. Three hours on, two hours in reserve, and then handover to another crew member.

Way over to the port side, the sky began to lighten. By six o'clock in the morning, it was daylight. *Brave Goose* had covered one hundred and twenty nautical miles. Their position had been noted on the paper chart. The sat-nav confirmed the navigation details.

Once Sally's excellent English breakfast had been consumed by all, Noel and Jock, who had worked between them all night navigating *Brave Goose* to her destination, left their post for breakfast. Jock took over from John, who stood in for Noel for the next two hours. Noel was up again for another two hours, then John, and so on, until they were in sight of Malta.

At ten miles out from Valetta, at five in the afternoon, Noel radioed Valetta Port Control on VHF Channel 12. He advised there was a berth awaiting for *Brave Goose* in Grand Harbour. This harbour was the third inlet to port when coming from the sea.

'Thank you, Sir. We have registered your arrival.'

Noel was requested to call again when they were one mile off the entrance.

Noel then called Grand Harbour dockyard on their call sign Channel 13, call sign Grand Harbour Marina. This was a dedicated section of the harbour for private craft: large cruisers and superyachts. It was a Camper and Nicholson-managed marina. They had been commissioned to carry out the inspections required by the Maltese authorities so that Maltese registration could be obtained.

A port police office was situated on the easterly side of the Dockyard Creek where pontoons had been established for smaller vessels. The creek also berthed superyachts and mega yachts on the easterly side. Where the creek widened, longer vessels like *Brave Goose* could moor stern-to.

'It's interesting, Noel, that the dockyard moorings have had to establish names for vessels of different sizes. Originally, all large motor yachts were simply superyachts; now, they have to accommodate mega yachts.'

'Yes, John. We are in the superyacht category, although somewhat smaller than some.'

'Okay, folks, this is stern-to mooring with lazy lines from the buoys out front. Jock and José, can you please prepare stern lines with heaving lines? The bow lines will be handed up on heaving lines by marinaras in their small boats. There will be substantial mooring buoys to attach our bow lines to. Please ensure you have a good purchase on the bow windlasses for both lines. Equally, when you have heaved the main stern lines on board, use the windlasses so we can square up. I will then have cross springs run out at the stern.'

'Wow! What a beautiful place, darling. It is fabulous.'

'It is. I am so glad we have a crew who know what they are doing. It isn't easy docking stern-to in a place you have never been to before.'

'Noel is good at this sort of thing. It looks as though there will be some good restaurants on the shore.'

'You are right on both counts, Fiona.'

Noel had instructed José and Jock to run out the passerelle. It was a gentle slope to the quay. The Maltese flag was flying from the stren. Following this visit, John hoped all the paperwork would be complete for their Maltese registration.

'John, Fiona, please don't rush on the quay. I need to accompany you to the port police so we can check in. We can then go to the Camper and Nicholson office to arrange the surveys. Don't forget your passports.'

The three of them left *Brave Goose* by way of the passerelle. They turned left and walked along the quay, backed by the Maritime Museum, heading for the port police.

'Ooh, I would love to go in there, John.'

'We can do during our stay here. We will have lots of time. It is a beautiful building, built of pale sandstone with lots of carvings on the façade. A place to visit, I agree.'

The port police were very helpful as they had been made aware of the reason for the visit, and realised that this new boat into the harbour was going to add to the island's coffers.

'We will be having our vessel surveyed while we are here so we can complete all the requirements of Maltese registration.'

'Yes, I understand, Sir,' responded the sergeant with three stripes on his white uniform.

'Will it be here we apply for a Nomad Resident Permit?'

'Yes, Sir. In the first instance. However, I can help you now. Here is a duplicate set of forms for you to complete. You may wish to look at the visa requirements before you complete the form. When you have completed the form, please return it to me here.'

The next visit was to Camper and Nicholson's office to get dates for the seaworthiness survey. As it transpired, due to the length of *Brave Goose* being in excess of 25 meters, she would have to go through quite a stringent process.

The swanky office of C&N, as one might expect, had a fantastic view of the harbour and the section they managed. John and Fiona gazed out of the window in the air conditioned board room.

'This must be the room they bring all the wealthy owners to, John.'

'Yes, I would love to hear what the walls have listened to over the years. Sales of mega and superyachts, contracts for charter and management of vessels on behalf of the owners. Insurance, all the paperwork associated with significant vessels.'

'This must be reserved for the over twenty-five-meter clients.'

A smartly dressed young lady wearing a light blue shift dress and white deck shoes approached. On her left lapel was a C&N logo with her first name engraved below it, then in smaller print, 'Manager of Legal Dept.' Her name was Camilla.

'Hello, you must be Mr and Mrs England?'

'Nearly correct. We have a wedding day at the end of next month, 30th June. I will be Mrs England then. But please call me Fiona.'

'Yes, I am John, just call me John.'

'As a sharp-eyed person will have spotted, my name is Camilla. I gather you need to register your vessel, *Brave Goose*, which is tied up almost below this window. What a beautiful yacht. You must be very proud of her?'

'We are,' responded Fiona.

'She has just had a re-fit at Pelaros's yard in Lefkas. She is looking her best. Do you need our captain here as well?'

'No, not at the moment. It's not too far for the captain to come should we need him.'

'Camilla, I am not sure this is within your remit, but Fiona and I were wondering about applying for a Nomad Visa. That would, as I understand it, allow us access to most EU countries without being hog-tied to 90 days in 180 days?'

'Strictly no, John, but we do come across this all the time. One of the requirements of the Nomad Visa is that you own or lease a property in Malta. As you would expect, we have a solution for that, as we assume most owners would like to remain on board their yacht.'

'That would be us, except while the surveys and service checks are being undertaken.'

'Oh, where will you be during the survey, John?'

'In a hotel, Camilla.'

'Okay, let's get through the yacht paperwork, then I can explain to you what we could do to help.'

Camilla opened a C&N folder packed with forms. John, Fiona and Noel would be involved in completing these. In addition, she gave John a list of the documents required for *Brave Goose*.

'In addition to these forms and documents we need from you, there has to be a survey of *Brave Goose*, attesting to its seaworthiness. In this pack is a certificate to be signed by the surveyor. As *Brave Goose* is longer than 25m, all the other documents on the list have to be provided. Once everything is in place, I will check the documents and then get them certified by the Malta Maritime Authority. Can you take these away and return them to me when completed, together with the original documents itemised on the list?'

'Absolutely. I am a solicitor, Camilla. We invented the art of creating paper and forms!'

Camilla laughed. Can you please pay one thousand euros as a down payment for the surveyor who I have booked to start work on

Monday? I will go off-duty at noon today as it's Saturday. If you need any help, the marina office remains open twenty-four hours a day.'

'Great, we look forward to seeing the surveyor on Monday.'

John and Fiona returned with the bundle of forms, which John immediately handed to Noel for completion as best he could.

'Noel, the surveyor will be here Monday morning to carry out the seaworthiness inspection.'

'Okay, John. That should not be a problem. Will you be staying on board while all this goes on?'

'No, we will book into a hotel. We are going for a walk round to see what we can find.'

'Okay, John. Everything will be fine here. Let me know where you will stay when you have decided, as a number of the forms will require you both to sign them.'

CHAPTER 23

FINN & CO

Kent Watson was congratulating himself on the turmoil he had created in the apartment belonging to John England. He was looking at photographs on his iPhone sent to him from Guy Miller, his hired help, who wanted to get his revenge for being handcuffed in the street by two coppers when England was having a discussion with Watson. The coppers had had to let him go, as he had not done anything. Well, not at that point. He was about to exact his revenge on England and his totty.

Guy was sure England's insurance company would cough up for re-furnishing the penthouse.

'Kent, it's Guy.'

'Yes, what do you want?'

'Some more money. I turned up in your office to sort out England, but I never got the chance. I have sorted out his apartment, so I think I am owed some more cash.'

'Do you indeed? That is where we differ. You will have to do something far more daring to get a further dollop of dough.'

'Like what?'

'I need some leverage on England to stop him trying to demand money from me. How about kidnapping his girlfriend?'

'So, if I did that for you, I would have to find somewhere to keep her?'

'She can go into the second-floor store where you were hiding out the other day. It's over my office, so it is secure, and it would be the last place they would think of looking.'

'What would you pay me for that?'

'The other five grand.'

'Not enough. I need seven grand. Do not forget I have already turned over the penthouse for no extra fee.'

'How would you go about this and get her here without anyone seeing you or her?'

'That's my problem, Kent. It will be late at night when I bring her to your place, so you just need to be there to open the office. I will also need a key as I'll need to get water and food for her.'

'Okay. Come tomorrow morning, and I will let you have a key. We can consider if anything needs to change upstairs.'

'I will be there. I need two thousand in advance so I can fulfil your requirements.'

*

Guy was true to his word. He arrived at Kent's office at ten the following morning, dressed in jeans, a T-shirt and a dirty navy-blue sweater.

'Kent, there are two flights of stairs to manoeuvre. I will, when the time comes, try to get help lifting her from my van to the top floor. She can't be very heavy. I will make sure she is unconscious when I deliver her here. Let's look at security; she will inevitably try to escape the minute she recovers consciousness.'

'Okay, Guy, let's go up and check what needs changing, if anything.'

Once upstairs, they looked around the room, a typical Victorian attic.

'There needs to be a substantial lock on the outside of the entrance door to the loft. A hasp, staple, and weighty padlock. The cast iron bed frame and old mattress are fine,' said Guy.

The two men retreated to Kent's office and Kent gave Guy an envelope containing £2000 in cash.

'I will give you a ring when the parcel has been delivered.'

Guy left, leaving Kent to his thoughts. He wanted to be far away when all this was going on. He had applied to close all his ISAs and when the money was released, he expected to receive at least £150,000.

CHAPTER 24

VALETTA

'Hello, Frank. Good to hear from you. Have you some news?'

'Yes, John, it's not very good. Mrs Wright has received a letter from Finn & Co., who say they are the solicitors to the trust. They go on to say there is no money left in the trust, and if she is paying for a solicitor to look into the matter, she is wasting her money.'

'Frank, I see this as good news. There certainly is money – there should be at least one £150,000 in the trust. The fact Finn & Co have written in these terms confirms my suspicion that the partner in charge, Kent Watson, has had his hand in the till all these years.'

'Okay, I will just tell her not to worry, and when you are back, you will sort it out.'

*

John's mobile rang as they were walking back towards *Brave Goose*. His travel agent advised he could get a balcony room looking over the harbour at Hotel 23.

'That sounds interesting. We will go and have a look.'

He turned to Fiona.

'Okay, darling. There is a hotel nearby where we can get a balcony room overlooking the dock, so we can stay there while the survey is done.'

Boarding *Brave Goose*, they found there was a visitor. A tall man with jeans and a leather jacket. John was sure this was the man he had seen waiting to join the aircraft in Manchester.

'John, this gentleman is Toby Partington. He is here to carry out the seaworthiness survey.'

'I see,' said John, now entirely in the picture. 'Was it you who flew out on the EasyJet flight from Manchester?'

'Yes, it was, and you are, Sir?'

'Oh, I am sorry, we are John and Fiona, joint owners of *Brave Goose*. I recall seeing you, but the plane landed at Prevesa in Greece. How is it you are here? We were in Lefkas marina and left shortly after arriving in Lefkas.'

'John, the marina here instructed me to undertake the survey, telling me you were berthed in Lefkas. So that's where I went. As it happens, I had another job in Lefkas, so I did that, then got the bus to Athens and flew to Malta. Here I am.'

'Very odd all that, but as it happens, we needed to come here to complete documents, et cetera. Where are you staying in Malta, Toby?'

'I don't have a reservation as yet.'

'How much of a disturbance will you make in the work you have to do, and how long will it take?'

'It will take a maximum of two days. I will work during daylight hours only. The work is inspection only, not pulling things apart.'

Fiona could read John's mind. 'Toby, why don't you use the spare single cabin. We can provide you with some food. Would that be a help?'

'It indeed would. I can start right now.'

'That's a deal. Look, let me introduce you to the crew, in particular Noel, the captain.'

Within the hour, Toby was settled in his cabin and making ready to commence his survey. He notified Noel he would be starting in the engine room and the bilge area, working upward methodically.

'John, I thought I should tell you that a surveyor from the registrar's office will call at some point to check I am fulfilling the requirements of the Maltese authorities.'

'That's fine, Toby, just tell Noel.

'This is a valuable development. We can take some papers back to the registrar's office for them to check through everything, and then we can return and sign in due course. I guess they will need to see the survey before confirming their registration. I have also discovered we have to cease registration in the UK, so I need to address that now and have them email me a document to terminate the current registration.'

Toby Partington finished his inspection of seaworthiness within two days, as anticipated. He told Noel and John that there were no issues whatsoever. He expressed his delight with *Brave Goose*, a beautiful gentleman's yacht. John and Fiona had managed a thorough perambulation of Valetta. John said it was a pretty town and the right size for a walk around, which they had managed twice in two days.

Once Toby had left, there was little else for John and Fiona to do but complete the registration. John had received the certificate of deregulation from London by email.

The two of them returned to the registrar's office, signed all the documents, and took copies of Noel's papers for the ship.

'Just the final issue, Sir, which I suspect is what brought you to Malta in the first place?'

'Would that be the payment of VAT on the valuation?'

'Correct, Sir. The survey also included a valuation. It is on that figure we will charge you VAT and certify its payment.'

'Okay, what was the valuation?'

'The valuation is £875,000.'

'That sounds realistic. How much will the VAT be on that figure? '

'The attraction of Malta to the yachting fraternity is the fact that our EU-recognised VAT rate is five point four per cent. That will make the VAT payable £47,250.00.'

John was delighted by the figure, which was over £150,000 less than the fee payable in Lefkas.

'How would you like me to pay?'

'Ideally, a bank transfer to the Maltese registrar's bank account. The details are here on the invoice.'

'Can you please bear with me for a moment while I call my bank?'

John and Fiona moved to a quiet area in the registrar's office, where John called his bank manager. He explained what he wanted to do straight away. John gave him all the registrar's bank details.

Half an hour had passed when the registrar called John and Fiona back into his office.

'Thank you, Mr England, the money has come through. Here is your VAT-paid certificate. Please keep this safe onboard as it will certainly be required by authorities in other EU countries.'

John and Fiona thanked the registrar for all his help. They returned to *Brave Goose,* holding the VAT certificate tightly. Noel was delighted to add this to his paperwork. John suggested he had a photocopy held with the papers and, unless demanded, not to show the original VAT certificate.

'Can I have all the passports, Noel? I am going to see what arrangements can be made for the Nomad Visa. Also, can you make me photocopies of all the documents I have just handed to you?'

John and Fiona arrived at the Port Police office. The same sergeant they had seen before was still there.

'Sorry, Sergeant, I don't know your name. We now own a VAT-paid and Malta-registered motor yacht called *Brave Goose.* What we would like to obtain now is Nomad Visas for ourselves and the crew.'

'Yes. They are called Nomad Residence Permits. I am not entirely sure they will be what you require. You can obtain a similar facility that allows you to travel unhindered in any Schengen area for as long as you wish. The cost here is quite high. I understand that Spain has a similar situation for property owners so long as you purchase their 'Golden Visa' at the time you purchase a property. Anyway, here are the details of the Malta scheme.'

'Thank you, Sergeant. We will give due consideration to this and be back in touch if we decide to proceed.'

Walking back to *Brave Goose,* John and Fiona discussed the visa situation. John was more interested in the Spanish scheme.

'We could buy a property in Mallorca, which seems to be the requirement. Mallorca would be more convenient for us. We need to think about this.'

CHAPTER 25

THE BALEARICS

'Fiona, why don't we fly to Mallorca, stay in a nice hotel, and then have a look around?'

'That would be lovely, John. If we kept *Brave Goose* there, or somewhere close, it would be easy for us to nip out regularly as there are flights many times a day, certainly in the summer.'

'Yes, it's a good idea. We could then move her back to Malta for the winter. By all accounts, the weather in the winter is usually very good.'

'Let's have a chat with Noel.'

'Noel. Fiona and I think we would like to sail around and look at Mallorca, Ibiza, and Minorca. We may want to buy a house there, together with a Golden Visa.'

'Okay. I will take *Brave Goose* anywhere you require. I will just need notice.'

*

'Kent, this attic will be okay for England's woman. It will just need some tidying up. The bedstead and dirty mattress will be fine. I will be able to tie her hands and feet to the bedstead.'

'Don't hurt her, Guy. We could be in enough trouble for kidnapping her. I don't want murder on my record.'

'I'm not going to hurt her, Kent.'

Guy met with Kent later in the day. He obtained a key to the office and the upstairs room.

'Look, Guy, I am about to go away. Here is my mobile number. When you have the woman tied up and before you lock her in the room, send me a photo of her bound up, and I would suggest gagging her too.'

'What then?'

'As I have told you, I will be away, so as soon as I see the photo of her bound to the bed, I will email you the number for the combination of the safe under my desk. You will find an envelope with your money in it.'

'How long are you away for, and will you be in this country?'

'I don't know how long I will be away, but I will not be in the UK. I will be in Europe.'

'Okay. If my money is not there, I will come and find you. When I find you, you will not like it.'

Guy was surprised to discover Kent's office was neat and tidy. He had made some significant changes. Guy thought he must have put most of the papers he had in storage.

'When can I do the deed?'

'That is a matter for you. I don't know where John and Fiona are right now. You will have to search for them.'

*

'John, before we go anywhere else, there is something I have to confess to you.'

'Good heavens, what has brought this on? What is troubling you, my darling?'

'I received an email yesterday requesting that I go for a scan in Manchester. John, I haven't been entirely honest with you. Much of the two recent so-called shopping trips have been to see doctors.

They think I might be suffering from cancer.'

'Oh, darling. Come here, let me hug you.'

'Don't hug me too hard, John. They think I could have breast cancer. I can't go any further with our wedding knowing this. I can't, in fact, marry you until this is sorted out.'

'Oh, darling, of course, you can marry me. This isn't going to change my mind. I hope it hasn't changed yours?'

'Of course not, John, but I cannot go through with the wedding until I know the prognosis and the implications the disease has for the future.'

'Fiona, you must tell me all about it. When did this first come to light?'

'It would be about eight weeks now. I had to wait three weeks to see a doctor and then another three weeks to see a consultant at the Christie Hospital.'

'Well, first things first. You are not going to be treated on the NHS with their waiting times and delays. You will see the best oncologist. I hope, if required, you will be operated on within a week or two at the outside. So I am going to change the flights from Mallorca to Manchester. If we can fly in the morning, that is what we shall do.'

'Oh John, I knew you would make a fuss. There must be lots of people in my situation. I can wait.'

'If there is one thing I know about cancer, it is that it needs catching as early as possible. As my nearly wife, I am in charge now. You will have the best. I will call Ian Birch to see how the apartment is going. If it's not ready, we will stay at the Midland Hotel.'

Fiona started to cry. She was shaking with fear. Every muscle in her body went stiff with fear. She had it in her mind that this would kill her.

'John, I want you to have this ring back. I have taken it under false pretences. I can't marry you when I'm a wreck and if I'm to be mutilated.'

'Don't be silly. This is so important; I will not stop searching for the best surgeon and the best hospital. Let me get to my office, and I will make some calls.'

*

'Ian Birch, please?'

There was no nonsense this time about holding on, that he was busy. John was put straight through.

'Ian, thanks for taking my call. I need some help. Fiona has just told me that she received today a text from her GP that she might have breast cancer. Do you know of the top oncologist in Manchester, the best hospital to treat Fiona?'

'Oh John, how terrible. I have your email address. I will drop everything and make some enquiries. As soon as I know what you need, I will email you. Give Fiona my best wishes.'

'Thanks, Ian. Looking forward to the contacts.'

'Hi, darling. I am waiting for some information on specialists and hospitals. I have changed our flights, and we are off home tomorrow. The flight is eleven in the morning.'

'Oh John, you are kind. I am sure I could have managed this without lots of money. However, you do make me feel reassured.'

'Well, I am sure your NHS route would have worked, but not as fast as I would like to move. I wish you had told me earlier rather than burying your head in the sand. That could be dangerous. However, we are back on track now.'

'I am sorry, darling, I thought you had enough to deal with. You are always fixing other people's problems.'

'Now I don't want any of that. I am fine. It's you we have to get fixed, the most important person to me. We must tell Noel that we are going back to the UK, and when we are coming out again. We will ask him to return to Lefkas. We can do our survey of properties in Mallorca when we have time. Perhaps in the winter.'

'How long is the flight, John?'

'Five and a half hours. We need a taxi to the airport at eight o'clock. We, and you especially, will be tired when we get home. That reminds me, I forgot to ask Ian Birch if the apartment was sorted.'

'Noel, can you arrange a taxi back to the airport here tomorrow at eight o'clock? We will not be going to Mallorca. You can remain here for a while and then travel back to Lefkas. Fiona and I have some urgent business to attend to in England. I will let you know when we get back to Lefkas. I hope you don't have too much difficulty with the Greek authorities regarding the VAT.'

'I will fix the taxi. Don't worry about us, we will be fine. We hope all goes well back in the UK.'

CHAPTER 26

HOME AGAIN

J ohn had been able to secure some extra leg room seats on the EasyJet flight. It appeared as though the flight wasn't full. Small overnight bags were all that they required, so leaving Manchester Airport was a speedy process. John had ordered a limousine to take them back to Peter's Tower. Ian Birch had told him that the penthouse had been totally refurbished. Clothes that had been scattered around had been dry cleaned and hung back in the wardrobes. Fresh flowers decked the living room.

At the reception area in Peter's Tower, they were delighted to see Sydney back on duty.

'Sydney, how lovely to see you back. Are you fully recovered?'

'More or less, Mr England. I have checked the penthouse. It does look good. I hope you enjoy it. Here are two new lift and key cards for you. The locks have been changed, and a new code for access has been added. The code is in this envelope.'

'Thanks, Sydney, that is excellent news. Please call us by our Christian names. Mr or Mrs England sound too stiff!'

'When did you get married?'

'It's fair to say we haven't yet got married, but any time soon.'

Going through the routine of accessing the penthouse via the right-hand lift, the couple were delighted they were able to stay in their home now that they were back in England.

John thought about carrying Fiona over the threshold, but in view of her medical condition, he thought better of it. The penthouse looked beautiful. Everything had been done to make it even better than it was before.

'Well done, Ian,' John spoke out loud.

'I agree, John, it is lovely. Better than I remember it.'

'Would you like a coffee, darling? While I do that, you put your feet up on the new sofa and think what you would like for supper.'

John plugged in a new coffee cartridge, and the machine made two cups of coffee. This replacement machine took extra large capsules and filled two cups at the same time. John was very pleased with it. He was carrying the coffee to the lounge area when the phone rang. He placed the cups on the coffee table.

'Hello. John England here. Oh, hello, yes, that would be excellent. We shall be there at eleven in the morning.'

'Who was that, John, and where are we going at eleven in the morning?'

'It was the secretary, Carol, to the senior oncologist, Mr Fairbairn, at the Christie Hospital in Withington. She has made an appointment for you to see Mr Fairbairn at eleven tomorrow. She asked if you would take some overnight clothes with you.'

'Why is that, John?'

'Mr Fairbairn may wish to keep you in following some investigations tomorrow.'

'Oh John!' Fiona drew in a stuttered gasp. 'That's all very fast. Is it necessary to move at this pace?'

'It is, darling. All the papers on this subject state without any doubt that the faster action is taken to deal with breast cancer, the sooner you can be cured and get on with living life. Is there something in particular worrying you?"

'There is, John.' Fiona took in a deep breath. A single tear ran down her cheek. 'What I worry about is that I know they may well want to remove one or both my breasts, my hair could fall out, and I keep thinking will you still love me when I am mutilated in this way?'

'Oh, darling. Don't even consider these things. I will always love you. I want to get you treated as soon as we can so that we can enjoy our life together.'

John brought the Range Rover to the front door of Peter's Tower the following day in preparation for the trip to The Christie Hospital. Due to the double yellow lines, John asked Sydney to keep an eye out for traffic wardens.

He explained he was taking Fiona to the hospital. It would be some time before they were back.

'I hope everything goes well, John'.

'Thanks, Sydney.'

Within fifteen minutes, John and Fiona passed through the reception. Fiona sat in the passenger seat, and John drove.

It was twenty past ten when the pair left Peter's Tower. Parking at the Christie in the reserved car park for private patients just off Wilmslow Road, there was ample space to alight, and they both walked arm in arm into the reception area.

A cheerful lady with a uniform and a name badge welcomed them both.

'We have come to meet with Mr Fairbairn. It's John and Fiona England He is expecting us at eleven o'clock.'

'Yes, that's correct. If you take the lift over there, someone will meet you on the second floor.'

*

'Mr and Mrs England, pleased to meet you. I am Carol. Mr Fairbairn's secretary. Can you please follow me to the waiting room? He has been delayed a little by an operation earlier this morning. He shouldn't be too long now. Would you like a tea or coffee?'

They both refused the offer. There was no one else in the waiting room. On their way into the hospital, Fiona had been struck by the number of people coming and going through the main entrance.

'Yes, darling, it is a busy place. It is, however, a hospital of excellence with regards to cancer treatment.'

They were sitting in a warm, well-furnished room, each quietly contemplating in their mind what was to happen next.

*

Back at Peter's Tower, Sydney was being confronted by a man, who he was sure was the same man who had knocked him out.

'What can I do for you, Sir?' enquired Sydney. At the same time, Sydney pressed the police alarm button which had been installed since the previous raid on the property.

'I just wanted to know if Mr England had returned to the UK. I understand from a mate of mine who works at the airport that they were on an EasyJet flight from Malta yesterday.'

'I wasn't on duty yesterday afternoon. I haven't seen the Englands yet, but if they are here, they will no doubt come down eventually. Would you like to take a seat over there while waiting?'

'That's very civil of you. I will.'

'Would you like a coffee?'

'Thank you. I would be very grateful.'

Guy Miller sat on this sumptuous black leather and feather-upholstered sofa.

True to his word, Sydney came from behind his desk, holding a hot cup of coffee. He was only feet away from Guy Miiller when two police constables burst in.

'That's your game, is it? You were just trying to keep me here until the cops appeared.'

Miller stood up, so much taller than Sydney. He ignored the

approaching police officers and came towards Sydney, who then threw the hot contents of the coffee into Miller's face. He shrieked like a scalded cat. While Miller was trying to recover, the two police officers grabbed and cuffed him.

Shouting and screaming, Miller said it was Sydney they should arrest for scalding him in the face.

'Quiet! You are under arrest.' One of the officers repeated the often-used warning to an arrested man, making it clear that anything he said would be taken down and used as evidence.

They dragged Miller out of the reception and placed him into a secure police van.

Half an hour later, Jon Kim, having been told of the arrest of Miller, rang John England's home phone. There was no reply, other than the answering phone, so he left a message to make contact when he could.

*

At the Christie, John and Fiona had nearly finished their coffee when the door opened and in came a tall, distinguished-looking man. He was over six feet tall and slim with a tanned complexion. He wore a blue chalk-stripe suit with a white shirt and no tie, but he had a silk handkerchief in his jacket breast pocket.

'Mr and Mrs England, I assume?'

'That is nearly correct. We are to be married shortly. John likes the sound of Mr and Mrs. I am Fiona Holmes at the moment.'

'I am John England, who will be responsible for all the costs associated with Fiona's treatment.'

'Well, I am glad we have that sorted out. My name is Fairbairn, but please call me James.'

'Thank you, James. We are John and Fiona.'

'Please come with me to my consulting room. We can then see what can be done.'

John and Fiona were in James' consulting room for over an hour. James instructed Fiona to go to the X-ray department, which was on the same floor. He gave her a slip of paper authorising the mammogram.

'When you have finished in the X-ray department, come back here. I will see you again when I have the digital mammograms. Would you like something else to drink or eat?'

They both responded in the affirmative, except that James said Fiona should have just water for the time being and nothing to eat.

'Oh, that's a bit unfair.'

'It may seem so, but if I need to operate today, you need to have fasted. Until I see the mammograms, I can't set out a plan. My secretary will pop back to see you both shortly.'

James left the room as if he were a soldier leading a parade.

CHAPTER 27

THE CALM BEFORE THE STORM

iona was corralled into the X-ray department, where she spent nearly an hour having mammograms. The X-rays were in digital format and sent straight to James's computer. Once released from the X-ray department, she joined John in the waiting room. She explained the process to John and how uncomfortable it was.

The door sprang open, and James joined the pair in the waiting room, inviting them to join him in his consulting room. He was gone before they even stood up. However, he hovered in the corridor, the door to his consulting room open.

'Come in, come in,' he requested. This man was not one for wasting time.

'Sit down, sit down.' He swivelled the monitor, so John and Fiona could see the picture as well.

'Now Fiona, these are X-rays of both breasts. On the right breast, as labelled on the X-ray, there are no signs at all of cancer. On the left breast, there are signs of cancer, but only minimal. The density of each breast is high, which can lead to cancer. Did you start your periods early?'

'I did, James. I can't recall exactly when, but I know it was well before fifth form when they started. Why?

'It is very often a symptom which can lead to cancer in later life.

As in your case, it would appear to be a correct assumption.'

'What do you advise as to treatment?'

'Fiona, there are options. We can give you structured medication over some time by way of injections designed just for you. However, these medicines are at a very early stage of development, and I can't give any guarantees as to their effectiveness.'

'And the alternative?'

'That would be a mastectomy on both breasts, which is what I recommend.'

'Oh, why both?'

'It is a known fact that when one breast has been invaded by cancerous cells, there is nothing to stop the other breast being affected. I recommend a total mastectomy, followed possibly by hormonal therapy, to ensure there is no spread and the disease has been stopped. At the moment, you are in stage one. There is a ninety-five per cent possibility of a total cure if swift action is taken now. If you only want me to remove one breast, then we can do just that and keep a close eye on you.'

'What about my figure? Can you replace the breasts?'

'Yes, certainly, Fiona. That would be in a month or so after the operation. It is a standard process. You will still look great.'

A tear trickled down Fiona's cheek.

'How long before you are able to operate, James?'

'Tuesday next week, I have a slot. We should get on with this.'

'Oh!' Fiona was taken aback. Her voice was tremulous; she was frightened though at the same time delighted that a possible cure was available.

'Don't worry, darling, I am sure James is right. It will be all over before you realise it.'

John got up from his chair to give Fiona a hug and a kiss.

'What is the procedure, James, from now on?'

'It's for you to tell me if it's one or both. My secretary will have a word with you now, book you in and make all the arrangements. Tell her what you have decided. Please do not be concerned. At this level of the disease, all will be well, and before the end of the summer, you will have forgotten all about it.'

'Thank you, James, see you on Tuesday,' John and Fiona said in unison as they departed his consulting rooms.

As the couple waited in the waiting area, Carol joined them and asked if they would accompany her to her office, which they did.

Once all the forms James required had been signed and the document to confirm payment of Fiona's stay in the Christie was signed by John, Carol advised that they needed to be at the hospital by seven o'clock on Tuesday morning.

'Will I be able to park my car for the day at the front car park, Carol?'

'Yes, John. Here is a ticket to place in your windscreen as long as your car is parked at the front. Now, Fiona, in this pack of information there are instructions on what to wear when you come into the hospital and what to bring with you. It also states what you can eat or drink up to twenty-four hours before you come.'

'Thanks, Carol. Look forward to seeing you on Tuesday.'

John and Fiona left The Christie hand in hand to go to the Range Rover.

'Wow, that was quite a morning, John.'

'Yes, darling. Would you like to go to the Midland restaurant for lunch? We are in no hurry, and it looks as though it may be a while before we can have fun again.'

'That would be great, John. Thank you for everything.'

'Darling, this is the very least I can do. How about getting married on Monday?'

'Can you arrange it that quickly?'

'I don't know, but I am certain I can try my hardest.'

The Range Rover swept into the underground car park at Peter's Tower and they parked up in its dedicated space.

'Morning, Sydney. We will be going out again shortly, so we may need a taxi. I will buzz you with the information.'

'Very well, Mr England. Happy to oblige.'

John phoned the registrar's office in Manchester to request an emergency wedding on Monday.

'Sorry, Sir, we usually don't do weddings here on Mondays.'

'If you check your records, you will find that I booked a wedding later in the month. However, my fiance was diagnosed with cancer this morning at The Christie Hospital, and they are going to operate on Tuesday morning. It is, therefore, imperative we arrange to get married before the operation.'

'Just a moment, Sir.'

Will twelve noon on Monday be suitable?'

'It most certainly will.'

John provided all the details the registrars required and confirmed they would be there at eleven thirty on Monday.

He then booked a table at the Midland for half past one as it was now twelve forty-five.

John sent an email to a number of people, requesting an early response to his invitation to lunch at the Midland on Monday.

Travelling down to reception, they stepped out of the lift to find Sydney having what they thought was a conversation, but as they drew nearer, it was an argument.

'Have you a problem, Sydney?'

'No, Sir, I can sort it.'

The person Sydney was talking to turned to see John and Fiona standing behind him.

'You are the person I need to see,' Guy Miller announced.

'Guy Miller – what are you doing here?' demanded John.

'I have an errand to perform for Kent Watson. I don't think I can do it now!'

'If it's us you need to see, tell me what you want, or please leave NOW.'

John was furious that this man, whom he suspected of being responsible for the raid, had caused Sydney to be concussed and taken to hospital, then had wrecked their apartment.

'You think because you have money, you can order people about!'

'I can order you to leave these premises, as they belong to me.'

Miller was now in a heightened state. His eyes were stormy. He didn't want to give in but realised he could be beaten by England. Sydney pressed the alarm bell, which requested an instant response from the police again to come to Peter's Tower.

Miller continued his tirade. 'I am supposed to kidnap you, Missus.'

Fiona narrowed her eyes to a slit, giving an unmitigated look of fury.

John grabbed the man by the arm and twisted it up his back, forcing him to the ground.

'I'm a boxer. I will knock your lights out, England. Wait till I stand up.' John was in automatic mode, remembering his Krav Magar training. He pulled Miller's arm hard as he kept him on the ground. Miller was now lying on his back. John had his wrist in a tight grip. With his right foot, John gave him an almighty kick in his balls.

John then twisted Miller's arm, pushing his hand hard against the regular rotation of the wrist. As John was wondering what to do next, in walked two police officers.

'Ah, over to you gentlemen. This is the man who wrecked our penthouse recently. You have the security video, which will prove it was him. He has just admitted that he was here to kidnap Fiona, my fiancée.'

The police officers handcuffed Miller. They placed him in a police van that they had parked outside the entrance.

'We need a statement from you, Sir.'

'Well, I promise to call at the station this afternoon and give you a statement. In the meantime, Sydney will give you a copy of the video of what happened here.'

'Who are you, Sir?'

'I am John England, and my fiancée is Fiona Holmes, shortly to be Fiona England. Chief Inspector Jon Kim will give me a reference should you need one. We have to go now.'

Once the pair had returned from their lunch, they went back to the penthouse.

John was delighted he had an instant response to his email. Everyone could attend. He confirmed the numbers for Monday to the Midland.

'I think you should have a lie-down, Fiona. You must be tired.'

'No, I'm not tired, John. I'll lie down on the couch and watch some TV or a film.'

'Quite a day, darling.'

Fiona was asleep on the sofa within ten minutes.

CHAPTER 28

DECISIONS, DECISIONS

'Fiona, I have just realised I have not bought you a wedding ring, and I don't think there will be time to buy one on Monday morning.'

'Don't worry, darling, it's the least of our worries.'

'I do have the wedding ring I purchased for Sienna. I am not sure how you would feel about wearing that?'

'It wouldn't worry me, John. What do you think about it?'

John went to their bedroom and opened his drawer, where he knew he had placed Sienna's wedding ring. After a short while of rummaging amongst ephemera, he discovered the ring.

'This is the wedding ring, darling. Will it fit?'

Fiona tried it on to the third finger of her left hand.

'It fits, wow. I would love to wear this, John.'

*

'Jon. Sorry to bother you on a Sunday. As you may have realised, Fiona and I will be busy next week. I wondered if you needed anything from me or her regarding Miller?'

'No problem, John. Pleased to hear from you. In fact, Miller is due in the Magistrates Court tomorrow, so I may miss the wedding ceremony, but I certainly will not miss the lunch!'

'That's good, Jon. I am looking forward to seeing you.'

'John, we have had a request from the Solicitors Regulation Authority, which has come to us following your concerns about Kent Watson and Finn & Co. I suspect your concerns expressed to the Authority have been looked into. We have received a request that Watson should be arrested and brought to court as a felon involved with the theft of clients' monies.'

'That is very interesting, Jon. They must have carried out further research through banks and auditors to come to this conclusion. Hopefully, my evidence may have helped.'

'I am sure you are right. We have checked flight departures, and so far, we have no evidence that Watson has left the county. There is a national arrest warrant out on him. Hopefully, some bright young Bobby will spot him somewhere.'

'Fingers crossed, Jon. Look forward to seeing you at lunch on Monday.'

'Is there anything you would like to do today, Fiona? I suppose you will be out of action on the shopping front, to say the least, after Tuesday.'

'No, darling. I am feeling so tired. Strange how the body reacts to a condition.'

'You don't need to apologise, my little one. You are suffering from a severe illness which needs stamping out. Have you decided if you want the other breast removed or not?'

'I have, John. I think it is sensible to take the advice of the specialist and have them both removed. It will avoid a further major operation later. There will, of course, have to be an operation to insert silicone implants. That should be a minor surgery.'

'I think that is a sensible decision. We had best tell James. You need to ring Carol first thing on Monday.

*

Fiona was awake at seven in the morning on Monday. She realised that the next few days would transform her life. Married and a double mastectomy all in the same week.

John rolled over in bed, realising Fiona was not there. He leapt out of bed, concerned she might be upset.

'Are you alright, darling?'

'Yes, John, I am fine. I want to speak to Carol as soon as possible in case there are some other issues they need to see me about before Tuesday morning.'

'What are you going to speak to her about?'

'I want the double mastectomy and the silicone implants during the same operation.'

'Is that possible?'

'I think so, darling. I have looked at the internet, and it is possible but it was on an American YouTube, so it might not apply to the UK.'

'Well, that would avoid a second operation later on.'

'That is what I was thinking. I will find out when I speak with Carol.'

John shaved and dressed and went to his office to see if there were any emails. There were. Quite a long one from The Christie. He read it on the computer and then sent the money they requested. He printed out the whole email and gave it to Fiona.

'Oh John, I had not realised how expensive this was going to be.'

'It's insurance, not an issue. Anyway, I have paid for it!'

'Thank you, darling. I will ring Carol now. It's nearly eight o'clock.'

Carol answered the call immediately. Fiona asked if she could go with the double mastectomy and at the same time have silicone breast implants.

'That should be possible, Fiona. I will check with James. You will have to come in this morning for measurements to be taken.'

'When shall I come?'

'Ten o'clock, please. See you then.'

The two of them immediately had breakfast and changed into some smart clothes suitable for a wedding.

At ten to ten, John's Range Rover parked at the front of The Christie Hospital.

Carol came to greet them in the waiting room, having been alerted by the reception team that they had arrived.

A man appeared, dressed in his blue scrubs, and invited them into his consulting room. He announced himself as Mark Harley.

'I am standing in for James today because he has been delayed. My word, you two look very smart. You look as though you are going to a wedding!'

'We are, Mark – ours at noon today!'

'Ah! So we had better get cracking. Now, Fiona, I gather you are happy to proceed with the advice that we should do a double mastectomy? I gather you would like us to insert transplants at the same time. Is that right?'

'Yes, Mark. If that is possible.'

'It most certainly is and, if I may say so, a very sensible decision. You will take a little longer to recover, but when you do, that will be that. Please follow me, Fiona. I will ask my theatre nurse to carry out the measurements. I realise you are in a hurry, and so are we. That is why I am wearing scrubs. I carried out one operation this morning, and another patient is waiting.'

Within half an hour, the theatre nurse had concluded the measurements required by Mark. Carol reappeared, as well as Fiona.

'Now, Fiona, here are your instructions for entering the hospital tomorrow. You are on a fasting diet for twelve hours before you come in and a light diet for the twelve hours before that.'

'Ah, okay, I will adhere to that. See you tomorrow, Carol.'

Walking out of the hospital at ten-fifty in the morning gave the pair forty minutes to get to the registrar's office. They would have to park the car somewhere.

'Let's go back to Peter's Tower, park the car there and get a taxi to the registry office.'

'Good thinking, John. We are cutting all this very fine. I am sure we will do it!'

Having parked the car in the underground garage, they were waiting for the lift to reception when, not for the first time, John was attacked from the rear by an unknown assailant. He received a sharp blow to his head, which floored him.

Fiona shrieked. The man was wearing a balaclava, a baseball cap, a dark top, and jeans. She saw him about to lash out at John's groin, though fortunately he was wearing trainers.

John had not been knocked out and was aware a further attack would be coming as he lay on the concrete floor of the garage. The assailant's foot and trainer were in the air when John grabbed the foot and twisted it as hard as he could. The attacker twisted over onto the concrete step to the lift. He hit his head hard on the edge of the concrete. He remained still, so John was able to stand, blood trickling down his face.

'Fiona, get in the lift and ask Sydney to get the police, and then get a taxi.'

John stood over the man, ensuring that should he decide to stand up, he would be ready for him. In the space before the police arrived, John removed the balaclava from the head of the assailant.

'My God!' exclaimed John. He couldn't believe his luck. It was Kent Watson. The man who he'd thought was frail and who was usually dressed in formal solicitor's clothes.

John saw the weapon Watson had used on him. A baseball bat, but a child's one. Smaller than the bats used in playing baseball. He had nevertheless caused a bruise and broken skin on the right temple of

John's head. Watson started to stir.

'Don't you move, you little bastard. The police will be here any moment. They need to speak to you, and I am sure they will arrest you for this. They will also rip your apartment to bits and your flat to discover where you have put the stolen money over the years.'

Two police officers, two ambulance crew members and a paramedic appeared out of the lift.

'What has been going on here?' enquired one of the police officers.

'This man assaulted me with this small baseball bat and gave me an injury on my temple, which has bled. He started to kick me, but my martial arts training kicked in. I grabbed his foot and twisted it hard. He fell over and hit his head on the concrete step.'

'Who are you, Sir?'

'I am John England. I am a solicitor, and I own this block of flats. I cannot stay here to discuss this as I am due to get married at half past eleven. At the moment, I may just make it. If you need a reference, please speak with Chief Inspector Jon Kim. He knows me well. I will give you a statement later today, but not now.'

'This is very irregular, sir. We shouldn't permit you to leave the scene of the crime.'

'Yes, I know the rules, officer. However, they didn't realise that the injured party had to be at the registry office in half an hour to get married when they drafted the rules. I need to wash my face, put on a new shirt, and take two paracetamol as I am confident I will develop a headache. Tell Jon Kim that you have arrested Kent Watson. That's who is lying on the ground.'

John pressed the button for the lift as the PC tried to explain he shouldn't be leaving.

Fiona was in reception talking to Sydney.

'I am going to change my shirt and wash my face. Is there a taxi to take us to the registry office?'

'Yes, darling, don't rush, we will be okay.'

At eleven fifteen, they both arrived at Heron House on Albert Square, only a short taxi ride from Peter's House.

John apologised to the receptionist for being late and gave a potted version of what had happened. The couple were escorted to a waiting area, where some of their friends and relatives were waiting. All eight of them.

At half past eleven exactly, the guests were invited to take a seat in the wedding hall. As soon as they were seated, the usher asked John and Fiona to follow her into the hall and walk to the front.

Once everyone was settled, the senior registrar, who was authorised to conduct wedding ceremonies, opened proceedings. The ceremony was performed and within ten minutes, John and Fiona were declared husband and wife. Fiona was moved by the announcement: a few tears trickled down her face. They kissed in front of the assembled company as spontaneous applause rang out.

The registrar asked for the two witnesses, George England and Edward Wright. Once the documents had been signed by John and Fiona and the two witnesses, an official marriage certificate was prepared and handed to Fiona.

'Off to lunch, everyone. Thank you all for coming,' announced John, then the couple walked down the centre of the chairs and out onto the pavement.

'Jump in a taxi to the Midland. I will pay for them when you arrive.'

John paid for his taxi, and then he and Fiona waited for the two other cabs to arrive.

As soon as the taxis approached, John paid each driver plus a handsome tip!

The party of ten made their way towards the restaurant, stopping at the cocktail bar to obtain a drink. Fiona decided water was to be her tipple for the day, and as to food, she had no idea. Maybe the menu would have some ideas that will help her.

More decisions, she thought. *I have made all sorts of decisions in the last few days.*

When the couple reached the penthouse in the early evening, Fiona was exhausted. She lay down on the settee and fell immediately asleep. John realised the events of the day and the forthcoming operation had become significantly exhausting for her.

A pile of mail was awaiting him, and as he was going to be tied up with Fiona at The Christie for a few days, he thought it best to deal with it now.

CHAPTER 29

PRELUDE TO THE OPERATION

T he post-wedding lunch was a great success despite Fiona feeling unable to join the festivities wholeheartedly.

'Sorry, everyone. I will get back to my old self as soon as I can after the operation tomorrow. I hope you will forgive us if John and I now depart. I have things to do in preparation for tomorrow morning.'

There was an outpouring of affection for them both, especially for Fiona.

In the taxi back to Peter's Tower, John received a call on his mobile. It was Carol, James Fairbern's secretary.

'I see, so the operation is postponed. Will you let us know as soon as you can when it is to be re-scheduled?'

'What was that all about, John?'

'I regret your operation is postponed. Carol says they don't have a date for the delayed operation yet, but she will advise us when a date is confirmed.'

'Whatever has caused this, John?'

'I don't know, darling, but we, or more properly, you, are in their hands.'

Back in the penthouse, Fiona decided a cup of tea and relaxation on the sofa would be appropriate. She switched on the TV just as the local news was about to start. They were surprised at how fast the day had gone as it was now five o'clock in the afternoon.

The opening news sequence was a crash on the M56 between two cars and a lorry. The lorry had gone off the motorway and ended in the ditch on its side. The two high-speed cars were tangled in a metal heap in the centre of the middle lane. The news footage showed fire engines, police and recovery trucks. It seemed the ambulances had left by the time the film crew arrived. The reporter explained it had been raining very hard and was still raining, which would not have been helpful to the rescue teams.

'There will be more information in a later bulletin. Now back to the studio.'

'That's is a terrible mess, John. It would be surprising if anyone got out of that crash alive.'

'More tea?'

'Oooh, yes, please. Did Carol say when she'd let us know about the operation date?'

'No, darling. But she said she would phone again in the morning.'

*

It was about three in the afternoon when the two cars referred to in the news report were driving down the M56, the drivers of both vehicles known to one another. The two men, James Fairbairn and Alfred Pilpot, were at the top of their game as consultant surgeons. James was an oncologist at The Christie Hospital, working for both the NHS and private patients. Alfred was an orthopaedic surgeon who specialised in hip replacements. He had a private practice at the Alexandra Hospital in Cheadle. The two men had been playing golf at Royal Birkdale Golf Club with two other consultants from Liverpool. The four had had a delightful weekend, with plenty of good wine and excellent food. They had stayed at a new hotel, recently opened to pander to the visitors and players at Royal Birkdale. It was only three miles from the course. All four men had their own large room facing out to sea. Car parking facilities were available, together with an excellent dining room.

Before dinner, some large gin and tonics had been consumed, two or three each. The maitre d' had spotted the party and offered them the à la carte menu and the specials.

'My, we are going to have a feast tonight.'

'Yes, James, I think you are right. I am ravenous. All I had today was the full English at breakfast and a cup of coffee. I am ready for a blowout.'

'Shall I choose the wines?' asked James, who, as usual, had taken charge of the event. They'd all played a full round in less than ideal weather. There was a southwesterly wind blowing strongly. It made some holes exceptionally difficult, as if the course hadn't been hard enough. The fourth hole was slap bang into the wind, a two-hundred-yard par three. On Sunday, they required three woods as opposed to eight irons on a calm day.

Despite the problematic weather, they'd all enjoyed the game. It didn't surprise anyone that James won the day. He played off a handicap of four, whereas the others ranged between eighteen and ten. As in everything in his life, James liked to play golf at speed.

They all changed in the locker room, placing clubs and damp clothes in their cars. They settled down to a few pints of beer in the club room, chatting with members who were keen to extol the merits of their course, which, of course, led to detailed examinations as to how each individual played some of the more difficult holes. They all returned to their hotel at about half past four, with the agreement that they would all meet in the bar at seven for an aperitif prior to dinner. They had discovered that their hotel had a Micheline star chef. The expectations of a beautiful dinner were high.

Once dinner was over, having consumed four bottles of exceptional wine between them, it was decided that they should retire.

'Unless you all have important business to attend to, why not let's have a putting match after breakfast tomorrow? Check out from here and then go to the golf club, have a light lunch, and then go home?'

That was agreed. The putting was full of fun, with no one making a par round. Before lunch, it seemed appropriate to have a few beers. Lunch was washed down with a couple bottles of red wine ...

*

Carol, secretary to James Fairbairn, was distraught. She knew she had a great deal of re-organisation to put in place, and she needed a surgeon. James had been quick and would carry out operations in about half the time of others. Her phone started to ring as soon as the news of James's crash became known. Luckily, she operated from a large office that housed the secretaries of other consultants so they helped field her calls. They knew she was in distress and came to her aid, offering their own consultants to carry out some of the work already booked for James during the week.

Her first job was, once she had recovered somewhat, to postpone all operations due to be carried out the next day. Most patients understood, except one who was furious.

*

The golfers had all left in their respective cars at about 2:45pm on Monday. The two consultants from Liverpool set off north while James and Alfred headed south, driving their sports cars. As soon as they were on the motorway network, they went on the M57, which was pretty deserted, so they had a short race driving between eighty and ninety miles an hour. Where the motorway joined the M62, they crossed over, heading towards Runcorn, which filtered them onto the M56. This road would take them both home.

No sooner had they joined the M56 than the heavens burst. There was a biblical rain storm, making it difficult to see where they were going, with the additional problem of spray from lorries. Despite the weather and the driving conditions, they were both satisfied that the

Aston Martin Volante and Jaguar XKR would meet the challenge. They didn't slow down. In fact, ninety was the speed chosen. Not to race but to get past all the slow-moving traffic. The three-lane motorway was heavy with commercial vehicles, so they stuck to lane three, the outside lane. Every now and again, they ploughed at speed through large puddles of standing water. Then it happened.

CHAPTER 30

HOSPITAL

The Jaguar hit a colossal patch of standing water covering nearly the whole width of lane three.

This threw it off the third lane and into the second lane, spinning several times and gradually getting closer to lane one. A large curtain-sided trailer and cabin arrangement as big as they come was in the second lane, travelling at top speed. The driver tried his best to avoid the Jaguar. This manoeuvre sent the rig into a slide, which sent it across the inside lane, bouncing off the back of another lorry, and being hit amidships by another truck, pushing the first lorry and its trailer off the motorway into the verge and down a bank leaving at least half the trailer still horizontal over lane one. Other vehicles coming up from behind realised they had to avoid the vehicles and swerved to the right, hitting Alfred in the Jaguar and James in his Aston Martin. Then more commercial vehicles added to the pile-up. The motorway became impassable.

The Jaguar and Aston Martin were caught up in the melé, and seriously damaged, their drivers pinned into their cars. The only way to distinguish the cars apart was by their colour as they had welded themselves together with the impact of the crash.

A lorry driver phoned for assistance as he could see from his cab that there were some serious injuries.

Within ten minutes, there was a queue of vehicles at least a mile long and getting longer by the minute. Eventually, sirens could be heard, and blue lights reflected in the rain. Squeezing up the hard shoulder was a convoy of ambulances, fire engines and police. The fire service used their hydraulic cutting equipment to release Alfred and James from their respective vehicles, following which they were attended by the paramedics who were confident that both men were severely injured and near death. Eventually, with help from the fire brigade, the two men were lifted from the wreck. They had been treated with Ketomin to help reduce pain. Once the medics could see the men, it was clear that each of them had broken legs. These were put into temporary splints. The driver of the Aston Martin was in a terrible mess. It was decided to call an air ambulance and take him to the neuro-surgical unit at Salford Royal Infirmary. The Jaguar driver was taken by ambulance to Warrington Infirmary.

While the recovery of the seriously injured men was being undertaken, removal trucks started to remove those vehicles blocking the third lane, which then permitted vehicles to pass the scene in single file along one lane of the motorway.

Two hours after the crash, two of the lanes of the motorway were open and running. The police were still in attendance, waiting for a heavy lifting crane on a massive vehicle. At midnight, the crash site was clear. The police were collecting their cones and returning to their base.

CHAPTER 31

OPERATIONS

'John England.'

'Mr England, this is Greater Manchester Police. I am DC Tanner.'

'Yes, Constable, what can I do for you?'

'I need you to come to the police station to provide a statement regarding the fight you had with Kent Watson.'

'Officer, my so-called fight with Watson was caused by him hitting my head with a small baseball bat. If you want a statement from me, please come to my home. I live in Peter's Tower, in the south penthouse. Let me know when you propose coming. I am not going to be very available due to my wife having to go into hospital tomorrow for a cancer operation. I can't say when I will be available.'

Okay, Sir. Would this afternoon be acceptable, say three?'

'Yes, I can spare you an hour then.'

*

'Hello, Carol, are you calling about the operation tomorrow?'

'Yes, John. I regret to have to tell you the operation cannot go ahead as planned tomorrow. James has been involved in a massive car crash on the motorway. He is seriously injured. He will be unable to perform any operations for quite some time, or indeed ever again.'

Carol was sobbing on the phone. John was taken aback at the information.

'I am sorry to hear this, Carol. Being selfish about it, what happens now?'

'I am trying to make alternative arrangements, but it will involve an initial consultation with a new consultant whenever I know who that will be. I don't expect I will be able to call you back for a day or two.'

'That has upset arrangements. Can you please see what you can do as soon as possible?'

'Yes, John, but every patient wants what you have requested. Some operations were potentially significantly more complex than Fiona's. I will be back to you within a few days, hopefully with some news.'

'Fiona, that was Carol from the hospital on the phone. James has been severely hurt in a car crash and cannot perform any operations for some time to come or ever again. So, my darling, we will not be going to the hospital tomorrow.'

'What happens now, John?'

'I guess Carol is running around to find consultants who have time in their diaries to stand in for James. It will be difficult as we have heard James was a high-speed consultant and could carry out more procedures than other consultants in a given time.'

'Oh, so I have just to sit here and wait?'

'Yes darling, I am afraid you do.'

The phone rang. It was Carol – could they be at the Christie at seven that evening?

John stood next to Fiona with his hand over the mouthpiece of the phone.

'Are you okay with that?'

'Yes, John.'

The message was transmitted to Carol, who was delighted.

When the call ended, John said, 'I have a police officer arriving at three this afternoon to interview me regarding the attack by Guy

Miller yesterday. He wants a formal statement.'

'Okay, darling, I will make us some lunch at about one o'clock.'

'Are you feeling up to it?'

'Yes, of course. I am not an invalid.'

*

At three pm, the PC was at the front desk. Sydney phoned to advise John that he was on his way up.

On arriving at the penthouse, DC Tanner introduced himself to John and Fiona.

'Mr England, can we discuss the fight you had with Kent Watson?'

'Certainly. Let me make one thing clear: I did not instigate the fight. Watson had been hiding around the corner of the lift shaft, which would have brought us up to reception. Without warning, he hit me on the side of the head with a miniature version of a baseball bat.

'I was not knocked out, but I stumbled due to the severe bang on the side of my head, then fell to the ground. I could see Watson's feet in his trainers nearby. I grabbed the leg nearest to me, his left leg, I think. As I did so, he lifted the leg, so I transferred my grip to his foot and trainer. I twisted his foot as hard as I could. With Watson standing on one leg, he had no option but to fall to the left, banging his head on the concrete step of the lift door. I stood up, with Watson in a daze on the floor. I decided to ensure that he wouldn't get up for more. I had solid leather shoes on, and so I kicked him in the balls, at which point he issued a loud screech.

'Within minutes of all this action, two police officers arrived and took control. They may have ordered an ambulance. I am not sure, as Fiona and I had to leave.'

'As I understand it, you were ordered to remain at the scene?'

'Yes, that is true, but as I tried to explain to the officers, my then-fiancée, now my wife, and I were on a tight schedule to get to Heron House in Peter's Square, where we were married at eleven thirty. If I am not mistaken, the attack took place at eleven.'

'I understand you are a solicitor, Sir?'

'That is correct, DC Tanner.'

'Then you, of all people, should know that it was an offence to leave the scene of an attack no matter who started it or who was right or wrong?'

'Look, detective, my wife and I were due to get married. We had to make our appointment. As a consequence of the unprovoked attack, I needed to freshen up, get rid of the blood all over my face, and put on a clean shirt. Once this was done, we had to go like the wind in a taxi to Heron House. That's why we did not stay.'

'The circumstances of your leaving are understood, but it is not an exception in law.'

'I assume you have Kent Watson in custody?'

'No, Sir. As a consequence of not having your side of the story, he was allowed to leave on police bail.'

'Where is he now?'

'I don't know at this moment.'

'So, as far as you know, he could return and finish me off?'

'That is theoretical. Now I have your side of the story, and we can issue a warrant for his arrest.'

'Good.'

'Is there anything else you wish to add to your statement, Sir?'

'No.'

'I will get your statement typed up and leave it with your reception as you need to sign it. Once signed, please deliver it back to our station.'

John let the detective out once he had returned the temporary lift pass.

*

No sooner had the police officer departed than John's mobile rang.

'Hello, Carol, any news? How is James?'

'I am not sure. James is in Salford Royal. They have an excellent neurological department there. He will get the best care. I am sorry John, the seven o'clock appointment for tonight has to be cancelled. I will get back to you with another date. As you can imagine, we have a serious scheduling job on our end.'

CHAPTER 32

THE WAITING GAME

Over the weekend, John and Fiona went to Tarporley to meet up with John's parents and explain to them all the issues they were dealing with. Audrey and George were very concerned and wanted to know what they could do to help.

'Why don't you try Clatterbridge Hospital, John? It is a specialist cancer hospital.'

'Great idea, Dad. Can I ring them from here?'

'Yes, son, no problem. Look them up on their website.'

John placed the call from the hall and came back in the room.

'What did they say, John?' asked Fiona.

'They say they are a specialist radiotherapy centre. They don't perform surgery.'

'Ah. I'll be having any post-operative treatment in the Christie's radiotherapy department. We shall have to wait to hear from the Christie after all.'

'Oh Fiona, that is a great shame. Let's hope the Christie can get their teams organised to admit you as soon as possible,' said Audrey.

'Yes, Audrey. It is a worry waiting. I am not sure what is happening to my cancer

in the meantime.'

*

Back at the penthouse on Monday morning, there was still no further news from the Christie Hospital about the date for Fiona's operation and who would be the lead consultant.

'If we don't get any information today, darling, I will ring the hospital in the morning.'

John was doing some routine work on his computer when an email arrived.

It was from an organisation he was aware of but had had no formal contact with before. It was an email from the Solicitors Regulation Authority (SRA). Amongst other things, they administered a compensation fund, which could be paid out in the event a solicitor does not have the funds or appropriate insurance.

It was an enquiry about the application made by John to the SRA about Finn & Co. on behalf of Mrs Wright and the funds the firm should be holding.

John replied to the email.

'I act on a *pro bono* basis. I have been fortunate in my life. I have inherited significant assets. I, therefore, decided to act as a *pro bono* solicitor for legitimate good causes who could not afford access to the law. I act for Mrs Wright, the widow of Frederick Eric Wright, who is recently deceased.

I am trying to recover the remnants of funds left in the estate. The Wright Trust has been managed for many years by Finn & Co, a firm of solicitors who were taken over some years ago by Fraser's Solicitors in Manchester. They moved the Finn & Co practice to a small office in Levenshulme, leaving the unqualified Kent Watson in sole charge of the estate and the accounts.

I have made enquiries locally, and I have discovered that in the last three years, £150,000 was released from the sale of farm buildings. Watson says there are no funds left. I suspect foul play here. The net funds should be at least £100,000, if not more; Watson provided me with a spreadsheet of rents and capital receipts. They show a net residue of nil.

Watson or another of Fraser's partners have been syphoning off money, believing there was no remaining beneficiary. Realising that I was on the case, Watson employed an ex-convict who attacked me recently. I am more than confident Watson and possibly one or other of the partners have helped themselves to the residual funds. Mrs Wright, now a widow in her eighties, has been relying on receiving the balance of the funds of the estate.

Your assistance in recovering these monies would be appreciated.'

A simple acknowledgement email was returned.

Carol called John to apologise again for the delay and to update him on James, who clearly was not going to be back at work in the near future, if ever.

'Oh, dear Carol. That is terrible and such a waste of a clever guy. So what is to happen about Fiona's operation?'

'That is why I am phoning John. We have another consultant who will take over the case, but he requires a whole new set of diagnostic information. Mark Harley would like to meet her on Thursday at three in the afternoon. You met him briefly last time you were here for breast measurements. Would that be possible?'

'Yes, Carol. We will be there.'

John relayed the information to Fiona, who was at least pleased matters were to progress.

*

'Look darling, I need to go to Boodles to purchase a wedding ring for you. I am not happy about you wearing Sienna's ring. I will take it with me as it's the right size and see what Boodles have.'

'That's great. I want to pop into Diesel and buy something, then I will pop over the road to join you.'

'Okay, let's go.'

John alighted at the entrance to King Street whilst Fiona waited until the taxi was nearly at the end of the street. A black Mercedes van had been following them. If John had been aware, he'd have seen that it had followed them all the way from Peter's Tower. Fiona got out and the taxi moved off. The van drew up opposite Fiona, and two men dressed in black jumped out of the sliding door on the side of the van. One covered Fiona's face with a cloth, and then the two of them carried her the short distance to the van, which departed at speed, turning left into Deansgate.

The van went southeast through the city via John Dalton Street, Princess Street, Upper Brook Street, then took a left fork to Plymouth Grove until they arrived at Stockport Road.

As soon as they were driving south on Stockport Road, they turned left into Barlow Road, then after a yard or two, left again into Cardus Street, which gave rear access to the Indian takeaway at the back door to Finn & Co's office.

The two men in black and the driver lifted Fiona out of the van, through the door to Finn & Co's office, up the flight of stairs and then to the further set of stairs.

*

John sauntered down King Street, assuming Fiona was still in one of the many dress shops. He hovered around, stopping to sit down on a chair for an outdoor coffee shop. He decided to order an Americano and wait until Fiona popped out.

He had finished his coffee, but still no sign of Fiona. He made enquiries at various shops, including Diesel. No one had seen her that morning. The last shop he tried said she had not been in but she had been seen being bundled into a black Mercedes van which sped off in a hurry.

*

'Jon, good morning. Sorry to bother you once more, but I suspect

Fiona has been kidnapped.'

'What makes you think that?'

John then explained the circumstances and the comment from the last retailer on King Street.

'Ok, John, I will get some officers down there. Any idea who might be responsible?'

'The only person I am having an issue with is Kent Watson over the money that should be in the Wright Estate bank account.'

'That was the man we met in Levenshulme, I assume?'

'Correct. I am sitting outside at the Costa Coffee. I will keep an eye out for your men. Thanks, Jon.'

As he finished the call, what seemed like an unmarked police car blocked off the end of King Street and two plainclothes policemen left the vehicle. They approached John who explained the circumstances to the two officers. After they had made some notes, one of them asked:

'Have you any idea where she might have been taken?'

'No, but the offices of the solicitors who are at the epicentre of my enquiries for the money from the Wright Estate, managed by Finn & Co. and due to a widow, are at the address I have given you in Levenshulme.'

'Okay, Sir, we will go there now to see if we can discover anything.'

John took a cab home to the penthouse to await developments.

CHAPTER 33

THE KIDNAP UNRAVELS

Back in the penthouse, extremely concerned for Fiona's well-being, John paced the floor. He knew in his heart that this was a put-up job by Kent Watson and the ex-con, Guy Miller. As he was considering what to do next, his mobile rang.

He raced across the lounge to the sideboard where he had become accustomed to leaving his mobile when he came in.

'Yes, who is this?'

'Never mind. Are you missing your new bride?'

'Whoever you are, what do you want?'

'One hundred thousand pounds.'

'And if you are asking me to provide that, what do I get in return?'

'Your wife.'

John now had mixed emotions. John was very anxious about Fiona, wherever she was. He was concerned it would not help her cancer. He was furious that this guy was seeking a ransom.

'Okay, so tell me, how do you expect to receive the money and when?'

'Mr England, it has to be in cash. Preferably used fifty-pound notes. I will tell you where to leave it when I ring tomorrow.'

The phone went dead.

John looked at the 'recent' calls on his mobile. The number used was there.

'Jon Kim, please.'

The formalities of phoning the police, except on a 999 call, took time. When Jon Kim was finally on the line, John explained what had happened and gave him the mobile number of the anonymous caller.

'Okay, John. Can you get this money?'

'Well, yes, I can. How sure will I be to get it back?'

'The first return must be Fiona. As to the return of the money, we can mark the notes to trace them.'

'Agreed. When I hear where they want it delivered, I will let you know. In the meantime, I need to get the money. When I do, where do you want it for marking?

'I will let you know later today. As it's Monday, the bank will have time to assemble the money.'

At the end of the call, John was distraught. His new wife of a few days has been kidnapped!

He poured himself a large scotch into a cut-glass tumbler. He opened the vast American refrigerator and put a few cubes of ice into the glass.

Where on earth could she be? He was convinced Kent Watson and his partner were involved.

John's mobile rang again.

'Mr England, this is the SRA in London. Are you free for a chat?'

'Yes, but I am rather distraught at the moment.'

'Oh, I am sorry to hear that. I hope it hasn't been caused by the issue we are investigating?'

'Well, yes and no. That is speculation, but I think Kent Watson is a crook, and he has an ex-convict working for him. They've kidnapped my wife and are trying to extort £100,000 from me to release her from their captivity, wherever she is. It is speculation on my part that Watson is the culprit but the police are now involved.'

'Would you prefer that I rang back, Mr England?'

'No, let's get on with it, whatever it is.'

'Mr England, I am Andrew Baker, head of compliance. If what you say is true, and we have no reason to dispute it, it would appear Mr Watson and one or more partners at Frasers have to answer some questions. I wanted to let you know that there will be a disciplinary meeting in two weeks. If you are free, then I would like you to attend.'

'In normal circumstances, I would say yes, and I would be there. However, I hope to get my wife released in the next twenty to forty-eight hours. She is suffering from breast cancer. Her consultant was severely injured in a car crash on the motorway on Monday and we are waiting to hear about an alternative surgeon. I regret, therefore, that priorities may mean I will be unable to come to London when you have this hearing.'

'Oh dear, you are having a tough time.'

'Yes, all because I am trying to help an elderly widow get the inheritance she is due. I believe that Watson and possibly others have stolen the money in the trust.'

'I understand, Mr England. They probably thought that there was no one to fight her corner and didn't expect to be asked to account for the money.'

'Andrew, you have it in one. Just proving it is the issue as they have all the evidence.'

'I will let you know when and where the hearing will take place. If you can attend, then that would be excellent, but I understand if you can't do that.'

John phoned his bank manager and explained the circumstances.

'The police would like the used fifty-pound notes to be marked invisibly, so there is every prospect of finding the culprits and having the money returned. The important part is to get Fiona back as soon as possible.'

The cash was duly marked and delivered in an unmarked car to John at Peter's Tower.

It wasn't long before his mobile rang again.

'Mr England, have you got the money?'

'Yes, I want to hear from my wife before I hand it to you.'

'Okay. I will call back in an hour.'

*

'Jon, the kidnapper, has phoned. They are calling back in an hour, so that I can hear Fiona's voice.'

Jon Kim made immediate arrangements for the call to be monitored and the location to be identified.

'As soon as we have a location, we will move in.'

'Look, Jon, I think Fiona is in danger. I want her back as soon as possible. I am happy to let you discover their location, but don't move in until I have Fiona.'

'Okay, John. We will put a trace on your phone in a few minutes, and we should be able to get to the location of the caller. We won't move in until we know you have Fiona safe.'

The next call on John's phone was from Fiona. Very distraught, crying and asking for immediate help to get her released.

'I will come and get you, darling. Put the man who called back on the phone.'

'Are you satisfied, England?'

'Yes, tell me where I can come and get her and I will bring the money.'

'Stay there. I will ring you back with instructions.'

John was all over the place, and he didn't know whether he was coming or going. Then his phone rang again.

'YES,' John said in a stern voice.

'Oh, Mr England,' said Carol from the Christie. 'Sorry, have I called at a bad time?'

'No, sorry, Carol, I was trying to deal with someone else. What news do you have?'

'I have a consultant who can see Fiona on Thursday at ten thirty. Can you do that?'

'Yes, certainly. We will be there. The same place?'

'Yes, see you Thursday.'

No sooner had John ended the call than it rang again.

'Place the money in a Waitrose plastic bag and put it into the first waste bin on the left on the approach to Piccadilly Station between five o'clock and half past this evening. Just put the bag in the bin and leave.'

'When do I see Fiona?'

'She will be on the six o'clock train tomorrow, Wednesday. The train stops at Levenshulme on its way to Picadilly. She will leave the train and walk down the roadway from the station. That will be about half past six.' The phone went dead.

'John, it's Jon Kim. We have got all that so leave it to us. You drop the money in the bin and walk away. Keep your mobile on, and I will keep you updated on what is happening.'

Jon's plan was to have a female and male undercover officer at Levenshulme Station meet the six o'clock for Manchester Picadilly. If Fiona was escorted onto the train, the plainclothes officer would join the train and advise Jon Kim.

'John, we will only act as soon as you tell us you have Fiona safely in your arms.'

Sydney called on the internal phone system, saying there was a courier at the front desk, and he required John's signature for the package. He decided to take his passport with him in case he had to prove his identity.

A smartly dressed young man with a battered and worn briefcase was waiting for him at the desk.

'Hello, I am John England. You are a courier for whom?'

The courier confirmed he was an employee of John's bank. He asked to see John's ID.

'Luckily, I put my passport in my pocket. Here it is.'

'Can I have a signature on this form, please?'

The courier handed John the briefcase containing a large number of bulging paper envelopes, which John knew contained the money.

'Can you please wait here.'

'Sydney, can I use the store for a moment?'

John took the briefcase in with him.

'The briefcase is for you to keep, Mr England.'

'That's kind. I will just check the contents if you don't mind.'

'That's perfectly acceptable, Mr England.'

John discovered five bundles of fifty-pound notes, valuing the total consignment to be one hundred thousand pounds.

Returning to the reception area, John thanked the courier who left.

*

It was just past five-thirty when John, as requested, placed the Waitrose bag containing the used fifty-pound used notes into the black rubbish bin at the start of the slope up to the station and platform level. John didn't wait to see who might collect it. He was sure that there would be some plain-clothed police officers around to witness whoever took the package from the bin. He walked up the slope to the main concourse of the station.

Jon Kim received a radio message from Levenshulme that an unknown male had boarded the train. Fiona was not with him. He relayed that to John, who was having a coffee in the concourse of Picadilly Station, looking carefully at the arrivals board.

Panic ensued. The police officer tried to leave the train as it was about to leave, but the doors were now locked. A message was sent to Jon Kim as soon as the officer realised what had happened.

CHAPTER 34

CAUGHT THE TRAIN

'John, it's Carol. Just confirming with you that Fiona is attending in the morning at ten thirty to meet Mark Harley.'

'Yes, Carol. I understand and we should be there.'

Realising that this was not the usual answer she expected, she asked, 'Is there a problem, John?'

'Yes, we have had an issue. Hopefully, I will be able to explain it tomorrow. See you then.'

John hung up, realising he was withholding information which might affect Fiona and her appointment. He was in a heightened state of anxiety. He needed his beautiful Fiona back, get her cancer sorted and then head away from all this, back to *Brave Goose*.

*

Fiona was being held in a room she did not recognise. The ceiling was at an angle and filthy. It couldn't have been decorated for decades. Her throat and mouth were dry and hurting due to the gag taped over her mouth. Perversely, she needed a wee. She was unable to move as her wrists and ankles had been secured to the bedstead on which she was lying. Her head was pounding. It was hard to see as the window was covered with cloth. It would never pass for curtains, but it assumed the role of a blackout, not fully dousing all light as she could see slightly. She could hear her heart beating in her chest. Her wrists and ankles ached, and she had cramps in her back and legs as she couldn't move.

What is going on? Fiona was asking herself. She had no idea how long she had been incarcerated.

She recalled being attacked on the pavement on King Street by two men, one of whom had covered her face with a cloth steeped in some chemical which had made her pass out immediately.

Now I am in this dungeon. It smells like an animal's cage. She must have peed without realising it. The urine was stinging her. She smelt awful. Surely, someone would come eventually. She sobbed, tears streaking down her face.

You wouldn't keep an animal like this.

Fiona thought it must be two days since she was abducted. Suddenly, two men burst into the room, cut her bindings, and stood her up. She was very unsteady and had severe cramps. They then ripped the tape off her mouth. She made a massive intake of breath but could hardly speak.

'Water, water,' Fiona croaked. 'Water, water.'

One of the two men handed her a plastic bottle of water, which she consumed all at once.

Both men wore black balaclava hoods. Their eyes were the only visible part of their face.

'More water!' demanded Fiona.

'We don't have any more, bitch. You have had your fill. Shut up, we are leaving.'

The two men bundled Fiona down two flights of stairs, out of a door and straight into the side door of a black Mercedes van. She could hardly see where she was but she could make out it was a street with little traffic and red brick buildings.

There was an old mattress on the floor in the rear of the van. She was told to sit on it.

'Where are we going? I need to see my husband.'

' You will see him soon enough.'

*

While all this was going on, a detective in plain clothes, Martha Payne, caught the Manchester Piccadilly train in Stockport. This train stopped at two stations on its way to Manchester: Heaton Chapel and Levenshulme. Martha was not sure where to sit, but as it was only a two-carriage train running in the middle of the day, there were hardly any passengers. She chose the last coach.

No one alighted from the train at Heaton Chapel. Four passengers got on. Three women joined Martha's carriage, looking as though they were off shopping. The man who got on chose the front coach. He made a total of three people in the first carriage. The next stop was Levenshulme.

As the train moved off, the man who got on at Heaton Chapel took a terse mobile phone call.

Martha left her seat in the last carriage and moved up the train to the front carriage. At the same time, two men in the coach stood up and restrained two men sitting opposite one another. There was no sign of Fiona.

'Stop, leave me alone,' said one of the men.

'And me,' demanded the other. 'Who the hell are you?'

'We are police officers. You are being detained for kidnapping a young lady in Manchester three days ago.'

'I did nothing of the sort,' said one. The other man also protested his innocence. 'Show me your warrant card,' demanded the second man.

Before anyone realised it, the train had pulled into Piccadilly Station. There was a posse of police officers in uniform on the platform. Amongst them was John England.

'You had better have a good story for your actions, officer. I am a solicitor, and this gentleman is a client of mine. We are going to Manchester on business.'

After half an hour of heated discussion, the two men were allowed to proceed on their way.

'So where is Fiona?' demanded John England. 'I was reassured that you would have had a police presence everywhere. Has the money been recovered?'

'Yes, John. It has.'

John's phone rang again.

'Yes, who is this?'

'Your wife will be at Manchester Piccadilly at six forty-five. You involved the police, so we had to adjust our plans. Thanks for the money.'

The caller hung up.

John relayed the call to Jon Kim, who had heard it anyway as it was relayed to him by the police listening in at the station.

'Is there a local train due in at six forty-five?'

'Yes, Sir', chipped in Martha Payne. 'It's the local train from Guide Bridge. It's a through train, so it will probably be on platform thirteen,' she speculated.

'Well done, Martha. Can one of you please check that?'

'Jon. You told me you had recovered the money, yet the thugs who have got Fiona said thank you for the money! What is going on?'

'We have your money, John. We substituted it for counterfeit money. It will be easier for us to trace, and it will save us time in marking all your notes.'

CHAPTER 35

THE CHRISTIE HOSPITAL

B y the time John and Fiona were back at Peter's Tower, it was eight o'clock in the evening.

'Oh darling, I can't tell you how good it is to be back home.'

'It's wonderful to have you back. I have prepared some supper as I guess you must be starving?'

'I am. Those bastards didn't give me any food, and I didn't get any water for ages. My mouth and throat were as dry as sandpaper.'

'Bastards. I hope Jon Kim and his men catch everyone concerned.'

'So do I. Any news of James and my cancer appointment at Christie's?'

'No darling, except you do have an appointment at half ten in the morning with Mark Harley, a consultant oncologist.'

'That's good, John. I was nervous that my incarceration might be detrimental to my cancer treatment.'

'I would hope not. It's worth telling Mark all about it.'

John's mobile rang. It was Jon Kim.

'Yes, yes, no, that can't be done, but probably later tomorrow afternoon. No, because Fiona has to be at The Christie at half ten in the morning. Okay, six tomorrow evening, then. I will let you know if we need to change the arrangement.'

'It's strange trying to understand what the conversation was about without hearing the other side of the conversation. So what's it all about, and who will be here at six tomorrow evening?'

'Possibly, Jon Kim and one or two detectives. They need to find your kidnappers as soon as they can. They need some information from you to help them find these people.'

'I can't recall too much, John. I was drugged at the beginning.'

'That would have been very frightening, darling.'

'Initially, it was. When I came round, I was tied to a bed with cable ties, my mouth was taped shut, with a bag over my head, and I couldn't see anything.'

'My god, you must have felt awful.'

'I did, and I do!'

'What would you like some of the spag bol I have made?'

'Yes, please, spag bol sounds perfect.'

'I can do that. I think a glass of Shiraz would be good to wash it down.'

'Yes, please!'

John got on with the final preparations for supper. They both ate well. Fiona was ravenous and ate everything laid before her and then some. The Shiraz was perfect.

'Was this all to do with the money you are trying to recover for Mrs Wright?'

'I guess it was. The man who was left in control of the trust and its money. The issue is that they were managing the trust, but instead of putting the money on deposit for the benefit of any legatees who came along, they took it. Kent Watson, the man in charge, was syphoning the money away.'

'That's illegal!'

'It is, darling. It's illegal for anyone other than the beneficiaries to syphon off money from a trust.'

'What will happen, John?'

'I am hoping the people involved, with your help and testimony, will go to jail when the police find them. The Solicitors Regulation Authority will be able to recover the missing money from the insurers of Frasers, the solicitors.'

*

A few minutes to ten, on Thursday morning, John had the Range Rover at the front door of Peter's Tower and they made the trip to The Christie Hospital in Withington.

'It's funny that with a name like his, he has become a consultant. Very appropriate!'

'What's the significance of his name, John?'

'Harley – Harley Street is the street of the medical profession in London.'

'I get it now, John. I never thought about that.'

John swung the Range Rover into the car park at the Christie Hospital with ease and parked in a bay allocated for private patients.

It didn't take long for Carol to join them in the reception area.

'Hello, Fiona, John. Mark will be along shortly. He had an operation this morning. It's always difficult to assess the timing of operations.'

'No worries, we are here now and have nothing to rush back for.'

The couple sat on a comfy sofa. No other patients arrived, so they sat in isolation for more than half an hour. Then, an hour. Carol returned.

'So sorry for the delay. Mark had to attend to another patient. He will be with you soon.'

Eleven o'clock came and went, and still no sign of Mark. It was noon when he appeared.

'I am so so sorry to keep you good folks waiting,' said Mark Harley in his soft Cornish accent.

'Sometimes things go to plan, and at other times they don't. This was one of those. Glad to say the outcome has been good, and the dear lady will be fine.'

'No worries, Mark. May we call you Mark?'

'Informality has been my life. Yes, Mark is just fine.'

'So let's get down to brass tacks. Do you both want to come into my consulting room.' It was a carbon copy of James's room. 'Now I have all the reports on you, X-rays and mamograms, et cetera, so there really is nothing more I need. When you come into the hospital, we shall do a further blood test and check your vital signs, but all that can be done is on the day of admission.'

'When will that be Mark?'

'I have a space on Tuesday next week.'

'That would be fine by me', said Fiona. 'Did you pick up on my request that when both breasts are removed, you will replace them with implants at the same time?'

'I can say yes to that, assuming there are no complications with the mastectomy.'

'Is that likely, Mark?'

'It is possible. Until we are in the throes of the operation, I won't know. I see we do have the measurements, so I will order them. We are ready to do as you wish if all goes well.'

'That sounds fine, Mark. What time on Tuesday do you want Fiona to come in?'

'Can you make seven-thirty in the morning? The operation will be at around nine o'clock.'

'Yes, we can do that,' John and Fiona confirmed in unison and laughed at their unanimity.

'Good, I will let Carol know. Looking forward to seeing you on Tuesday. Have a lovely weekend.'

As they were about to walk out of the department, Carol caught them.

'Hello, can I give you all this, please?'

'Oh, what is it?' enquired Fiona.

'There is a pamphlet on the hospital, a form for you to sign, and I assume one for you, John, as well as a first payment slip. Then there are the details about what to bring with you. Don't hesitate to ring me if you have a query.'

They thanked Carol and went home.

CHAPTER 36

THE NEXT EXCITEMENT

D espite the delayed consultation, they were back at Peter's Tower at one-thirty.

'Would you like to pop along to the bistro for a light lunch, darling?'

'Yes, what a good idea, John.'

As the pair walked out of Peter's Tower reception and along the pavement to their local bistro, John was conscious of being followed. They walked along a little further, by which time a man overtook them. The man stopped right in front of them and turned to face them.

'Do you want something?' enquired John.

'Yes, another pile of notes like the last lot.'

'Well, we are just off for lunch, so why don't you join us so we can discuss this? The bistro is just here?'John replied in a calm and clearly unexpected way to the unknown man.

'No, you will be up to your tricks.'

'It's up to you, but I am not standing on the pavement discussing this. We are hungry.' John started to walk, moving around the man, keeping himself between him and Fiona.

As John opened the door to the bistro for Fiona, he pulled his mobile phone out of his pocket, swung around and took a photograph of the man.

'Thanks, that will be a good photo. Do you have a name to go with it?'

'Not for you, I don't.' The man turned and ran back towards Peter's Tower. John decided he was not going to follow him.

'Oh John, not more hassle?'

'Just a little. He is one of Kent Watson's foot soldiers. I will send Jon Kim the photo and a synopsis of the conversation. If we are going to be stalked, then the police need to know and try and apprehend these people. Now, what would you like for lunch?'

'You are amazing, my darling. Anyone else would be in a state about what has just happened. Here you are, as cool as anything.'

'That is what they want, to get me all annoyed and het-up. As soon as the opposition starts to be annoyed, abuse and physical attacks are likely.'

'Can we have a bottle of the house rosé, a menu, and some still water?' requested John as the waiter handed him and Fiona a menu.

'Are you alright, darling? Your hands are trembling?'

'I don't know how you can sit there, order wine and remain as cool as you are. Don't you realise what has just happened? Why are we still here? We should have gone straight back to the penthouse. This is very alarming, John. It's not surprising my hands are trembling.'

'Sorry, my love, there is nothing to be frightened of. We were in broad daylight and were on a public pavement. The man didn't dare do anything as he would have come off worse. Some other member or members of the public would have come to our aid if he had tried an assault.'

'You are very sure of yourself, Mr Husband, but I love you for it.'

'Thank you, but let us enjoy our lunch and think no more of it.'

Once lunch had been consumed, the two walked back to Peter's Tower and their beautiful penthouse. It was a summer day with a blue sky and high wispy cloud. The view from the penthouse was, as always, magnificent.

John opened the patio doors wide-open onto their large patio. John had decided it was too big a space to be called a balcony.

'Feels like something's missing out here, John.'

'What do you mean?'

'I mean, it would be nice to have sun loungers, patio table and chairs, a settee, and perhaps a gas BBQ.'

'Yes, they would all be a great addition.'

'If the weather is fine, it would be perfect for me recuperating after my operation, John.'

'I must phone Jon Kim and tell him about the man who attempted to secure more money from me. When I have done that, I will look for a retailer in garden furniture who could furnish our patio.'

*

'Jon, I have just text you a photo of a man who tried to apprehend Fiona and me as we were going out for lunch. Luckily, we were nearly at the restaurant entrance. What was also odd was that he demanded some more money, another one hundred thousand pounds.'

'Ah, he has to be a member of Kent Watson's team.'

'What makes you say that, Jon?'

'The forensic department had at least one hundred thousand pounds in used counterfeit fifty-pound notes. We swapped your genuine notes for these. They must have discovered the difference. Any bank that would scan the notes would quickly discover that they were not genuine and would confiscate them.'

'I guess that is why they would like 'real' money. What have you done with the real hundred thousand I gave to the police?'

'That is still here, Jon. Where would you like me to send it?'

'Can a courier or police officer deliver it to Peter's Tower for my attention, Jon?'

'Once we have rounded up this gang, in particular Kent Watson, then we will put them before a magistrate in preparation for a criminal trial.'

'Okay, Jon. I will await developments.'

John then searched for a local supplier of garden furniture and BBQs.

He discovered a company with a showroom in Wilmslow. He decided to take Fiona with him.

They viewed a selection of attractive rattan garden furniture sets in various designs and styles. Eventually, they decided on what they would buy: a U-shaped seating arrangement, a couple of stools, and a few different coloured scatter cushions. They didn't sell BBQs, but they had plenty of dining tables with eight chairs. They chose an oval table. John explained the delivery issues, but the retailer was not daunted by the task. They would send two men.

Where to go to get a barbeque was the question.

The salesman in the showroom suggested a large B&Q store which they would find near the A34 on their way back to Manchester. They stopped there only to discover the large barbeque they wanted was out of stock.

The showroom where they bought the furniture had also suggested Amazon. John found that for nearly £600, they could buy a hybrid barbecue which ran on gas or charcoal. You used the gas burners to light the charcoal. It seemed ideal, so one was ordered with tools and a cover. He also ordered a storage box. Covers would also be needed for the furniture.

'That was a productive excursion. Everything should be here tomorrow,' John said then notified Sydney of the impending deliveries. As a precaution against damage, Sydney placed protective lining around the walls of the lift.

It was a waiting game now until the purchases arrived, but they were both excited like expectant children at Christmas.

'We didn't order any covers for the furniture to protect them against the rain.'

'No, John, but the cushions will go into the storage box. It would be a good idea to have the covers, which we can keep in the storage box until needed. I will ask Sydney if he knows of a bottled gas supplier and I will order a bottle.'

CHAPTER 37

KENT'S MEN

Kent Watson was considering his next move when his mobile rang. He didn't recognise the number, and neither did his phone.

'Yes?'

'Is that Kent Watson?'

'Who wants to know?'

'It's Jon.' It was Detective Inspector Jon Kim, but Watson assumed it was John England. It was a helpful ploy on this occasion.

'What can I do for you?'

'I ran into a friend of yours the other day. He was wanting another hundred thousand from me. What's all that about? Have you finalised your accounts so the authorities can decide if I am right?'

'Huh, I am surprised you have to ask. The notes were all counterfeit, and I need full compensation for releasing your wife.' There was a loud clicking noise on the phone.

'Well, I am not in the habit of paying crooks for illegal acts like kidnap. Where are you, Kent? I need to come with others to run over your books, business and personnel so we can ascertain where the money has gone.'

Kent ended the call. He realised that the loud click could be a tap on the line and that the police were trying to find his location.

*

'Guy, it's Kent. I am getting nowhere with the Englands, and the police have had a tap on my phone. I need you to cause some havoc in the England household. Can you do that?'

'I can. It will happen tomorrow. I need to get some equipment.'

Guy Miller went to see a friend who was a known armourer in the criminal world. Marcus was his name, and he was based in Manchester. A quick call allowed Guy to make arrangements to meet him.

'Hi Guy, what can I do for you?'

'I need some explosives and a detonator with a radio-controlled trigger.'

'Ah, that's relatively easy. We use the mechanism from a small TV. I have one made up. It's not cheap.'

'How much, Marcus?'

'Off the shelf, it will be a grand.'

'Okay, I'll get Kent to send the money now. Let me have your details.'

Guy took the details, then he gave the information about where he wanted the explosives to Marcus.

'Will this be a big bang?'

'It depends on what you attach to the explosive.'

'What would be best?'

'A bottle of gas. That will shake the neighbourhood.'

'Okay, so how far away can I be to trigger the explosion?'

'No more than a hundred meters. That is quite a long way, and you will be safe that distance away.'

'Okay, double-sided sticky tape would be the best way to attach the explosive.'

Marcus put everything Guy needed in a small cardboard box, and off he went.

*

'Did you get a triangulation on the signal?' Jon asked his technical team.

'Very nearly, Jon. We are able to establish a signal to within half a mile of his office.'

'I think that could be his flat. I will get in touch with the local authority to see if he is on the electoral roll or if he appears on the local authority's records, like council tax, et cetera.'

Once the information was received, which came a great deal quicker than Jon expected, he rounded up some troops for a raid on Kent's flat.

'Look, I think we should have a stake-out at this address to see if people are going in and out. Here are photographs of the man behind the fraud and kidnap of Fiona England – Kent Watson – and his main sidekick, Guy Miller. And this is the man who stopped John England yesterday, no name.

'So can you organise a rota to stake out this address and keep an eye open for twenty-four hours? If Watson and Miller are both there, we will launch a raid. Keep me posted, please.'

Jon Kim had a conversation with the commander on duty to advise him of his plans.

'Seems like a plan, Jon, but do you know if these people are armed?'

'No, we haven't been alerted to that possibility.'

'Well then, I will notify the armed response unit to have a team on standby in the event you mount a raid.'

'That will be reassuring, Sir. Thank you.'

Jon Kim rang John England before he went off duty.

'John, just to let you know in view of the attempt to recover more money from you, we have decided to arrest Watson and, if possible, Miller and any other members of the gang we discover once we gain access to Watson's flat.'

'He isn't very bright if he remains in his flat while trying to extort money from me.'

'If criminals were bright, we would be out of a job!'

'Thanks for letting me know. I won't tell Fiona as she is stressed enough by what happened on top of the operation she is due to have on Tuesday next.'

*

'Mr England, it's Sydney. I have a large van and three men here with your furniture.'

'Thanks, Sydney. I will keep an eye out for the delivery men.'

One of the delivery men soon knocked on the penthouse door, having been provided with a temporary lift pass that would expire in six hours.

'Mr England, I am the foreman of the delivery crew. We have all your new patio furniture for you. Can you please show me where it is to be placed?'

John opened the front door, which was very wide for this very occurrence. He then opened the large patio doors and explained where the furniture was to go.

'Did you bring the protective covers with you as well?'

'We did, Sir. My word, what a wonderful view.'

'Yes, it sold me the apartment!' John thought it unnecessary to explain his connection to the block.

Within an hour, three men had assembled the furniture and removed all the packaging, which they took away. John gave each of them a ten-pound note to say thank you for the care taken in setting up their new furniture.

"Wow, this looks fantastic, John! And now the sun is out we can sit outside.'

*

Guy Miller was hanging around outside Peter's Tower when another van arrived. The driver went inside to speak with Sydney.

'Are you busy, mate?'

The van driver came out of the reception area and realised he needed help with all the stuff.

The internal phone rang. Sydney advised there was a man with a barbeque and a gas cylinder. Should he send him up?

'You need to go to the top floor, which is where the penthouse is,' Sydney told him.

Seeing Guy hovering around, the driver asked him, 'Are you busy? If not, would you mind giving me a hand with this lot, which has to go to the top floor?'

Guy Miller couldn't believe his luck. He accepted the invitation. He asked if he could leave his parcel inside in case it was pinched on the pavement. 'No, put it in the van. It will be locked when we go upstairs.'

The two men put both parts of the barbecue carefully in the lift. There was only room for one man at a time in the lift.

'Look,' said Guy, 'I will stay here and keep an eye on my parcel, which is quite valuable. While you are dealing with the barbecue, I will move the gas cylinder on the trolley to the lift so you can load it quickly when you come down. I can't hang around too long. I have someone to meet.'

It was agreed. The delivery driver appreciated the help very much. He gave Guy his parcel from the van before he went up in the lift.

'This is your new barbecue, Sir. Would you like me to assemble it and connect the gas? The gas bottle is still on the ground floor. It wouldn't fit in the lift with the barbecue and me! With regards to the gas, Sir, since the tragedy at Grenfell Tower, we have to advise clients in apartments to get approval for the use of a gas cylinder from the block owners before its use or connection, so I regret that I will be unable to attach it for you.'

'That won't be a difficulty as I own the whole block. I can give myself permission to use one!'

'That is a first for me, Sir. Sorry, I wasn't to know. Would you like me to assemble everything and make the gas connection? I can demonstrate how it all works.'

'No, that's fine. How were you to know?'

Before the man left with all the surplus packing materials, John gave him a £20 note for his trouble and care in establishing the barbecue.

'How thrilling, John. We will have some fun with all this stuff. I haven't any steak in the fridge, but I do have some burger pates.'

'Sounds good, darling.'

'Do you want a barbecue tonight, John? It looks as though it will stay fine.'

'Yes, why not.'

'I will light the gas, which, according to the instructions, will light the charcoal. I prefer the taste if it's been cooked on charcoal.'

It would be another half an hour before the barbecue was up to temperature. John and Fiona enjoyed unwrapping all the tools for cooking on the barbecue. The gas bottle stood by the side of the barbecue and was working well.

CHAPTER 38

EVERYTHING'S COOKING

G uy Miller thought to himself how fortunate he was in being able to establish the explosives on the bottom of the gas bottle delivered to the Englands. The issue now was to find a place opposite the tower and at the same height where he could activate the remote signal to set off the explosive.

Fortunately for Miller, there was a multiplex cinema on the other side of the street. He bought a ticket for a film he had no intention of watching. What he did know about cinemas was that there would have to be fire exits in at least two places for each of the six mini-cinemas. He wondered how high he was as he stepped on the third set of escalators. At the top, he realised the escalators had run out. The cinema on the top level did not indicate any film was showing. So, at the end of the escalator, he started to explore how to get to cinema six.

The area was unlit except for some security lights. He wandered along a corridor, which he had worked out ran alongside the cinema. The corridor provided an escape channel for people exiting from the front of the mini cinema, leading them to the escape stairs and the exit doors to the external part of the cinema. It is from there that the fire services could rescue stranded people.

Guy wandered down the stairs again and out under the first lit exit sign. This led to a door with a push bar to open the door. There, a sign announced the door was alarmed: 'DO NOT OPEN EXCEPT IN AN EMERGENCY. ALARMED DOOR.' Miller was sure that if he opened it, there would be an instant response from the security staff and the alarm.

He wondered if the same system was in place on the floor below. He wandered down using the 'down' escalator to the large foyer and landing. There were two kiosks, but as the films were playing, these were not in operation. Between the two kiosks was another alarmed fire door.

He worked out that all the exits had to be on the same circuit. If a fire was in one area, the whole place would be cleared. It made sense that if one door sounded its alarm, they would all go off. If he was right, there would be a light against each re-set button on the main panel. So what should he do?

He decided to wait until he heard the film finish. There would be a rush of people leaving then. He would try to open the door on this level, and once it was open, he would run upstairs and undo the escape door there. The sound could be deafening. The cinema's staff would assume someone leaving the cinema had tried to open the wrong door.

He could open the top door and then trap the circuit breaker with an ice cream carton he picked up out of a waste bin. He could then leave the top door open.

Guy opened the fire door on the landing where the escalator finished. An almighty noise emerged from sirens all over the cinema. People were rushing out of the cinema. Guy ran up the stairs and opened the fire door at the top. He left this door slightly open. He would need to get back the same way.

Once through the fire door, he was in open air, standing on a grating, his back to the wall. If he walked much further forward along the grating, he would encounter a set of escape steps. They were hinged, and as anyone stepped on them, they folded down to the balcony at the next lower balcony. The fire escape followed on until the third level when the stairs hit the ground floor.

Standing on the balcony at the highest level, he was level with England's apartment balcony one floor lower than the penthouse. The balcony for the penthouse faced south, whereas Guy was now facing east. He could see the glass surrounding the penthouse balcony, which was where he assumed the barbecue would be located. He couldn't see it or anyone on the balcony.

He wasn't here to assassinate people; he just wanted to cause damage. So he pressed the control button. Nothing happened.

Oh my god, I have been to all this trouble only for the thing not to work!

Could it be a fault with the buttons? He discovered how to get into the back of the handheld unit to discover the batteries were protected by a plastic membrane, which would stop the batteries running down and a possible unexpected detonation. Clearly, the membrane had to be removed. The grating he was standing on was not ideal. Dropping one of the AAA batteries would prevent the whole thing from working at all. He spread his handkerchief on the grating and placed the unit on it. He carefully removed the batteries one by one and cleared the plastic film. He reassembled the battery pack and replaced the battery cover with the buttons.

He placed his handkerchief back into his pocket. As he did so, he dropped the button unit.

Blast, damn it! All this trouble and I have let the buttons go.

The crowd below were assembled around the front of the cinema and the buttons dropped amongst them.

Guy decided to get off the fire escape as soon as possible. Someone would undoubtedly look up if they saw the unit fall. He couldn't risk being spotted. He shot through the fire door, closing it properly behind him. He rushed down the now stopped escalators to join the crowd. Just as he got to the street, there was an enormous explosion above. It was the bomb planted under the gas bottle left on the balcony of the penthouse. Whoever in the crowd had found the unit must have pressed the buttons, causing the blast. If he had known the little button unit would work at this distance, he would have had no need to go on the fire escape!

Miller walked away briskly from the throng as fire trucks, police officers and an ambulance came hurtling into the area.

CHAPTER 39

AFTER THE BOMB

'That was quick!' shouted Sydney as two policemen came into reception.

'We are not here for you; the cinema's fire alarm has gone off. But then we heard your alarm as soon as they switched the cinema alarm off. What has happened here?'

'I don't know, officer. According to the panel, the alarm that triggered the activation is in the penthouse on this side of the block, but the owners are in. You will need a card to use the lift.'

'Can I have one, please?' requested the constable. Sydney provided the card that was needed. Once at the top of the tower, the police didn't need any further help in tracing the apartment. The moment they stepped out of the lift, the lobby was full of acrid smoke. The door to the penthouse was open. The two police officers went in to see what had happened.

No explanation was necessary. The glass patio doors were broken to pieces. The patio furniture was on fire, and the gas bottle attached to the barbecue was in pieces, some of which were in the lounge. As they were inspecting the wreckage, two people emerged from the kitchen.

'That was swift work, officer. I am John England, and this is my wife, Fiona. I think we need the fire brigade to quell the fire and some first aid as we were lacerated by shards of glass, as you can see.'

'We have both services on the street outside, and I will call them in immediately.'

*

Within half an hour, the fire service had extinguished the fires on the patio. The ambulance and paramedic crew were attending to Fiona and John and said they would take them both to A&E at Manchester Royal Infirmary.

By seven o'clock, both patients had had their wounds attended to. They were stitched and bandaged up after careful surgery had removed the shards of glass from their bodies.

'We gather it was your apartment that had an exploding gas bottle, which in turn broke the large patio windows? Is that correct?' asked the attending doctor.

'Yes,' John uttered in response. He felt as if he was back in Bosnia again.

'Well, you are both fit enough to go home. We shall need to see you in outpatients on Wednesday next week.'

'I don't think our apartment is capable of being lived in. I will make arrangements for alternative accommodation,' said John. 'I will need a taxi as we arrived in an ambulance.'

'Our welfare officer will come and see you in the waiting room. She will make the arrangements for you.'

'Thank you, doctor, you have all been very kind.'

'It's what we are here for, Sir. If I may say so, it didn't look as though this was the first time your body had received shrapnel.'

'You are correct, doctor. The first lot was collected in Bosnia. That event had rather more force behind it as I was closer to it.'

'I hope you will find we have done a decent job for you. I am experienced in this sort of trauma as I worked in Belfast General Hospital during the Troubles. As you can imagine, we had our fair share of injuries.'

'Thank you, doctor, we are extremely grateful.'

A woman came into the waiting room about half an hour after John and Fiona got there.

'Hello, are you John and Fiona England?'

'We are.'

'My name is Joanne. I'm a welfare officer here at the MRI. Can I do anything to help you?'

'Can you arrange a taxi for me to take us to the Midland Hotel please? However, before that, I need to make some arrangements. Do you have a phone I could use?'

Joanne took John to a nurses' station nearby, which had a landline.

'Sydney, quite an afternoon. Can you book us a room at the Midland tonight for at least seven days? Then can you put some bedclothes and some day clothes into a bag for Fiona and me, our toiletries and my mobile phone and charger? Are you okay, Sydney?'

'Yes, Mr England. Your penthouse is in a state. I will call Mr Birch on Monday for you when the police have finished. For now, I will lock up and go home.'

'Oh, what are the police doing?'

'They are mainly forensic officers, Sir. They think there is something suspicious about the explosion.'

Once settled into the Midland Hotel and feeling very sore and painful, the couple took some analgesics they had been given by the hospital to quell the pain.

'It's taking Sydney some time to bring our stuff, isn't it?'

'Oh, John, he must be extremely worried. He has had a bad day as well.'

The words were hardly out of Fiona's mouth when someone knocked on the door.

John opened the door to see the last person he expected: Jon Kim.

'My god, Jon, what has brought you here?'

'You have. When I heard there had been an explosion in Peter's Tower, I was concerned about you. I was correct to be concerned. The gas bottle explosion was not an accident. We found an explosive under the bottle.'

'My God, whatever next!'

'We will get to the bottom of it. So I wanted to come and tell you that your wonderful man in reception, Sydney, asked if I would mind bringing this case for you. Sydney says apart from clothes and toiletries, your mobile phone and laptop, complete with chargers, are also in there.'

'He is a wonderful man. I have no worries when Syndey is on duty. So what are the next steps, Jon? When can you release the property to me so I can arrange a clean-up and repair?'

'I don't know yet, John. As soon as I do, I will let you know. I am glad to see you are both still with us. Let's see if we can trace the person responsible.'

CHAPTER 40

FORENSIC EVIDENCE

'Fiona, did you ask the surgeon in A&E if you could go ahead with your operation on Tuesday?'

'I did, darling. He said it was up to me. It very much depended on how I felt. He could not think of a medical reason why the operation should not proceed.'

'That's good. How do you feel about it now?'

'I feel pain, the same type you get if you have cut your finger but a hundred times worse. If there is no medical reason why the operation should not proceed, I am up for it.'

'Good. I will pass the news on to the Christie via Carol.'

'Ian Birch, please.'

'He is tied up in a meeting.'

'Is that a meeting with staff or an external client?'

'I gather it's a staff meeting, Sir.'

'This is John England. Please see if he will take the call.'

'Hello, John, how are you both?'

'Not well at the moment. Thank you for taking the call. We had just taken delivery of new patio furniture, including a dining table and chairs, and then came the new barbecue, followed a little later by a gas bottle.

'Fiona and I were carting food, wine glasses, cutlery, and some wine when the gas bottle exploded, setting fire to the new patio furniture, smashing the patio doors to the penthouse, and covering me and Fiona with shards of glass. The apartment is in ruins, yet again, so we are staying at the Midland following a couple of hours in A&E where we got patched up.'

'Whatever are you two going to face next?'

'I don't know, Jon. What I do know is that the police suspect foul play. The whole penthouse is swarming with crime scene officers trying to find clues as to who might have been behind it.'

'Oh, I see. So this looks like another claim?'

'It will be when the apartment is released to us for cleaning and refurbishment again.'

'Okay. Let me put you in touch with a firm that specialises in cleaning after events like this and then the interior furnishing company that fixed everything up before.'

'Thanks, Ian. Can you email me their details? I will get back to you when the police have finished.'

John then phoned Carol at the Christie to advise her about Fiona. She said she would inform the consultant.

'How are you feeling at the moment, darling?'

'I just want a sleep.'

'Good, you go to sleep. I will sit in the armchair and work on my laptop.'

John had an idea, which he would explore when Fiona's operation was over. He thought it would enable them to live a pleasant life free of stress, whether it was at home or on *Brave Goose*.

*

'Hello, can I help you?'

The police constable behind the counter of Bootle Street Police

Station in Manchester was addressing a young man, say twenty-five or thirty years old. He was holding a small white box with ten buttons on the top, more like a TV remote control unit, but it was missing all the other buttons TV remotes have.

'Well, Sir,' the young man said, politely addressing the constable. 'It's regarding this box.'

'Yes, what about it?'

'My fiancée and I were at the pictures yesterday afternoon when the alarm went off. The instruction was to vacate the cinema by the nearest fire exit, which we did. When we were outside, the fire brigade and some police cars arrived. There was no obvious sign of a fire. We were in a crowd of people standing at the side of the cinema, as that was where the fire exit led us. We would have been standing there for ten minutes when this hit me on the head. I looked up but there was no one there. Above was a steel balcony with an escape ladder attached. This had not been activated.

'It's only a light box but it hurt quite a bit when it hit me. You can see the scar here.' He pointed to a red scar on his forehead. 'It fell on the floor, so I picked it up, not knowing what it was.'

'Did you try any of the buttons?'

'No, Sir, not intentionally but I guess I must have pressed some in picking it up.'

'What happened next?'

'There was a deafening explosion from high up, not in the cinema, but from the flats opposite.'

'Did you think the buttons may have had something to do with the explosion in the flats?'

'No, I didn't. Not at the time.'

'What happened next?'

'My girlfriend put the box in her handbag, saying she would hold onto them so I could hand it in today, which is what I am doing now.'

The police constable put some gloves on and placed the box in an evidence bag.

'Can you please wait a moment, Sir? I need to speak with someone.

The constable advised the forensics team of the item handed in and the conversation he had had with the young man.

'Thanks, constable,' the forensic officer said. 'Please don't let the gentleman leave. We will need his and his girlfriend's fingerprints so we can eliminate them from our enquiries. I will be down in a minute to take them.'

'Thank you very much for bringing the box in,' said the officer to the man. 'The forensic team are delighted that it has turned up. It will be a piece of evidence for the police to investigate. Regrettably, we will need your fingerprints and those of your girlfriend so you can be eliminated from our enquiries.'

'Oh, you will need my girlfriend as well?'

'Yes, Sir, is she in town?'

'Yes, we were due to have supper together.'

'Can you please call her and ask her to come here as soon as she can?'

No sooner was the call made for the girlfriend than the forensic officer appeared with an electronic pad to collect fingerprints from the couple, Bill and Ann. The forensic officer took Bill's first, and then when she arrived, Ann's prints as well. The police took their contact details and address and thanked them for their assistance.

'Oh, I have one more question before you go. Have you opened the box and removed or replaced the batteries on the inside?'

'No, not at all.'

The couple left, leaving forensics to search the box for fingerprints, eliminating Bill and Ann's prints. There were three prints which didn't match theirs.

'The detective I have spoken to suggested some names for whom we do have prints. I will check to see if they match the ones we have.'

It took no time at all for the forensic officer to find the prints inside the box, and the batteries matched the person he and the detective suspected.

Within the hour, the forensics officer had identified the fingerprints inside the box, which belonged to Guy Miller.

Jon Kim was delighted at the news. He called a meeting at six in the evening of all the officers and police administrative assistants. There was a plan to set out for the next day regarding the explosion at Peter's Tower and the money Kent Watson had embezzled from the Wright Family trust. He was convinced the issues were linked.

CHAPTER 41

FIONA'S OPERATION

I t was half past seven when John and Fiona drove into their parking space at the front of the Christie Hospital. John carried Fiona's overnight bag and escorted her to the reception area for private patients.

The receptionist welcomed them and asked John to sign the contract and make a payment amounting to half the fee for the operation, as well as an overnight stay or more if needed.

'If you take a seat over there, a porter will escort you to your room.'

Sure enough, in no time at all, a porter arrived and picked up Fiona's overnight bag, and the three of them walked quite a way down a corridor and then up two floors in a lift. Another corridor and they were shown to Fiona's room.

'This is your room, Madam. There is an ensuite bathroom here. It has an emergency pull string. If, when using the bathroom, you need help, please pull the string, and someone will come to your aid. The same applies to the bell push button lying on the bed. Please don't hesitate to contact us with anything you need. We are here to help you. The bed can be adjusted up and down, and the backrest can also be adjusted. The buttons are to control the TV.'

'I can't see a TV. Is it hidden?'

'Ah, pressing the 'on' button will bring the TV into view. It's the mirror, which turns into a TV and back again when the TV is

HEAD IN THE SAND

switched off.'

'That's clever,' said John. 'It's a big screen if it's the size of the mirror.'

'I am sure you will enjoy playing with that, John.'

'A nurse will be along shortly to see you.'

The porter left. Fiona noted the gown and paper pants laid out on the bed.

'I guess I will have to dress up in that stuff.' There was a knock at the door, and in came a lovely nurse who said she was from St Lucia.

'I have to get some details about you, Madam.'

'Okay, press on. I am in your hands.'

'I am one of several nurses you will meet during your say. I am on all week, so it will mainly be me. My name is Christina. I need to weigh you, take your measurements, and then get some blood.'

'Will you be staying, Mr England?'

'Yes, unless Fiona would prefer I didn't.'

'I would like John to stay. If he is in the way, you can ask him to move. He is very good at doing as he is told,' said Fiona with a wide grin on her face.

Christina started taking Fiona's details and soon realised she had a large number of plasters and wound dressings in various places on her arms, legs and neck.

'Oh dear me, whatever has happened, Fiona?'

'It's a long story, Christina. We live in a penthouse in Manchester. We had a new barbecue delivered on Friday and a gas bottle to go with it. The bottle exploded as we were carting items out to the patio prior to a barbecue. The explosion shattered out large patio doors. Shards of glass were sent in every direction. John took the primary blast, but some shards found their way to me. We were looked after by the Manchester Infirmary A&E department.'

'Good heavens. I need to refer this to Mr Harley. He will need to inspect these wounds. I will carry on, but until Mr Harley sees you, I can't assume the operation will take place today.'

Christina completed her job by taking some blood samples from Fiona in two vials. She also attached a plastic bracelet to her left arm, bearing Fiona's full name and birth date.

'You might like to get into bed wearing the pants and gown.'

Christina left. She sought out Mr Harley, who was just arriving at eight-fifteen.

'Mr Harley, when you have a moment, and before you speak with Fiona England, I need to have a word about her.'

'Come back in a quarter of an hour, and you can tell me all about it.'

'What do you think will happen, John?'

'I don't see any relationship between a mastectomy and a number of shards of glass penetrating other parts of your body. I think he will want to know what happened but I think he will proceed.'

Fiona, dressed in paper pants and a theatre robe, was in bed when Mr Harley knocked on the door and came in.

'Fiona, I gather you have been in the wars?'

'Yes, Mark. It was totally unexpected, and the police think it was a deliberate act.'

'Tell me what happened, and then show me the wounds you have suffered.'

Mark studied her wounds.

'So the police think this was a deliberate act? Is someone after either you or John? If so, I think we need to know about this. We don't want any violence in the hospital.'

'I can put your mind at ease by asking Detective Chief Inspector Jon Kim to call you now.'

'Okay, that would be a good idea. I have to pass this information to the hospital manager. All patients in the hospital are owed a duty of care. It's with that in mind we must be sure this hospital will be safe.'

John provided Mark Harley with Jon Kim's phone number so he could ask the appropriate questions of the police.

Mark made the call to Jon. After a quarter of an hour on the phone, Mark was reassured by Jon Kim that Fiona and John were no risk to the hospital as Jon's officers had just arrested the perpetrator of the explosion who would be remanded in custody.

Placing the phone down, Mark said he was satisfied with what he had heard.

'We will proceed,' he said. 'Now let me have a closer look at you, Fiona.'

Mark examined Fiona all over. 'It's lucky your breasts were not caught by the shards.'

'Yes, Mark, that thought occurred to me yesterday. Did Jon Kim tell you they had arrested the culprit and offered you a police guard?'

'He did, but there was nothing about police guard.'

'To be fair, he offered that to us, but as they have now apprehended the culprit, it seemed unnecessary to place a police constable on duty.'

'Good,' said Mark. 'I have had a text to say the blood tests are okay. We will proceed with the operation. If all goes well, you can go home on Friday. A nurse will be in shortly to complete some of your critical signs. A porter will then wheel you up to the operating theatre.'

Fiona thought it would be about ten to nine. She was wheeled now by two theatre orderlies into the anti-room to the theatre. She met a charming man dressed in scrubs and wearing a mask.

'Fiona, I am the anaesthetist. I will look after you throughout the operation. My name is Charlie, so we can start the process now. Have you had an operation before?'

'Yes, Charlie. It was in the MRI after I was raped several years ago.'

'Oh, what was the operation for?'

'I was given an abortion as I couldn't stand the idea of giving birth to a child whose father was a rapist.'

'What stage of the pregnancy did this happen?'

'Twenty-three weeks, I am pretty sure, but they gave me a sedative or possibly an anaesthetic.'

'Oh, well, have you told Mark that?'

'No, I don't think so.'

Charlie left the ante room and went into the theatre to speak with Mark. He told him about the terminated pregnancy following a rape.

'If it was more than twenty-four weeks, which it sounds like, then the milk ducts could have been active, but as the pregnancy was terminated, the milk glands would never been in action. Could that be the cause of her cancer?'

'Yes, thanks for that. I took over this patient when James Fairburn was killed in a car crash. He may have known.'

Charlie returned to the anti-room. 'I think you must have told James about your abortion?'

'Yes, I did.'

'That's okay now. I have told Mark about it. So let's get cracking.'

Charlie inserted a cannula into the back of Fiona's left hand, having established she was right-handed.

'You will feel a warm sensation in your arm in a moment. Can you keep talking to me? Tell me where you are living.'

Fiona set off chatting about the penthouse.

'The ... the gas ... ga ...' She was under, so Charlie wheeled her into the theatre.

'I am ready now for the anaesthetic, Mark, when you are.'

'Charlie, we are removing both breasts and then replacing them today with breast implants. The cancer is less than grade one, so this should be a safe procedure. It's half past nine now. Theatre nurse, please log the time and vital statistics, and we will begin.'

By eleven o'clock, the operations had been completed. The prosthetics were placed once the breast tissue had been removed. Fiona was sewn up again. She looked bruised and discoloured, but that was normal.

'In a month, she will look as if nothing has happened. Thank you, everyone.'

Mark left the theatre, and Fiona was taken to the recovery room.

By noon, Fiona was still drowsy but alert enough to realise what was happening. A senior nurse attended to her, occasionally providing her with a drink of water. She was wheeled to her own room where John was delighted to see her.

The ward sister came to see Fiona.

'You seem to be doing just fine, Fiona. Are you hungry?'

'Yes, I am a little.'

'Would you like a small mug of tomato soup and a chicken sandwich?'

'I would, thank you. I am still plugged into some machines. Will that last for long?'

'I doubt it. I think it should be possible to remove all the cables and lines sometime tomorrow.'

The sister went to get Fiona's food.

'Darling, how wonderful to have you back.' John gave her a big kiss.

'I am glad that is over.'

'Are you any pain?'

'No, not at the moment. This is the button I have to press if I feel pain. The machine will provide me with a hit of morphine. That will be helpful, especially at night.'

Fiona's sandwich and a cup of soup in an easy-to-drink cup, the sort you would give a baby, arrived.

'Have you had anything to eat, John?'

'No darling, they have a café here. Once you have had your lunch, I will go and get mine.'

No sooner than Fiona had finished her soup and sandwich than she dozed off.

Time for me to go and get some lunch, John thought and went to the hospital café.

CHAPTER 42

POST OPERATION

J ohn was eating breakfast at the Midland on Friday morning when
his mobile rang. It was Jon Kim.

'Hello, Jon, I am just being lazy and only now finishing my
breakfast.'

'Oh, sorry, John, should I ring back?'

'No, no. It's perfectly fine. I suspect I will be off to the Christie
shortly. Fiona may be allowed to go home today. Well, *home* is a bit
of a stretch. It's been the Midland Hotel for us for a while.'

'Oh, that sounds good. She will be pleased to be on the right side
of the operation.'

'Yes, she has been a wonderful patient. When can I get workmen
back to the penthouse? Have your forensic guys finished?'

'That's the purpose of my call. Yes, forensics have finished. You
can set to with the clean up.'

'That is fantastic, Jon. I will make arrangements straight away for
that to commence.'

'The other thing I have to tell you is that Kent Watson and Guy
Miller have both been arrested. We put both of them before
magistrates, and despite the fact Watson was not a participant in the
explosion but was clearly behind the organisation of various
attempts to do damage to you and Fiona, they have both been held in

custody until their attendance in court. We are awaiting a date for their preliminary hearing in court. It is unlikely they will be given bail.'

'That's all good news, Jon. I will organise the cleaning up of the penthouse so we then will have our home back.'

On returning to his room, John dug out the details of the glaziers and the 'tidy-up' company.

Both companies could come on Monday.

Back at the Christie, John went to Fiona's room to find it empty. Her suitcase was standing in the room, but no sign of her.

On inquiry, the sister on duty said she had gone to the scanning department. As he walked back to her room, she reappeared, looking so much better.

'Hello darling, how are you today?'

'I am feeling so much better in myself, but I feel sore.'

'Not surprising, really.'

'You're right, John.'

'When can you come home? Well, back to the Midland?'

'The nurse said I could go after my scan and whenever you arrived.'

'Can I give you a hug?'

'Best not, I think, at the moment. That's where I am sore. You can kiss me, though.'

'I will settle for that. Brilliant.'

As the two were having a long, lingering snog, the door burst open and in walked Mark.

'That tells me all I need to know. You must be feeling better?'

'Oh, Mark. We were just catching up on lost time.'

'Perfectly understandable. I have just been looking at your scans. Everything looks just fine. I have a prescription for you. If you call at our pharmacy on your way out, they will give you a starter supply of a drug you must take every day at the same time, a time of your choice. However, you must take it at the same time every day for five years.'

'Wow, that is quite an order. What is it?'

'Tamoxifen was discovered by an English doctor, Craig Jordan, who worked in America but used to live in Bramhall, not far from here. I heard he has just died, aged 77. He was very highly regarded, and he popped in here now and again when visiting his elderly mother, who by this time was in a home. He still has relatives in the area. His work with regard to breast cancer was acknowledged by academics globally. He was made an OBE on the Queen's Birthday Honours list in 2019 to honour his services to women's health. Craig later worked for the University of Texas, where he was a professor of molecular and cellular oncology. Tamoxifen had been developed by ICI for a different purpose, but it was found not to work. Jordan unearthed the drug, realising its preventative properties. His later work branched out into the prevention of multiple diseases in women, having discovered the drug group SERMS (selective estrogen receptor modules.) He will be keenly missed by people like me who use his knowledge and discoveries every day.

'You must come and see me once a year for a review. Have a good journey home. It's been a pleasure meeting you both.'

Before heading back to the Midland Hotel, John stopped off at the hospital pharmacy. The 'perpetual' prescription for Tamoxifen was handed over to the pharmacist who looked at the quantity and immediately said he could not dispense such a large amount and he would have to order them.

'I can give a two-week supply,' he said.

'But my wife has to take one pill every day for five years.'

'The best I can do for you, Sir, is to sell you a year's supply on this prescription.'

'Okay, if you can do this on this prescription, let's go for it.'

'I will need a hundred pounds deposit. I will have them in by Wednesday. When I know the actual cost, you can then pay me the balance.'

Back at the Midland Hotel, the couple rested in front of the TV in their room. Fiona fell asleep on the bed.

CHAPTER 43

FUTURE HOME

There was nowhere to go or sit outside. They were prisoners in a posh hotel in the middle of Manchester.

'I wonder how long it will take to fix the patio doors on the penthouse, John?'

'I don't know my love. I also wonder how the contractors might get the glass up to the penthouse? It certainly will not fit in the lift.'

'That's a thought; maybe that was never considered when building the place?'

'It's not proven as easy living in a super penthouse as we had hoped. Would you consider moving and living in the countryside?'

'Yes, John. I would like to have a lawn, flower beds and a vegetable garden where we can grow our own fresh vegetables.'

'How do you feel today, darling?'

'I am okay, I have felt better, but I guess I will gradually improve. You have something on your mind. What are you thinking about, John?'

'Well, it's a lovely day. This a very nice room but I would far rather be outside in the sunshine.'

'Me too. Where do you suggest we go?'

'I would like to drive out to the village of Prestbury and get some lunch there and have a look around the area.'

'I am up for that, so long as you don't drive too quickly and we find a pub so we can sit outside and have a snack lunch.'

John realised he didn't have a car handy so they got a taxi to Peter's Tower where he collected his car keys. He had a quick snoop at the penthouse, which looked – unsurprisingly – as though a bomb had hit it.

Back in reception, where Fiona had waited, they went to the underground car park and left in the Range Rover.

'Prestbury it is. I need to put it on the sat-nav as it's been many years since I have been there.'

'Will we go back to *Brave Goose* some time this year, John?'

'Yes, darling. I think I will ask Noel to bring her to Mallorca. Port de Pollença, to be exact. It will be easier for us to get there; it's only a two-and-a-half-hour flight, and there are planes every day from Manchester.'

'Sounds like a plan.'

'I will phone Noel tomorrow. *Brave Goose* is still in Valetta. It will take them a week to get to Port de Pollença. I think it's about 750 nautical miles. At eight knots non-stop, it's roughly four days. Noel will need to book a stern-to mooring on the outer mole in Pollença.'

'That sounds lovely, darling. We have nothing else to do once I am signed off. I would love to spend some time in our other home.'

'That's what I like to hear.'

As they were talking, John drove into Prestbury village.

'Gosh, this is beautiful, John. I love the white buildings and old black and white houses and the beautiful church.'

'Yes, darling, but because it is so pretty it gets jam-packed on occasions.'

John parked the Range Rover near the church in a large car park. There was plenty of space. He could imagine some days it would be heaving. They walked down a narrow path to the edge of the village towards the church, passing as they did, a firm of estate agents.

They gazed in the window to see what was for sale. Hardly anything below a million, and many more at prices higher than that.

'Hey, look at that one. I am sure that is where my parents used to live. Let's get the details just out of interest,' said John.

A pretty girl seated behind a desk stood up immediately. They walked over and she introduced herself as Joyce.

'Could I have details of the house you have for sale in Mottram St Andrew, please? I am pretty sure it used to be my parents' house.'

'Of course, I will also give you details of another property in Mottram, which is quietly on the market. The owners are not in a hurry. They would like to sign a contract with someone who is in a position to buy, then they can move with confidence to buy a smaller house. Are you ready to move, Sir?' enquired Joyce.

'Yes, we can move whenever it suits us.'

'Is your house for sale now?'

'No, we own it and don't need to sell it to buy. So we are in a good position to purchase.'

'May I take your contact details, Sir?'

'That's kind. I will give you my email address and phone number.'

'Do you have a mortgage and a solicitor lined up, Sir?'

'Good question, Joyce. I am a solicitor, and we are cash buyers.'

'Lots of people tell us that, Sir. Do you mean you will not need any borrowing at all?'

'Yes, Joyce, that is what I mean. If I may say so, you are very thorough. We will go and have a snoop at the two properties we have details of once we have had some lunch.'

John and Fiona wandered off down the main street, past the church and along. Opposite was a traditional-looking pub, the Admiral Rodney.

'Let's cross over and have lunch there.'

The two placed their order for lunch. As it was warm outside in the sunshine, they chose to sit outside. John had a pint of Old Speckled Hen, and Fiona ordered an orange and lemonade. The two of them enjoyed their snack lunch, John his beer and Fiona her drink. They were keenly reading the details of the properties they had been given.

'I like the look of this one, John; it's not as big as the house your parents used to live in.'

'Correct, and it will have a beautiful view over farmland to the rear.'

'Perhaps we can go and have a look at the outside when we have had lunch.'

'This could be an expensive lunch!'

'Ha ha, yes, but it was your idea.'

'True, I like the idea now that we could be living in a rural community. There must be lots of people who do the chores and gardening, so we will be well served by all that sort of thing.'

'Will there be wi-fi here, John?'

'Looking at the size and price of most houses, I am sure that is a certainty.'

'Turn left at the Bull's Head and go down Priest Lane, past the school, and take the first left.'

'How did you know all that?'

'On the house details, the agent has written the directions to Oak Road.'

'Clever! I just thought you were an expert on map reading.'

'I am, John. I was taught by Noel on *Brave Goose.*'

'You were looking at nautical charts on the boat – no roads on the sea!'

'Ah well, I am only doing my best.'

'Perfect, it is, too, as we have now arrived at Oak Road. I am going to park at the side, and we can walk around.'

'It looks to me that the gardens at the back of the houses on the right face west. So that is perfect on a summer's afternoon.'

'How do you know that, John?'

'Look where the sun is. It's high and over there,' said John, pointing over the houses to the southwest.

The two wandered down the lane to where it was restricted in width by two houses. They were probably built in the eighteenth century when only horse and cart transport needed to pass.

'You are quite right,' said a man who emerged from the house they were interested in. He had overheard their conversation, realising they had some estate agent details in their hand.

'Do you know the area? My name is Jim, by the way.'

'Well, I should, but it's testing my memory. I used to live over there at the corner house. My dad put up the stables, and he kept two horses here.'

'Yes, and your parents' name, and yours, of course, is England?'

'That is amazing! You must have lived here a long time, Jim?'

'I have – about fifty years. My wife died last year, and that's why I am proposing to sell. I see you have a copy of the details in your hand.'

'Oh dear, I am sorry to hear that. I am John, Jim, and this is my wife Fiona.'

They all smiled at one another and shook hands.

'Kind of you, John. My wife was not well and went downhill quickly. She refused to go to the doctor for ages. It was breast cancer that got her in the end. She was in terrible pain. It was awful to see her at the end.'

John and Fiona looked at one another in a knowing way.

'Would you like to look round?'

'If that's not inconvenient, Jim.'

'No, it isn't. The problem is that I will not even start looking for a place to move to until I have sold this. So I hope you are not in a hurry to move?'

'No, we are cash buyers, but we don't have anything to sell. Where are you looking to buy, Jim?'

'Well, I am not going to buy a property again. I would like to rent a flat, ideally in Manchester, as I am very keen on classical music. I like art galleries, and I don't have long to live. I am eighty-five now.'

John and Fiona looked at one another again with a knowing look.

'Shall we remove our shoes, Jim?'

'Oh heavens no. I know this place needs upgrading to modern standards, but I don't have the spare cash to do that. The money I get from the house sale will pay my new rent and send me on all sorts of trips.'

John and Fiona were excited to look around the house. It was, as Jim had admitted, not up to modern standards, but it was spacious and could be remodelled to make it a fantastic home.

'Can we go out to the back garden, Jim?'

'Yes, of course, my dear fellow.' Jim unlocked the back door, and John and Fiona wandered out to a significantly large garden with plenty of room to make a vegetable garden. To the right of the house was a stone embankment, some of which had been rendered and painted with climbing plants. Then, on the left-hand side of the rocky area was the long lawn.

'Fiona, that rendered area was where the opening to the mine used to be. In the brickwork, there used to be a timber door to give access to the mine. Someone has rendered the brickwork since Frank's escapade down the mine. You know, darling, we could make this into a fantastic house with a value of at least twice the asking price for an expenditure of about half a million. What do you think?'

'Is that right, John?'

'Yes. Would you like to live here?'

'I would, John. I think the plot is fantastic, and the house could be remodelled to be a wonderful property.'

'Jim, are you free for a chat?'

'Yes, John. How remiss of me! I haven't offered you a cup of tea.'

'No, we don't need a tea. Thanks anyway, Jim. We have just had lunch and a pint at the Admiral Rodney in Prestbury village. Considering it's a Saturday, it wasn't as busy as I had expected.'

'Okay, well, let's go and sit in the lounge.'

'Jim, I want to make you an offer.'

'Oh, I don't think I can afford to take an offer. As I have explained, I will have rent to pay for a flat in Manchester.'

'Let me explain, Jim. Fiona and I own a large block of modern apartments in Manchester just off Deansgate and close to the trams, as well as The Bridgewater Hall, home of the Hallé Orchestra.

'What I would like to offer you is a two-bedroomed modern apartment that would be rent-free for the rest of your life. You would have to pay a contribution to the insurance, but other than the Council Tax, you wouldn't have any more costs. For that deal, I would give you £900,000 for your house.'

'Oh, my word! I need to think about that, and I need to have a look at the apartment.'

'Let me give my receptionist a ring.'

John took his mobile phone out of his pocket.

Hi, it's John England. Do we have an empty apartment?'

'Yes, Sir, it's on the third floor and faces south. It's fully furnished.'

'Okay, don't show anyone around today. I will be coming over shortly.'

'That's okay, Sir, as we have another unit to let as well.'

'Thanks.' John finished the call.

'I know this is a bit out of the blue, but would you like to look at an apartment we have available at the moment? I will happily take you there now and bring you back.'

'Wow, John. This is almost too good to be true. Yes, why not? Let's go.'

Within the hour, John turned his car into the underground car park. All three of them got out.

'It's pretty quiet today. The football season hasn't started, and folks are on holiday in the main,' said John.

'Jim, as a tenant-resident, you are entitled to a car parking space. It will have a number that coincides with the apartment number. You also get an electronic key, which lifts the barrier gate to the car park. The lift from here goes up to reception and there you have to change lifts.'

'Afternoon, Ben, can I have the key to the empty apartment? I think it's on the third floor.'

'Thanks, Ben,' said John as he was handed the key, complete with a swipe card for the lift. On the bundle was the electronic key for the underground garage.

'You have to swipe the card on the pad so it will call the lift and automatically stop on the third floor.'

'What happens, John, if you share the lift with someone on the fifth and third floors?'

'Good question, Jim. The lift will stop at the third and then take the remaining passengers to the fifth and then return to the ground floor.'

'Looks like the owners have thought of everything.'

John realised Jim had not fully appreciated that he and Fiona owned all the apartments in the block.

'Yes, it has been well thought out, Jim.'

All three of them came out of the lift, and there was a choice of only two apartment doors.

'The apartment we want is 3a, which is nearest to the lift.'

John opened the door.

'Here it is, Jim. Hallway, two bedrooms, each with an en-suite bathroom, a cloakroom and WC, a lounge, a kitchen with dining area, and a patio with French doors from the lounge. The heating is electric underfloor. There is an electric fire in the fireplace in the lounge, and there is a living flame. Bathrooms and cloakrooms have electrically heated towel rails. All the furniture you can see is included. Bed linen, et cetera, is for you to acquire. There is a utility room off the hall. Let me show you. The washing machine and dryer are plumbed in here. There is also a waste shoot, so you don't need to bother taking waste down in the lift. The waste goes in green or blue plastic bags – green is food and degradable waste, blue for all other waste.

Jim went into every room with a beam on his face that was getting larger by the minute.

'So, what do you think, Jim?'

'John, I think this is just great. How can you afford to pay the rent on this for me for the rest of my life? It could be ten years, John.'

'I don't think you quite realise, Jim, that Fiona and I own all fifty-two apartments. We just won't charge rent to ourselves. We do have a penthouse on the top floor, which is twice the size of this apartment. That is where we live.'

'Oh, I see. Blimey, you must have one heck of an income.'

'Well, there are plenty of costs and staff. But I admit there is a worthwhile surplus.'

'Fantastic. This is a dream come true.'

'When you worked, Jim, what was your job?'

'I was a Ships Chief Engineer. One down from Captain on various ships of the Cunard liners.'

'How interesting, Jim. I look forward to doing the deal and to having a long chat with you about marine engines.'

'John, let me sleep on this, please. I am nearly certain I will go ahead. I just want to check with my son Marcus to see what he thinks.'

'Okay, Jim, let me know tomorrow afternoon. Here is my card with my mobile on it. I need to drop Fiona back at the Midland Hotel, but I will take you home after that.'

John placed Jim in the passenger seat and Fiona in the back. She hopped out of the car as soon as they arrived at the front of the hotel.

'Bye, Jim, looking forward to seeing you again,' said Fiona.

CHAPTER 44

SHORT CRUISE

A s soon as John arrived back at the Midland Hotel, he sent an email to Angela, his letting agent, who had an office in Deansgate, Manchester. John advised her that apartment 3a was currently off the market as he had a potential long-term let.

'I need to chivvy up the cleaners and glaziers so we can get back to our penthouse as soon as possible,' he muttered to himself.

As soon as John had terminated the calls, his mobile rang.

'Hello, Jon. What news?'

'Ah, I am glad to have caught you in. Both Miller and Watson have been arrested. They are in detention now pending being put before the Manchester Magistrates Court on Monday.'

'Have you managed to get a case together to enable you to get a conviction on Kent Watson?'

'We hope so, John. We have employed a forensic accountant which has turned out to be very useful as he has spotted numerous items that required further investigation. We found lots of areas where Watson held money personally. We have so far been able to recover eighty per cent of the funds he squirrelled away. We are still looking for the remainder.'

'Brilliant, Jon. I hope you achieve a conviction against Watson. Sometimes, courts hesitate to put financial criminals into custody. But Watson's involvement in using his office as a prison for Fiona when she was kidnapped will go against him. Will you need me as a witness, Jon?'

'I very much doubt it. We might need Fiona though.'

'Oh, that's a blow. We were hoping to go away for a month in July.'

'I will have a chat with the CPS lawyer once he has digested the case.'

*

It was nearly two weeks since John had spoken with Jon Kim regarding the possibility that either John or Fiona would need to attend court. John could undoubtedly see the benefit of Fiona attending court. After all, she was the one who had been kidnapped. John's attendance was less important as he had not been in direct contact with the kidnappers.

Jon Kim rang and spoke to them about court attendance.

'I suspect you will be on holiday at *Brave Goose* when the case goes to court?'

'Yes, it looks that way, Jon.'

'What sort of electronics do you have on the boat?'

'It is easier to say what we don't have rather than what we do have. What do you need, Jon?'

'I understand that the court might be persuaded to use Zoom on this occasion. The issue as I have explained to the CPS is that Fiona has recently undergone a large operation. She needs some recovery time.'

'Yes, Zoom can be made available on *Brave Goose,* so we can join in with the court proceedings using that system.'

'Good. I will try to get that agreed upon. I will let you know, John.'

*

'Noel, how are you doing with your passage to Mallorca?'

'All good, John. In fact, we are halfway there. We haven't stopped; we are on course for getting to Barcelona on Thursday this week, with a view to being in Port de Pollença on Friday.'

'Seems an odd way to go, Noel?'

'It might be, but fuel in Mallorca is very expensive, with it being an island. In Barcelona, like the rest of the mainland, fuel is much cheaper.'

'Good thinking, Noel. When do you expect to arrive in Port de Pollença?'

'I hope to be stern-to on the Yacht Club mole by Friday afternoon. Once we are tidy and clean and stocked up with food and drink, we will be ready to welcome you any time from next Monday.'

'That's excellent, Noel. I will let you know when we will be with you.'

*

'Jim, I have just picked up your message; sorry we have been out and about, busy tidying our personal items following the repair to our patio windows, and the damage to furniture and decor.'

'John, I have spoken again to my son Marcus and my solicitor, all of whom are suspicious as the deal sounds too good to be true. So I am no nearer giving you a decision.'

'Oh dear. Look, let me get my solicitor to send your man and your son a formal offer, which is will be valid for up four weeks. What I really wanted to speak to you about was to invite you to spend a couple of weeks on our motor yacht. She is based in Mallorca at the moment. She is called *Brave Goose* and has twin Gardner Diesels, one thousand horsepower each. I thought you would be interested in going on a boating break. Don't worry; I have a resident engineer on board, as well as a captain, deckhand, and stewardess-cum-chef. You will be our guest. Fiona and I will be on board too, of course. What do you think? We plan on flying out next Thursday.'

'Wow, that sounds extremely attractive. How big is *Brave Goose* John?'

'She is 140 foot in length and just over 300 tons gross weight.'

'Wow, John. You certainly are a man of means!'

'Can you let me know over the weekend if you would like to come?'

CHAPTER 45

BRAVE GOOSE

'Hello, John, it's Jim. I hope this isn't too early for you on a Sunday?'

'No, not at all,' John lied, having just woken due to sound of the mobile ringing. 'Have you arrived at a decision, Jim?'

'Yes, John, I would love to accept your invitation to join you on your motor yacht.'

'That's great, Jim. I'll be in touch with regards travel arrangements as soon as possible.

Shall I drive to either the airport or your apartment?'

'We have limited parking spaces. All are allocated except for 3a at the moment, so just park there. Feel free to come here, and I will ask the receptionist to let you in. I will send you a text with the time you need to be here?'

'Thanks John, looking forward to it.'

'Ah, how do you feel today, darling?'

'I think I feel fine. Why have you woken up so early? Its Sunday?'

'Jim rang to say he would love to come to *Brave Goose.*'

'He must be an insomniac, calling at this early hour. Good idea to put him in a guest cabin well away from us!'

'Good thinking. I am going to get up now as I am wide awake.'

'Have we any plans for today, darling?'

'No, we could go and have a look at the penthouse. You may need to collect a few things before we go away.'

'Yes, that would be helpful. I have been thinking about the house in Mottram St Andrew. Should we get an architect to have a look at it for us and give us some suggestions on the re-fit. Like we did with *Barve Goose*?'

'Despite the fact you have just woken up, you are full of bright ideas this morning. Yes, I agree with you. I will see who I can find who would be good at that.'

John and Fiona made a list of the jobs to be done in the penthouse.

'I will contact Ian Birch tomorrow to get the name of the firm that did the refurbishment last time. They would be ideal for refurbishing the house at Mottram St Andrew. Always assuming Jim goes ahead with the deal.'

'Oh, I had hoped for a different interior designer for the house. The very modern furnishing of the penthouse is ideal for that space, but not country enough for the new house.'

'Okay, darling. I will go and get some Sunday papers, and at the same time, I will pick up a few house magazines so you hopefully can choose a style to give the designers a guide.'

Fiona spent the whole of a drizzly Sunday going through all the magazines. She cut out a few pages to create a design mood board for the house.

'What do you think of these ideas, darling?'

'You are not just a pretty face. These are great. They will go wonderfully in the house. All we have to do now is to buy it!'

*

'Hello, Noel. Good to hear from you. Where are you?'

'We are tied up in Port de Pollença. I have booked this berth for four weeks on the basis we might come and go over the next month.'

'That's great, Noel. Did *Brave Goose* run well?'

'She did, never a stutter, very smooth. We ran at eight knots despite the normal cruising speed being twelve knots.'

'Good. We will have a guest with us for the first two weeks. He is a retired marine chief engineer. He used to work for Cunard, on the 'Queens'.'

'I had better tell Jock then. I guess they will have a great deal in common.'

*

'Jim. John here. *Brave Goose,* is now moored in Port de Pollença, Mallorca. When would it suit you to fly over?'

'Would Wednesday be okay but for just one week?'

'Yes, certainly. Although you are most welcome to stay longer.'

'You are too kind, John, but I have lots to do at home.'

John didn't pursue the question.

'Jim, we will meet you what is your surname so I can tell my staff at the apartments?'

'Strong, Jim Strong!'

'I won't forget that, Jim. Thanks. See you at eight-thirty on Wednesday morning at Peter's Tower. Do you have an email address?'

'Yes, John. My email address is my name @sky.com.'

'Okay, Jim, I will email you the travel details. Can you please send me a copy of your passport's front page? I need this to book your flight. See you Wednesday morning.'

*

At eight o'clock on Wednesday morning, John and Fiona checked out of the Midland Hotel, taking a taxi to Peter's Tower.

'Sydney, good to see you. We are still at the Midland, waiting for the glaziers to fix the patio windows, then clean up and replace the

267

furniture and re-decorate. They should be finished when we get back in a month.'

'Very well, Mr England. I will try to make sure they finish before you get back. Have a great time.'

Jim, true to his word, arrived at reception from the lift and straight into reception.

'Are you okay pulling your suitcase to the tram stop just around the corner, Jim?'

'Yes, I am quite used to travelling. I don't usually pack much. When my wife was alive, we needed a removal lorry for her cases.'

'I know what you mean, Jim,' said John, grinning at Fiona.

A half-hour trip had them at Manchester Airport departures by nine o'clock, ready for the ten-thirty flight which would get them into Palma at noon Spanish time.

They boarded the EasyJet flight, and as they were mid-week travellers, there was room in the extra legroom seats for all three of them.

The plane touched down at noon as predicted. After checking through customs and arrivals, they found a Mercedes taxi to take them to Port de Pollença. They arrived at the end of the leading pontoon at the marina at one-fifteen.

Noel and the crew were all dressed in white shirts, blue shorts and white deck shoes.

José was down in a flash to collect the luggage, which followed the owners and guest to the quarterdeck and placed in their respective cabins.

Introductions took place, and Jim was escorted to his cabin so he could freshen up before they enjoyed a salad lunch prepared by Sally.

John and Fiona appeared first in shorts and *Brave Goose* tops with gold braids on the lapels. Then Jim followed them in white shorts, with a white belt and figure of eight brass buckle, a short-sleeved white shirt and three pips epaulettes, a white peaked cap with gold trim and the Cunard badge, which was a rampant horse holding a globe surrounded by gold acanthus leaves.

There was a stunned silence.

'My word, Jim, you certainly are doing us an honour in your Merchant Navy uniform. Thank you.'

'I promise I won't make a habit of it, but frankly, I don't own a light rig as you have. We used to be dressed up most of the time on the 'Queens'.'

'Not ideal for visiting the engine room, Sir!' commented Jock.

'You, I gather, are Jock, the engineer?'

'I am, Sir, but I usually wear blue overalls.'

'Jim, I hope you won't be offended, but I insist the crew call Fiona and me by our Christian names. Will you be happy with that?'

' I am delighted.'

With that comment, Jim removed his cap.

'Would you like some wine, a beer or a gin and tonic, Jim?'

'A gin and tonic was my tipple and still is; with ice if you have it?'

'We do, Jim. I think we had a new ice maker installed during the re-fit last winter.'

'Excellent, less to go wrong for the engineer, and an ideal drink for guests.'

The assembled company laughed and realised they had a 'real' sailor in their midst.

'Let's sit down,' said John. 'There will be four of us for lunch. I have invited Noel, our captain, to join us.'

'Perfect,' replied Jim. 'How long have you been captain, Noel?' he enquired.

'When a man named Goose purchased her in 2018, he kept all the crew. I had been working for the previous owner until his death in the spring of 2018 for ten years. Mr England and Fiona purchased *Brave Goose* in 2020. They too kindly kept all the crew, which was terrific. Shortly after their purchase, the former owner, Goose, was shot in the back and went into hospital in Barcelona. He was in a bad way, but he finally left the hospital and rejoined *Brave Goose*. He joined us for a short cruise to where we are now, Port de Pollença. While we were having dinner at the Yacht Club, someone, who we later identified for the police, had come onboard and finally killed Goose.'

'Oh, not a happy time?'

'No, Jim, but Goose had already sold the boat to Fiona and me. As I had taken his last will and testament, he wished to be buried at sea. The local regulations required the body to have been cremated, and the ashes could then be scattered. Again, there were regulations attached to that, but we fulfilled his wish. He was a rogue of a man, but once you got to know him, he was quite a character.'

'Tell me, Jim, what ships were you attached to?' asked Noel.

'I served on a number of Cunard ships up to 1987. When I was 36, I was appointed the Chief Engineer for *QE2*. It was a fantastic ship with a lot of teething problems. Fortunately, we overcame these. She was built by John Brown shipyard on Clydebank in 1967 and she was well ahead of her time. When I joined her, the first thing we had to do was to give her a re-fit. In 1982, she was part of the armada to the Falkland Islands in the South Atlantic as a troop ship. You can imagine the state she was in when we got back to the UK. Anyway, it was an excellent opportunity for me to specify the replacement of an up-to-date kit. All at the expense of the MOD. I served on her until 2008, when we sailed her to Dubai. When I got off the *QE2*, I was 65 years old, and Cunard retired me. That's when my wife and I sold our house, bought the old spoil tip on Oak Road in Mottram St Andrew, and built our home.'

'Quite a story, Jim. I could tell you quite a story about the site where you built your house,' said John. 'I will keep that for another day. Let's have lunch. Red or white wine?'

CHAPTER 46

NOT THE ENDING EXPECTED

ollowing lunch, Jock invited Jim on a tour of the engine room.

'Thanks, Jock, I would love that. Just let me change out of my whites because knowing engine rooms as I do, they will not remain white long.'

Within a few minutes, Jim reappeared, dressed in much older, casual clothes, and he walked straight to the engine room access. No one had told him where it was: experience sent him the correct way.

'Hi Jock, are you down here?'

'Yes, Jim, come on down.'

'Well, goodness me, Jock, what a beautiful engine space you have. It looks brand new, but I know it isn't. Tell me what you have done.'

'Starting with the basics, the sides of the ship, bilges, engine mounts and the ceiling have all been repainted white with epoxy paint. The lighting has all been replaced with LED tubes, which provide an outstanding working light. Then we had all the electrics re-wired. Something no one ever notices, but you and I would!'

'You are so right, Jock.'

'The engine controls have all been converted to electronic controls rather than manual cable controls. The hydraulic steering is new. There are two new generators, 25kva each, both Cumming machines. Then, we renewed all the fuel lines and twin water separators for each engine. The day tank and the four main fuel tanks have been emptied and cleaned. Once all that had been done, we renewed the fuel gauges with repeaters on the bridge. We had the fuel tanks filled, including the day tank. We used the glass tube gauges to see the levels as we filled. We took the fuel reading from the pump on the dock and adjusted our gauges to read the correct quantity of fuel in each tank.'

'That, Jock, is a comprehensive overhaul. The main item you have not mentioned is the two magnificent Gardener diesel engines.'

'Yes, Jim. They were not forgotten. I broke the engines down and sent all twelve cylinders back to Gardner. I wanted the cylinder caps enamelled as they were in the old days. I specified the maroon colour. While the cylinders were away, I had the chance to check fly belts, chains, and sumps. I gave them a good clean. I polished all the pipe work, which sparkled. It all looked even better, as did the beautiful enamelled cylinder caps. We had just completed a long trip from Malta to here, and the engines purred like a cat all the way, non-stop for nearly five days. The fuel consumption is twenty per cent lower than previously, despite the non-stop nature of the voyage.'

'That all sounds wonderful, Jock. I suppose if she had been re-antifouled during the re-fit, that would have helped improve the fuel consumption, but the cleaning of tank pipes and the cylinders having been overhauled would have added to the economic fuel consumption. John must be pleased.'

'He doesn't know yet, Jim!'

'I guess he will when he checks the fuel costs.'

'Yes, you are probably correct. So what is your overall impression of this little ship?'

'I think she is a little beauty. I am very envious. I have the bug again coming here.'

'Yes, it wasn't just the engine room that received the treatment. I wrote the spec for the work here. We have some new bits I haven't pointed out. One is a new wastewater purifier system, which is fantastic. Sally is thrilled to bits as we put in a waste compactor.'

'So all in all, she is a very tidy ship!'

'Thank you, Jim. Coming from you, that is a compliment indeed.'

*

Sally found Jim wandering around the quarter-deck.

'Can I help you, Sir? You look lost.'

'Sally, it's Jim – in accordance with John's instructions,' he said with a wide grin. 'I'm looking for John and Fiona. Do you know where I might find them?'

'Yes, Jim. Fiona has not been well of late, so it is probable they will be having a siesta. They normally re-appear about four.'

'I am sure you will know what has been arranged for dinner tonight.'

'I do, Jim, because I have a night off. I gather you will be eating at the Yacht Club.'

'That sounds just fine. I will go up to the boat deck and have a siesta myself.'

*

It was five-thirty when John reappeared.

'Hello, Jim. The last time I saw you, you were disappearing into the engine room. Did you enjoy it?'

'I did, John. Jock has ensured you have a most efficient and tidy engine room. His work, I gather, has saved you about twenty per cent on fuel cost, based on the figures for the trip from Valetta.'

'Wow, that *is* a saving. He is a good man, Jock.'

'Yes, I think you have found a beautiful boat with an excellent crew. A hard trick to pull off. I am glad I have seen you, John. I can't

273

tell you how much I appreciate your offer. However, I do need a million for my house. I understand I won't be paying rent. I would if I had done what I was planning which was to find a smaller and cheaper flat. The million is essential to me. I have two grandsons I want to give some money to. The million will allow me to do that.

If you agree to a million, I will move in three months, subject to the lawyers, and sooner if they do their jobs quickly.'

'Okay, Jim. Three months and a million tenancy at no rent for life for apartment 3a. Is that the deal?'

'It is, John. Are we agreed?'

'Yes, Jim, we are agreed. Do you want to shake hands on it? Oh, and when the spirit moves, you let me know, and you can come back to *Brave Goose* with pleasure.'

'John, for someone I have just met, and vice versa, this is an exceptional deal, and I am sure we shall get on famously.'

'Can you let me have your solicitor's details in the morning, as well as the full address and postcode for your house?'

'I will, on one condition?'

Feeling slightly apprehensive about the potential additional condition, John responded cautiously, 'Yes, what's that?'

'Can I use your computer to allow me to email my solicitor what you have emailed yours? Can you let me have printouts of all the emails?'

'Of course, my dear fellow. Do you want a gin and tonic or a glass of champagne?'

'John, that's wonderful! Our arrangement deserves champagne.'

Fiona appeared on the quarterdeck to meet Jim.

'Hi Jim, I thought John was with you?'

'He was. He has just gone to get a bottle of champagne and some glasses.'

'Oh, what's the celebration?'

'We have just shaken hands on the deal. I will move out of Quarry House, which is my house's name, in case you haven't spotted it, in three months. I hope the solicitors will get their skates on so the time scale can be met.'

'Gosh, how exciting, Jim. Your dream has come true much earlier than expected.'

'Ah, you two have found one another? Have you heard the news, darling?'

'I have – how wonderful.'

John poured out two glasses of champagne after the cork had exploded out of the bottle and landed in the harbour, bringing Noel running onto the quarterdeck.

'Is everything alright, John? I thought I heard a gun?'

'No gun, Noel. Just champagne.'

'Ah, that's fine. Are you celebrating?'

'Yes, Noel, we have just bought Jim's house. Having seen and inspected it, we invited him here for a short holiday while we both contemplated the deal, and we have now concluded it. It's just up to solicitors now to tie it up now.'

'Well done to you both. I will get back to my paperwork for the Port Police.'

'John, do you think it would be possible on exchange of contracts for me to enter into the lifetime tenancy of 3a Peter's Tower? It would enable me to move some of my belongings into the flat away from the house. Much of the furniture will need to go to charity or to auction for the few antique pieces,'

'I don't see a problem with that, Jim. Once you are living in the apartment and not the house, may I have a key to the house, even though there will still be stuff for you to move? I would like an architect to come and have a look and make some preliminary

275

sketches of what we want to do. Don't ask me what that is because I am asking the architect to come up with ideas.'

'Have you booked return flights, John?'

'For you, Jim, but we were planning on staying longer.'

'Oh dear. I have a problem, John. I have come away with an insufficient supply of my pills. Should we go back?' said Fiona.

'Well, let's see what we can arrange. I am sure we can organise a delivery here without having to return to the UK simply to pick them up and return them.'

'Have you ever been to Menorca, Jim?'

'No. I don't think I have ever been there.'

'Okay, let's plan on sailing to Ciudadela Miniorca. We will have to moor off and take the tender in, but it will be worth it. I am going to phone my solicitor – let me know if you want to do the same. When I have finished, you can use my study.'

'Did you manage to organise some more pills, darling?'

'I did. I spoke with Carol, and she is arranging to send 4 week's supply of Tomoxifen to be delivered to the Yacht Club, together with an international prescription for 56 tablets.'

'That's great. I have ten days left, but if we stay for a month, I will run out. It's a change in habit. To think I have to take one of these pills every day for a minimum of five years is amazing.'

'If it keeps cancer at bay, it's not a great burden.'

'You are, of course, right, as you always are!'

'I am going into the clubhouse to speak with the receptionist. I need to warn them of the arrival of a small parcel by DHL.'

The pills arrived as a medical emergency. John picked them up from the Yacht Club just in time for their departure to Menorca.

'I think we should go back earlier and start to plan what we want to do to the house in three months.'

The next few days flew by as the crew, Jim, John and Fiona travelled to Menorca and then back to Mallorca, travelling along the magnificent east coast of the island, then finally berthing in Palma at the Club de Mar. This proved to be a suitable place to leave *Brave Goose*, allowing a short taxi ride to the airport for all three.

'Well done, Noel and crew, for getting a berth at this famous marina.'

Fortunately, they occupied a berth alongside the mole on the opposite side of the marina pontoons. The taxi was ordered in good time for the journey to the airport and was able to draw alongside *Brave Goose* where José had deployed the starboard side boarding stairs.

A cheery wave from the crew saw them off.

Once back at Manchester Airport, a tram ride virtually to the front door of Peter's Tower enabled all three to achieve access to their future apartments.

'Morning, Sydney. How are things here?'

'Mr England, good to see you and Fiona back again.' He looked at Jim knowingly. Sydney was sure he had met him before but couldn't give him a name.

'Let me introduce you to Jim Strong. He will be the new tenant of apartment 3a. I'm not sure when he will move in, but when he does, it will be indefinitely. Can you let Jim have some keys so he can go and work out what he needs to bring, or not as the case, may be?'

'Oh, Mr England. There was a firm working most of last week and up until yesterday. They were repairing and cleaning your flat.'

'Have the glass patio doors been replaced yet?'

'Yes, Sir, they have. I went up yesterday, and everything seems fine now. There has been new furniture delivered. The decorators were working for four days last week. It all looks fine to me.'

'Tell me, Sydney, how on earth did they manage to get the huge glass doors up to the patio?'

'The glaziers came last Monday and prepared everything. The replacement glass doors were delivered last Tuesday after you had left.'

'Okay, Sydney. But how did they get the glass up there?'

'That was probably the easy bit. The contractors used the window cleaning cradle. It is strong and was able to carry all four doors up at once. They were delivered to the patio and carried by hand, one by one, to be fitted in the existing frames, which didn't need any work on them. The doors fitted the first time.'

'Well, I had not thought of that Sydney. Clever. I have my keys with me. We shall go and have a look.'

'Are you going to have another look at your apartment, Jim?'

'Yes, shall we share the lift?'

'Will I see you before you leave, Jim?'

'Yes, good idea. Can I get up to your penthouse, John?'

'Yes, you will be able to do that. Let me get you a temporary lift card. When you have finished, give it back to Sydney. It won't work at any other time. It's a one-off card for today only.'

In the lift, Jim thanked John and explained he would come up and say goodbye when he had completed his viewing.

It was nearly two hours since John and Fiona had said farewell to Jim, who promised he would come and say goodbye before he left.

'Sydney, has Mr Strong brought the keys back for 3a, and if so, has he gone?'

'Yes, Sir, he left over an hour ago. He dropped the keys back.'

'Thanks, Sydney.'

'Well, what do you make of that Fiona? Jim has left the building after leaving the keys for 3a behind. You would have thought he would have come to see us before leaving, wouldn't you?'

'It isn't all that surprising, darling. Don't forget that the person who must have run the house, the finances, taken out insurance, and had the car serviced must have been his wife. He spent his life living in the lap of luxury, sailing the world in one of Cunard's flagships, the *Queen Elizabeth the Second*. His wife, I am sure, held their home together, made all the decisions, and paid for the electricity, gas and water. He would have never been there. I suspect when he was on leave, he expected a menu so he could choose what to eat for dinner, as he did when on board. She did what every wife does most of the time. Her husband wasn't around!'

'I think you have hit the nail on the head, darling. They would not be a team. He was the money earner but spent very little. I bet she chose the plot on which to build the house she wanted. It was furnished by her. He came home on leave to enjoy it.'

'I think he finds it very difficult to make a decision, hence the call to Marcus, his son. If you think about his working life, he would never have had to make a decision. The ship went where it was told to go. If it was short of fuel, he had it refuelled. The dials in the engine room would tell him that. He would record the temperature of the engines while at sea, the output of generators, and the record of engine oil consumed. He would even have someone else take all the readings. He might check them from time to time and record them in the ship's marine engine record ledger.'

'Of course, you are right, John. He has never had to make a decision on anything as valuable as his house in his life. It would have been a joint decision. He has no wife now; he has to make a decision himself, but he can't. His HEAD IS IN THE SAND.'

ABOUT THE AUTHOR

Since 2009, Robert has been writing novels of various genres, mainly to do with different types of crime. The first five books he wrote are referred to as the 'Wall's Saga', a story about a family's trials and tribulations following the unexpected death of the head of the family, Peter Wall.

In between writing the five books in the series, Robert wrote his own autobiography, which was not published but given to members of the large Jordan family, as well as to his friends. He also wrote the family tree in 2018 as a present for family members at Christmas.

During the Covid pandemic, he wrote two short stories in which proceeds and donations were given to the NHS nurses charity.

Once the pandemic was virtually over, he wrote more books involving some of the main characters from the 'Wall's Saga'. The later books are very much on a theme but each one is a novel in its own right. This novel, *Head in the Sand*, starts with a look back to the childhood of John England, the central character in most of the books.

Towards the end of the book, one of the central characters develops breast cancer. There are various twists and turns to get her operated on and come out smiling. This element of the book triggered the idea of asking readers to make donations through the R A Jordan website to the work of Breast Cancer UK, a charity to which a moiety of the sale price of this book will be donated. For those who wish to make a more significant donation, please visit the author's website to donate.

All the R.A. Jordan books can be purchased from Amazon. The easiest way to find them is to click on the website name, which will take you to a list of the books. Clicking on the front cover of the website will take you straight to the Amazon page holding the book of your choice. All books are available on Kindle.

The website is: www.rajordan.uk

Donations to the Christie Cancer Hospital, Manchester

That's it – nothing else!

AUTHOR'S NOTE

I have not written an obituary for anyone, but in view of the Breast Cancer connection to my cousin V Craig Jordan, who died on 6th June 2024 at the age of 76, I felt his career was so exceptional I had to include it in this book, somehow. I urge you to read this biog. It is incredible how much effect one person has had on a single disease for the better.

Virgil Craig Jordan, CMG, OBE, FMedSci (July 25, 1947 – June 9, 2024) was an American and British scientist specializing in drugs for breast cancer treatment and prevention. He was a Professor of Breast Medical Oncology and Professor of Molecular and Cellular Oncology at the University of Texas Houston, Texas. Previously, he was Scientific Director and Vice Chairman of Oncology at the Lombardi Comprehensive Cancer Center of Georgetown University. Jordan was the first to discover the breast cancer prevention properties of tamoxifen and the scientific principles for adjuvant therapy with antihormones. His later work branched out into the prevention of multiple diseases in women with the discovery of the drug group selective estrogen receptor modulator (SERMs). He later worked on developing a new Hormone Replacement Therapy (HRT) for post-menopausal women that prevents breast cancer and does not increase the risk of breast cancer.

Jordan's paper, *The Effect of Raloxifene on Risk of Breast Cancer in Postmenopausal Women: Results from the More Randomized Trial*, was one of the top 20 most cited papers in breast cancer research from 2003 to 2004.

Early life

Born in New Braunfels, Texas, Jordan moved to England with his family as a child. He went to school at Moseley Hall Grammar School in Cheshire before attending the University of Leeds, where he received BSc, PhD and DSc degrees in pharmacology.

Research career

Jordan began working on the structure-activity of anti-estrogens as part of his PhD program at Leeds University. During that time, he met Arthur Walpole, the patent holder for the drug that became tamoxifen.

In September 1972, Jordan became a visiting scientist at the Worcester Foundation for Experimental Biology, Massachusetts. While there, he began researching the idea that tamoxifen, a selective estrogen receptor modulator (SERM), could block estrogen receptors in breast tumours. Estrogen receptors in breast tumours attract estrogen, which is then absorbed into the cancerous cell and encourages the cell to divide, causing the cancer to grow. Until this time, the treatment for this type of breast cancer was oophorectomy.

Jordan returned to Leeds University as a lecturer in Pharmacology between 1974 and 1979, after which he spent one year at the Ludwig Institute for Cancer Research at the University of Bern, Switzerland.

In 1980, Jordan joined the University of Wisconsin–Madison where he started to look at the effects of tamoxifen and another SERM, raloxifene, on bone density and coronary systems. This was needed because of the concern that long-term use of SERMs could lead to osteoporosis and heart disease. Jordan's research showed that post-menopausal women who took these drugs did not suffer from a lowering of bone density or an increase in blood cholesterol. Raloxifene is now used to prevent osteoporosis. Jordan gained a full

Professorship at Wisconsin in 1985, the same year his alma mater awarded him a DSc.

In 1993, Jordan became Professor of Cancer Pharmacology at Northwestern University Medical School in Chicago, IL., and director of the Breast Cancer Research Program at the Robert H. Lurie Comprehensive Cancer Center of Northwestern University. He was the inaugural holder of the Diana Princess of Wales Professor of Cancer Research (1999–2004).

He was appointed Officer of the Order of the British Empire (OBE) in the 2002 Birthday Honours for services to international breast cancer research.

In January 2005, Jordan was the inaugural Alfred G. Knudson Chair of Cancer Research at the Fox Chase Cancer Center in Philadelphia, PA. He has recently published work showing that estrogen, given at the right time, causes the destruction of cancer cells rather than feeding their growth. Jordan was the Scientific Director of the Lombardi Comprehensive Cancer Center, Professor of Oncology and Pharmacology, Vice Chair of the Department of Oncology, and the Vincent T. Lombardi Chair of Translational Cancer Research, Georgetown University, Washington, D.C., prior to moving to Texas.

Jordan was appointed Companion of the Order of St Michael and St George (CMG) in the 2019 Birthday Honours for services to women's health.

Personal life and national service

Jordan was the father of two daughters, Helen and Alexandra.

Military Service: Captain Intelligence Corps (V) (On the staff of the Deputy Chief Scientist (Army) UK (1971–75)), Attached NBC Officer Region 1 US Mobilization Designee, DEA Officers' Course and UK Police Narcotics Squad Training (1973–78), 23 Special Air Service (1975–79) (Commanding Officer Rory Walker (1975-1978)),(Commanding Officer Tony Hunter-Choat(1978-1979)),

(Director SAS Group, Brigadier Johnny Watts (1975-1979)), RARO SAS (1979–97). SAS Regimental Association (2008–present).

Jordan died at his home in Houston on June 9, 2024, at the age of 76.

Awards

2020 Honorary Doctor of Science degree from the University of Wisconsin–Madison

2019 Companion of the Order of St Michael and St George (CMG) for services to women's healthcare.

2012 Louis S. Goodman and Alfred Gilman Award in Receptor Pharmacology, American Society for Pharmacology and Experimental Therapeutics

2011 St. Gallen Prize for Clinical Breast Cancer Research, Switzerland

2008 David A. Karnofsky Award from the American Society of Clinical Oncology

2006 American Cancer Society Award and Lecture from the American Society for Clinical Oncology.

2003 Kettering Prize

2002 American Cancer Society Medal of Honor for basic research.

2002, made an Officer of the Order of the British Empire by Queen Elizabeth II for services to international breast cancer research.

2001 Umberto Veronesi Award for the Future Fight Against Breast Cancer (2001)

2001 Bristol-Myers Squibb Award for Distinguished Achievement in Cancer Research.

2001 Doctor of Medicine, honoris causa from the University of Leeds

1993 Cameron Prize for Therapeutics of the University of Edinburgh

1993 ASPET Award from the American Society of Pharmacology and Experimental Therapeutics.

1993 The Gaddum Memorial Award from the British Pharmacological Society

1992 Brinker International Breast Cancer Award for Basic Science from Susan G. Komen for the Cure.

Printed in Great Britain
by Amazon